Her Daughter's Eyes

Her Daughter's Eyes

Jessica Barksdale Inclán

NAL Accent
Published by New American Library, a division of
Penguin Putnam Inc., 375 Hudson Street, New York, New York 10014, U.S.A.
Penguin Books Ltd, 27 Wrights Lane, London W8 5TZ, England
Penguin Books Australia Ltd, Ringwood, Victoria, Australia
Penguin Books Canada Ltd, 10 Alcorn Avenue, Toronto, Ontario, Canada M4V 3B2
Penguin Books (N.Z.) Ltd, 182–190 Wairau Road, Auckland 10, New Zealand

Penguin Books Ltd, Registered Offices: Harmondsworth, Middlesex, England

Published by New American Library, a division of Penguin Putnam Inc.

First Printing, May 2001
10 9 8 7 6 5 4 3 2

FICTION FOR THE WAY WE LIVE

REGISTERED TRADEMARK—MARCA REGISTRADA

Haiku by Issa on page 10 from *The Essential Haiku:*
Versions of Basho, Buson & Issa, edited and with an introduction by Robert Hass
copyright © Robert Hass, 1994. Reprinted by permission of HarperCollins Publishers, Inc.

LIBRARY OF CONGRESS CATALOGING-IN-PUBLICATION DATA:
Inclán, Jessica Barksdale.
    Her daughter's eyes / Jessica Barksdale Inclán
      p. cm.
    ISBN 0-451-20282-1 (alk. paper)
    1. Teenage girls—Fiction 2. Teenage pregnancy—Fiction. 3. Single parent
families—Fiction. 4. Motherless families—Fiction. 5. Sisters—Fiction. I. Title.
PS3559.N3332 H47 2001
813.6—dc21   00-053284

Printed in the United States of America
Set in Simoncini Garamond
Designed by Leonard Telesca

PUBLISHER'S NOTE
This is a work of fiction. Names, characters, places, and incidents either are the products of the
author's imagination or are used fictitiously, and any resemblance to actual persons, living or dead,
business establishments, events, or locales is entirely coincidental.

For Rebecca and Sarah,
no matter what

ACKNOWLEDGMENTS

I first need to thank Kris Hults Whorton, a thoughtful, generous reader who guided me through every stage of this book with good humor and critical, useful words. Julie Roemer eagerly read my manuscript in its various forms and provided me with a resounding, emotional response that helped me enormously. Darien Hsu challenged me with gracious, critical readings and also whipped me into an editing formatting fervor, which hasn't worn off and for which I am grateful. Beth Moore, legal whiz and dear Stairmaster partner, gave me sound family-law advice and read three drafts with eagerness, joy, and encouragement in the truest sense of the words. I also thank Anita Feder-Chernila, Cristina Garcia, Marcia Goodman, Gail Offen-Brown, Jackie Persons, Kristen and Alan Obrinsky, Basudha Sengupta, Marissa Gomez, Mara McGrath and George Pugh, Maureen O'Leary, Meg Bowerman, Susan Browne, Leonore Wilson, Judy Myers, Joan Kresich, and Diablo Valley College. Connie Hughes and Michelle Smith always believed it would happen. Everyone at Pam Bernstein and Associates—Fiona Capuano, Shana Kelly, Donna Downing, and Pam Bernstein—was supportive, energetic, and critically dead-on. I don't think I could have asked for a better editor for a first novel than Carolyn Nichols—she taught me so much and gently guided the process from start to finish. Far more than all this, and just about everything, my special gratitude and love to Jesse, Julien, and Mitchell Inclán, Carole Jo Barksdale, and Bill Randall.

The Silence
Between Them

Of course, it wasn't a typical nursery. No one would expect any mother on Wildwood Drive to furnish such a room without multiple visits to I Bambini and Cradle in Arms, scooping up plush cotton and soft pastel wools and quilted bedding. But here, in this particular room, on the same sycamore-lined street, no one had festooned a bassinet with lace and ribbons or painted giant moons on the ceiling over a crib. There were no stacks of crisp bleached diapers or fuzzy sleepers, no fancy oak furniture, no fluffy stuffed bears or musical mobiles. But in the closet, empty now of Air Jordans, Doc Martens, and hairballs, Kate and her fifteen-year-old sister Tyler had made a crib out of a cardboard box, a camping pad they'd washed and cut to fit, sheets Kate had bought at the Goodwill for fifty cents, and an old baby blanket she'd found in the steel chest in the basement. The blanket, once bright pink but now faded to the color of melted peppermint ice cream, was one of the many things their mother had been unable to give or throw away. "They are my memories," Kate's mother Deirdre used to say, smiling, folding up a baby tie-dyed shirt, a tiny sundress, or a pair of overalls one of them had worn and worn until the fabric was like their own skin, all the happy times somehow grown too small and slipped off them and locked away in their grandfather's army trunk for later viewing.

Now, though, her mother dead, her father Davis at work or on most nights of the week at his girlfriend Hannah's, Kate sat quietly in her closet, the door closed, only a fractured round of light coming in at the handle. She breathed in, still tasting the dust in her nose and mouth, even though she had spent hours in here with a bucket and handfuls of rags. She had thought about using Pledge or lemon ammonia but then wondered if the liquids were poisonous, yellow watered flecks somehow worse to breathe than the dusty air itself. But despite the dust and the dark, Kate sat, the slats of the hardwood under her thighs, the smells of her recent childhood in her throat, the softness of her clothes touching her cheeks, forehead, hair.

Kate heard the front door close. Before she stood up, she lifted her shirt, almost as if to say good-bye, rubbing her hand over her belly, the soft stretched skin, the puckered belly button. She had learned how babies were made, but it would have been impossible for someone to really show her what pregnancy was like, unless they had been able to transport her to this body, leaving her old, thin one behind. Month after month, even though no one but she could have noticed at first, she saw her skin stretch and distend and then move, a miracle that even sex could not explain, her insides churning with feeling that no other human thing could compare with. Right now Kate could feel what she thought was the baby's rear, an arc of bone under her skin moving under her fingers. Other times, a triangle of elbow or knee would ripple across her abdomen as she felt the baby turning inside her. She imagined this baby, this body, outside her, in the world, and she pictured herself holding it in her arms, bending over the box and setting it down on the blankets, just like any mother.

"I'm back," said Tyler as she pushed into Kate's room. "What are you doing?"

Kate pulled down her shirt and lifted herself up. "Just thinking."

Tyler swung her hair out of her face and laughed. "In the closet? About what? About the crib?"

"Yeah, about the crib." Kate walked over to Tyler, taking the paper bag her sister held. "What did you get?"

Tyler smiled, pulling the bag away from Kate, then taking off her sweater. "You will never believe how cute some of this stuff is. Guess. Guess what I got."

"I don't want to guess."

"Come on! I was gone all morning. The least you could do is guess."

Kate sat down on her bed, her head and body heavy. "I don't want to. I'm hungry."

Tyler shook her head and closed her eyes, turning finally to Kate, her arms folded across her chest. "You know, I don't have to do this, but I am. Right? All I want you to do is look at what I found. Okay?"

Kate knew she should be grateful, but all she wanted to do was eat and sleep. Just standing up in the closet had tired her, and she didn't care about the baby stuff Tyler found. Kate felt her body go quiet, some faded curtain falling over her as it did each early afternoon. She was awake but still, as if the blood in her head were going to all the organs that really needed it: heart, liver, uterus, kidneys, placenta. Kate felt she could hear her heartbeat in every vein, in every cell; she could almost see blood throbbing at the backs of her eyeballs.

Tyler kept talking, and Kate knew that she should be more grateful because Tyler had given up her friends and cheerleading and even her homework for Kate and the baby. But something made her want to shove the bag off the bed and scream. She could yell, "The goddamn crib is in the fucking closet. Who cares about anything else? It's all wrong," but she didn't because she didn't want to believe the words herself. She couldn't bear it if Tyler slammed out of the room like she did when Kate told her about the baby in the first place. Now, so late in her pregnancy, Kate couldn't stand any more days of silence and confusion and fear, desperate to know someone was going to help her. She didn't want to be any more alone than she already was.

"Okay, fine. What did you get?"

"Look," said Tyler, pouring small plastic and fabric things on the bedspread. "This," she said, holding up a blue rubber bulb, "is a nose thing. For boogers, I think. For getting them out."

"Yuck," said Kate, holding the thing in her hand, squeezing it flat, and listening to the squeal of air as it expanded back to its original shape. "It's like a baster. Well . . . here, let me try on you."

Tyler pushed her away impatiently. "Don't you want to see everything? I mean, look at all this. Here. These are little booties. And these are little mittens. The lady says babies sometimes scratch themselves. And this is a clip to hold a pacifier to an outfit or something . . . They didn't have pacifiers. The lady said we've got to buy those new, like they can be dangerous and stuff. Anyway, she said that babies really shouldn't have pacifiers, but I had already bought it . . ."

As Kate listened to her sister, "What lady?" she said finally, interrupting Tyler, who was twirling a water-filled teething ring on her index finger.

"What do you mean?" Tyler turned toward Kate, her brown eyes the color of cracked amber marbles.

"You said, 'The lady said.' What lady? What lady said what?"

Tyler hid her face under her blond hair and began putting everything back in the bag. "Oh, the lady at Second Time Around . . . I'm going to put this all in the closet. Are you still hungry? I can make us some melted cheese sandwiches and milk shakes. Did the school call again?"

"Tyler, what lady?" said Kate, the pounding in her eyes stronger, the room pulsing with her body.

Tyler sat down on the bed, running her hand on Kate's arm. "It's fine. It's just that I went to the clinic on the way home. I'm just worried. Nobody knows what is going on here but us. You're so tired all the time. I think . . . I'm scared, Kate. I don't think I can do this."

Tyler leaned her head on Kate's shoulder, but Kate stood up suddenly, Tyler still at a right tilt on the bed. "You went to the Oak Creek Clinic? What did you say? Did you give them your name? What if they call, Tyler? What if Dad finds out?"

Tyler righted herself and stood up, her hands on her hips. "Well, so what? What's the big damn deal? So what if everyone finds out? It's not like this stuff never happens or anything. Like, no one has had a baby? It's not like you're the Virgin Mary or something."

"You just don't get it, do you?"

"No, I don't get it. I've never really gotten it. Why do we have to do it this way, Kate? You don't have to have the baby in Oak Creek or even Concord. We could run away to Point Jerusalem or even Briones and go to a hospital there when you go into labor. Dad wouldn't even know we'd left. We'd come back and everything would be normal. I mean, we could still hide the baby, but you'd both be fine. I'm scared to do it here. I don't want to do it here. I don't want to be all by myself, Kate." Tyler looked up at her sister.

"Can't you please tell me what else there is? Why we have to do it this way? I won't tell anybody even if it's"—Tyler breathed, then swallowed—"something awful. I swear."

Kate wanted to say, "Of course, I'll tell you. Oh, God, I want someone else to know," but she said, "I can't tell you, Tyler. I just can't."

"But why? Who would I tell? Why don't you trust me?" said Tyler, raising her arms in a sad question, then letting them fall slowly to her sides.

Kate started to say, "You *are* the only one I trust," but then said nothing, the air in her mouth useless, her vocal cords tense with coiled words. She didn't have anything left to give her sister, nothing that Tyler wanted, no reassurance, no secret plan, no ardent boyfriend waiting with a fast car, lots of cash, and excuses for everybody. She could not dredge up a happy ending. There was only each day of the pregnancy, the moments leading up to the birth, and then there was nothing but the hope that somehow, with a baby in her arms, everyone would forgive her.

Tyler waited for a word, and then sat down on the bed when Kate said nothing and lay down on the pillow, her hands over her eyes. Kate stood over her, remembering when Tyler was younger and they'd play house, Tyler always the baby even though they were only one and a half years apart, Kate the mom or the dad, but always the one who took care. Mostly, she was a good parent, tucking Tyler and sometimes their best girlfriends Alicia and Brittany into the play beds, making pretend stews in mismatched Tupperware from her mother's kitchen, reading stories even when she couldn't actually read, making up the story as she turned the incomprehensible pages. And later, when she had learned to read, and much later, after her mother had died, Kate would find books like *Heidi* or *The Secret Garden* to read to her sister before they fell asleep, lulling Tyler with the old, predictable happy endings.

Kate sat down, and held Tyler's ankle in her hand, fingers and thumb crossing over the thin bones as if searching for words from her sister's body, something that would comfort them both. "I'm sorry. You've done so much for me, Tyler. I probably don't deserve it. And I'm scared, too. But, I don't want anyone to know. I can't take the chance that some lady from the clinic won't think she's really helping out by calling Dad. Then he'll come racing home and surprise us. See me like this, or worse." Kate grimaced, imagining a birthing scene, blood everywhere, her screams, her father opening the bedroom door to a brand-new baby. And then there would be questions, and Kate didn't know where any of her answers would lead. She needed time. She needed time to think, and she needed the baby before the words would come that would make all of this better. "Listen. We just have to do this. We are going to read all the books. If something bad happens, we'll call 911. Really, at the first sign of trouble. But nothing will. I swear, nothing is going to happen."

Tyler looked up, her hair across her face. "But what about later? What's going to happen then? How long can we keep the baby here, Kate?"

Kate stood up and walked toward the closet, staring down at the crib. *Maybe the baby would never even sleep in here,* she thought. *Maybe they will find me out and take me to a home. Maybe they'll make me give it up.* The day she moved into the body of the baby's father, her body brilliant with new breath and sound and blood, Kate didn't think about this confusing day, staring at a closet crib, worried that a nosy clinic worker would lead a charge to their house, rousing the neighbors who would whisper, "That family is cursed. Nothing has been right since their mother died." Kate shook her head, wishing her mother were here to tell her what to do and whom to trust. But Deirdre wasn't there, and she never would be again, and Kate knew she had to hold her baby, hold it tight, keep it to her until there was the time she could say, "It's mine. The baby is mine." Just as her mother had held Tyler and her, every day, almost until the very last minute she was alive.

"I don't know," said Kate. "I . . . you really just need to trust me, okay? Somehow, it will all work out. I swear."

Later, in the kitchen, Kate and Tyler sat at the tile counter, sipping the chocolate milk shakes Tyler had made out of two pints of Häagen-Dazs vanilla and Hershey's syrup. Kate had eaten two cheese sandwiches, melted cheddar in stringy lines on her plate. Outside, the Anderson kids, Jamie and Jessica, walked past the open kitchen window on their way home from the elementary school two blocks away, turning onto their front path, kicking a soccer ball between them until finally, waving to kids across the street, they went inside to do homework or watch television. It was sunny for a change, this strange spring soggy as any January, the sun glinting against the green, oak-studded hills only for hours a week. But now a miracle of spring air, full of plum and acacia, moved into the kitchen, sunlight and breeze twirling dust motes and children's voices around the girls. Tyler followed the kids with her eyes, and Kate wondered what part of her life she was mourning for.

"Oh, that was good," said Kate, interrupting Tyler's silence, slurping loudly with her straw, making the sound their mother had always given them a raised left eyebrow for, whispering, "Stop it" in restaurants.

"Do you want another?" asked Tyler, jumping off the bar stool. "I love to make these." She stood on the other side of the counter, and Kate watched her sister, the pensive look of just seconds ago gone. Even though Kate knew it wasn't true, Tyler seemed to have already forgotten about their fight, the upcoming delivery, ready to jump into shake making and diaper buying. *I wish I were more like her,* she thought, knowing that parts of her mind were stuck in times she should have forgotten or pushed aside by now: her mother's illness, the hospital visits, the day her father met Hannah, the day a man first touched her and she wanted him to do it again and more. She wanted to be like Tyler, to switch on and off, forgive and go on, move into each day without dragging the past behind her like sin.

"Well?" said Tyler.

"No. I'm full. That was really good, though," said Kate, tipping the glass up to her mouth for the final milky drops.

"Okay, then. What else for today?"

"I'll do the dishes."

"No," said Tyler. "I mean for the baby."

"Oh. Okay. I got these books from the library. Dr. Brazelton, Dr. Spock . . ."

"Ha! The Vulcan. What does he know about babies?" said Tyler. "Live long and, hah, deliver!"

Kate stood up and carried her dishes to the sink. "Not *Mr.* Spock. Just get the books from my room. Under the bed in my book bag."

Tyler went for the books and Kate filled up the sink with hot soapy water, looking at the plaque her mother had nailed to the cabinet the year before she died: MY HOUSE IS CLEAN ENOUGH TO BE HEALTHY AND MESSY ENOUGH TO BE HAPPY. And certainly, their house had been cleaner then than it was now: the floor mopped once a week, her grandmother's silver polished before company arrived, the ceiling fans dusted, corners vacuumed of spiderwebs. Now, thought Kate, almost laughing, spiders lived long happy lives, their children born and setting up house in the same spot, clumps of wrapped dead insects dotting the ceilings, doorways, nooks. She thought of the haiku Mr. Edgar, her English teacher, had read earlier this year:

> *Don't worry, spiders,*
> *I keep house*
> *casually.*

But sometimes, when they knew their father would be home, she and Tyler spun through the house, widening the small clean path they had created for themselves in his absence, a narrow walkway from bedrooms, bathroom, and kitchen, the rest of the space filled with leggings, underwear, homework, glasses, Power Bar wrappers, Coke cans, and microwave popcorn bags.

"Here," said Tyler, her hair pulled back in a ponytail, her cheeks red. "God, it was dusty under there."

"We'd better clean today."

"Let's read first. Okay," she said, sitting down and opening the pages of *Baby and Childcare.* "Where do we start?"

They had read all about meconium, jaundice, and vitamin K shots and were working into umbilical cords and cradle cap when Kate and Tyler heard the rumble of the garage door opener. "Oh, shit," said Tyler. "Quick, get into bed. I'll say it was a short day, two-ten, and I came home early, and you were home sick with cramps. Go."

Kate ran into her bedroom, her right hand cupping her abdomen, her stomach gurgling with milk and cheese. She threw a blanket over the makeshift crib, hiding the bag of baby supplies and clothes, and then slammed the closet door and shoved shoes and books under her bed. Before she got into bed, she opened the window, letting in the early spring air and the already disappearing sunlight, as if sun and spring could change everything.

Under her covers, a copy of *The Great Gatsby* in her hands, Kate heard her father's voice, the clanking of dishes in the sink, the back screen door opening and closing. For a minute it sounded like home, the old sounds when their mother was alive, when everyone was always home, and the house was used and taken care of. With her father talking to Tyler, she could imagine, as she fell asleep, that her mother was in the next room, too, that she was still a part of the house, holding her father's shoulders and kissing him, drying the dishes that Tyler handed to her, coming into Kate's room and stroking her forehead, hugging her, rubbing the ball of Kate's stomach, talking through skin to her grandchild.

❧

When Davis opened the door of Kate's room, he almost walked right back out, turning his heels on the Berber carpet, escaping down the hall, through the kitchen, and back into the garage. Davis never knew exactly what would upset him, every single thing in the house a memory, not just her clothes and silver earrings, wedding and birthday photos in wood frames. Twice he had opened a drawer— one makeup, the other ski wear—and found a note, a question and statement no one, no doctor, certainly not Davis, had ever answered for her. *Why now?* Deirdre had written in black Sharpie pen. The other note was in ballpoint, written on the bottom of a lunch bag, stuffed between apricot blusher and cotton swabs. *Sanjay,* was all she wrote that time. Underlined. Davis didn't know what to do, stilled questions on his tongue. *How can I answer these?* he wondered. Why did she write this? What was this question? This neighbor's name? Should he walk outside, cross to the house left of his, ring the bell, and show his neighbor the scrawl, ask, "What the hell does this mean? Why did she leave your name behind?" But each time Davis held the notes in his hand, not knowing whether to return them to the drawer or crunch the paper in his hand, swiftly, and toss the note away. The words seemed so ugly, so sad, language with no voice, no song, no body behind them. So, Davis folded them back as they had been, imagining his wife's movements as he slipped paper between cosmetics and wool, his movements briefly bringing her back. If he could not answer her or even understand what she had meant, at least he felt her now, felt her hiding her fear and questions and wonder about the years of illness and hurt.

The last note Davis found in their room was tucked in a *Sunset Western Garden Book,* a page saved by a dirt-smudged shopping list. Davis had grabbed the fluttering paper but wanted to let it go as soon as he felt it. The paper was dry and cold, dirt like powder under his fingers. But instead of dropping it, he brought the list to his nose, breathed in beyond the pencil and dust, past the paper, hoping for a whiff of vanilla or musk. And why Davis finally slipped the paper back in its careful page—*Aptenia, Arabis, Aralia*—and closed the book, then the door, was that there was nothing left at all, just simple elements, carbon, wood pulp, soil. Nothing of his wife. Nothing of Deirdre. Just the paper reminder that she was once alive, in this room, writing down the words *topsoil, fish emulsion, lime, compost.*

Soon, Davis thought now, sighing, he would stay outside altogether, walk the perimeter of the lawn and patio, call into the house, and talk to his daughters from behind screens, curtains, and window blinds. Then there was just Wildwood Drive, his car, a few square blocks of lawns watered automatically and parks full of colored play structures and baseball diamonds, and then Highway 24 that led eventually to Oak Creek and Hannah's house. In the cool air of his Dodge Ram, he would be able to breathe again, imagine that his seventeen-year-old daughter did not look exactly like his dead wife. Of course, even before Deirdre found the lump in her breast, Davis had recognized the resemblance between her and Kate, watched his daughter's light brown hair turn darker, her thin girl body transform into adult flesh, breasts, butt, and thighs, her voice melt into Deirdre's same timbre, low and gentle. Sometimes, when he called home from Hannah's, Kate would answer, and he would start to talk to her as if she were Deirdre, his mouth desperate to form the exact questions he'd asked his wife: "How are the girls? How was work today? Should I pick up a bottle of wine?"

But now, Kate asleep, her cheek pushed up by her hand and her hair lying across her face, one strand wrapped under her nose, her body reminded him of Deirdre's, long and full. Davis wondered how it would feel to touch Deirdre one more time, just once, to rub the length of her body, feel her under his hands, the woman he had known for so long.

He swallowed and closed his eyes, pushing into the room, knocking gently on the open door.

"Kate? Kate?" He moved around the room, trying not to look at Kate in her bed, touching white dresser tops, plastic horse manes, wildly colored CDs, rubber bands, cotton balls. Davis remembered when Kate had been wild about the horses, her floor turned into stables and ranches and farms with building block and Lincoln Logs barns and fences, the stiff horses frozen in perpetual motion, Kate and Tyler making whinnying sounds, and then giving the horses voices, roles—mother, father, child. Now, Davis thought, they were both too old for playing house, and he realized he didn't know what they did in here anymore. He knew he didn't know anything about the music Kate or Tyler liked, picking up a CD and reading the group names: Smash Mouth and Matchbox Twenty. Davis didn't know or really even think about what Kate read at night or for school. He bent down to pick up the book on the floor by her bed, running a finger along the edge of the large triangle fold she'd made for a bookmark.

"Kate?" Davis said again, looking at her shoes, big white Keds with clunky heels. He imagined her walking like Frankenstein, lurching through the halls at Las Palomas High School with all the other Frankensteins in their matching shoes. He thought about how he and Deirdre wore polyester shirts and pants when they were at U.C. Berkeley, one pair of hers so tight she had to lie down to zip them up. He remembered the coke spoon necklaces, the disco music at the frat houses on Saturday nights, and then suddenly the punk rock and peg-leg jeans, and the nights in his Cutlass, Deirdre's naked body gleaming in the streetlight. How he had a condom, then—no! he didn't, but how they had sex anyway, right there, in his car, because his bedroom at the frat house was always occupied by his roommate Neil and his girlfriend Sammy or Jane, and Deirdre lived at home with her mother in Monte Veda, and there was nowhere else to do it. And then there was Kate.

Davis sighed and put down Kate's book, right where it had originally fallen and softly sat at the edge of the bed. Kate slept through the lurch, just moving the hair off her face, her eyes still closed. "Kate?" he whispered, looking at the posters of strange-haired music and movie stars, the books on the shelves—Hemingway, Steele, Shakespeare, Crichton, Woolf. He looked toward the closet, wondered what she was wearing these days besides the impossible Keds. For so long Kate's and Tyler's clothes were huge, shirts down to their knees, pants the entire family could fit into. Now, as he drove past the high school, the girls looked like the girls of the early seventies, hip huggers and neon orange polyester, thin horizontal stiffed T-shirts, shades of green he thought only belonged in Florida. He bent down toward her face and looked at his daughter, this almost Deirdre.

"Kate?"

He stood up as Kate moaned, stretched, opened her eyes. "Dad? Is that you?"

Davis looked down at his daughter. What a question, he thought. What a terrible question.

᠂᠊᠂

."You're awake?" her father said, taking a step back. "How are you feeling? Cramps again?"

Kate tugged the blanket away from her body, yanking a pillow in front of her stomach. "Where've you been?"

"What do you mean?" said Davis. "You mean today?"

Kate raised her eyebrows and bit her lower lip "No. I mean lately."

Davis walked to the window. "I've been at Hannah's, Kate. You know that."

Kate watched her father, his body long and firm from the Nautilus machine he used, now set up in Hannah's garage, or so Kate imagined. "You haven't been home at night for a while," she said, just as Davis asked, "What are you planning for dinner?"

"What? Dinner?" asked Kate, sitting up and leaning against her headboard. "I guess that's my job now, huh? I plan dinners. And everything."

Davis turned from her words as if his back could deflect the sound itself. "Well. I just wondered . . . What I meant to say was, I brought over a Domino's pizza. Hannah and I just picked it up. I thought we could all grab a slice together." Davis moved from the window, keeping his eyes just about Kate's head as he spun toward her. She thought about standing up and pulling off the blankets, just so he could see her and her round hard stomach, her full round breasts. She wondered if he would make her plan dinner then. What kind of dinner would he ask her to make if he could see what had been going on inside her for months? What would he do? Kate wondered. She thought about doing and saying it all, making her father listen to the whole long story, but she wasn't sure if her legs would help her do that.

Davis looked into her eyes briefly, then said, "I guess you're feeling better now. Let's have some pizza."

Soon, Kate knew, Davis would be gone, Hannah in the truck cab beside him, speeding down Highway 24 toward her boys and her house. And there she and Tyler would be, with some leftover pizza, the cheese slightly hard, lukewarm, and stuck to the box like glue.

❧

Tyler washed dishes, her hands sliding in the too-big rubber gloves, hair unmoussed by steam and dangling in front of her face. She knew she was holding a glass, then a spoon, now a plate, but she was really thinking about what was going on in Kate's bedroom while simultaneously ignoring Hannah, her father's girlfriend, who sat at the red tile counter drinking a diet Coke.

"So, how is school going?" asked Hannah, swirling the Coke in her glass.

Tyler shrugged, refusing to turn around and meet Hannah's eye, secretly flipping her off under the soapy water. Tyler wished she could do it to Hannah's face. She wished she could spit and tell Hannah what she was really worried about was if Kate had closed the closet, had hidden the bags and blankets. And what if she hadn't, a bootie or bib somehow on the floor, her father asking, really asking what it was. "Kate," Tyler imagined him saying, his voice deep and thoughtful. "What on earth is this for? Come here! Stand up. Oh, my God. Are you pregnant? Who did it? He did! We need to go talk to him and then take you immediately to the doctor for a checkup."

Tyler sighed and swirled her gloved hands in the water as if to erase her anger. She wanted Hannah to shut up so she could listen for noises in Kate's bedroom.

"So, has Kate been feeling sick for a while?" asked Hannah as she finally stood up, bringing her empty glass to the sink.

"Nah. Just cramps," said Tyler.

"Seems like she gets those bad. She needs to go to the doctor."

Tyler turned to Hannah, holding a wet fork in her hand. Hannah's thin pale lips were in a worried smile, her blue eyes wide and intense. *She's looking for the secrets in this house,* Tyler thought. *Now that Hannah has Dad, she wants everything we have.*

Tyler almost wanted to laugh, to say, "Yeah. I think a doctor would be a great idea about now!" She wanted to tell Hannah about the Goodwill and the used-clothing stores and the Oak Creek free clinic on the west side of town, where Tyler picked up pamphlets about premature babies, breast-feeding, stages of labor, and home-birthing alternatives. She thought about leaning her head on this woman's shoulder for one minute, until she remembered that it was because of Hannah and Hannah's relationship to her father that he wasn't here anymore. It was because of her two small children, Max and Sam, and how they needed stability and security now that their own father had left them, that Tyler and Kate had lost theirs. Tyler narrowed her eyes and wondered how this woman could be more important than she was. Or than Kate was.

"It's, like, no big deal. She has been to the doctor's. She has always gotten really bad cramps. The doctor said it would probably all change after she had babies," Tyler said, rinsing off the plate.

"Well, she has a ways to go before that," said Hannah, walking to the screen door that led to the backyard. "What's up with that lemon tree?"

Tyler shrugged to herself, but then took off the rubber gloves and walked over to the window. The last time she had looked outside, she was sure the tree looked like it always had, skinny, but with glossy green leaves and perfect lemons, but now what leaves were on the tree were sallow, small green fruit on the ground.

"Wow," said Tyler. "Must be all the rain."

"Yeah, it's El Niño. At least we have the weather to blame for everything. It's probably something with the soil," said Hannah, opening the door and walking outside.

Tyler watched Hannah walk to the tree, grab it around the trunk, and shake most of the leaves to the ground with one gentle sway, fruit dropping at her feet like marbles.

⁂

Kate, Tyler, Davis, and Hannah sat around the dining room table, chewing through thick cheese. Kate wondered if her father was even swallowing, this fake dinner just for show, the real dinner later, at Hannah's, with her two boys. Davis saw Kate looking at him, and he smiled, chewing in exaggerated motion to show he couldn't talk.

"This is sooo good," said Tyler, pulling the crust from her mouth, strings of cheese like long teeth coming from her lips.

"It's really the best pizza around," said Hannah. "You'd never believe it. But look how thick the crust is."

Kate smirked, wondering how thick crust could be a substitute for anything. "Yeah. It's great. I think I've eaten five thousand pizzas in the last two years."

Davis swallowed and looked up. For a second Kate saw that look, the look he had the night her mother died, the first time he came to check on them after spending the night at Hannah's, the look he had whenever Kate said, "Dad?"

"Maybe we can do a big dinner here this weekend," said Davis, putting down his slice. "Maybe we can do an early barbecue or something. Or what about spaghetti?"

Kate felt Tyler's foot under the table, nudging, nudging her. Kate looked down at her lap, knowing that he couldn't come back now—it was too late. "I've got a big test next week . . . and I'm going over to Erin's to study on Saturday night. And I think we might study all Sunday afternoon."

"Yeah, Dad," said Tyler. "I've got stuff, too. Like a big test. And there might be a sleepover at Megan Riley's."

Davis looked at Hannah, who shrugged. "It's not a good weekend, Davis. The boys have so much going on."

"Okay. But don't complain about pizza then," said Davis, smiling, relieved that he asked, relieved that he didn't have to do anything.

"Look at the time," said Hannah after seconds of silence, picking up her plate and bringing it to the sink still full of soapy water. "We've got to go get the boys."

Kate looked at Tyler, who was wagging her head side to side, mouthing, "The boys, the boys."

"Well, we're off. I'll call tomorrow. Don't study too hard," said Davis. "And where is this sleepover?"

Tyler looked down. "Oh, I think Megan Riley's. It might be canceled. I'll call to let you know."

"All right, you two. Have a good night," said Davis, putting a hand on each, catching a shoulder, a back, and Kate watched her father leave, close the door, move into the life he made without them.

The first time Davis had called home from Hannah's, Max and Sam playing cars under his feet, the phone felt like a cold, broken bone in his hand. He couldn't stop touching it, pressing it, searching for the fracture, trying to understand this pain between him and his girls.

"You're staying? At her house?" said Kate. "Why?"

"Kate!" said Davis. "That's a ridiculous question."

"Is it?" Kate answered, her anger sluicing through the receiver. "Oh, I'm sorry. I just thought it was normal for dads to come home at night. I just thought that maybe we'd have dinner here, you know?"

Davis listened to her breath, imagining the kitchen, Kate leaning against the counter, her hair tucked behind her ears just like Deirdre's. He imagined the emptiness, space he could never fill himself. "I'll be home tomorrow. It's just one night, Kate. It's not like I'm never coming home."

Kate snorted, half covering the phone with her hand. "Dad's not coming home. He's staying at Hannah's," she called to Tyler. "Yeah, really."

"Kate! Kate! Listen, just heat something up. There's plenty of casseroles in the freezer. All the directions are taped on."

"Fine," said Kate, her voice still, the echo of sound so Deirdre, so his wife, that Davis wanted to hang up.

"I'll call you from work tomorrow. We'll do something. I promise. Really."

"Fine," said Kate.

"Do you believe me?" said Davis. "Don't you believe me?" Davis stopped talking, but he wanted to say, "But haven't I been there all along? Haven't I always been there? Can't I have this one night away? Can't I just stay here in peace for one single night?" But he didn't, swallowing air and sadness, kicking a Matchbox car from under his feet.

"I believe you," said Kate, flatly. "Sure."

"Okay. Then I'll see you tomorrow. After work."

"Fine," said Kate. "Sure."

"I promise," said Davis.

"I believe you, Dad," said Kate.

"Okay. Bye," said Davis.

"I love you, Dad," said Kate, but Davis was hanging up, and he couldn't bear to pick the phone up again and redial, even though he wished he could tell Kate that he loved her and Tyler more than anything he had left. But the phone was cold and ugly, his hand still full of his tight grip of it, and then Max and Sam were on him, and Davis forgot.

Now, sitting in his truck cab with Hannah, the garage door open behind him, he wondered if he should put the car in park and go back inside.

"What is it?" asked Hannah. "Why are you stopping?"

"I don't know," said Davis, shrugging and looking toward the door to the kitchen. "Something."

"What?"

"They just seemed upset. There's something going on."

"You mean Kate's cramps?" asked Hannah. "Tyler says she gets those all the time. I think she needs to see a gynecologist. If you want me to, I'll take her sometime next week."

"Maybe that's it," said Davis. "I really think it's something else. I think . . . I think I shouldn't be gone so much."

Hannah sighed. "Those girls are fine. It's not like you aren't here, Davis. We come by all the time. And after all, Kate's almost eighteen."

Davis looked over at Hannah, her blond hair brushed smoothly across her head, her eyes blue, and full of light, and sincere. "But don't you think they need me here, now, at home?"

Hannah put her hand on his thigh. "We've talked about this so many times. You know what it will mean to us, Davis. I thought you made a decision."

"I know. I have."

"I've said it before, Davis. I can't have Sam and Max uprooted right now. I can't bring them over here at night. They've been through too much with the divorce. They need stability. They need their home. It wouldn't be right. And anyway, Kate and Tyler are teenagers. They are just about grown-up, Davis. Sam and Max can't take care of themselves like the girls can."

Hannah moved her hand to his shoulder. "And you know the girls wouldn't want my boys around, all the noise and toys and crying. They are really better off here, I think. They can have their own space and quiet for studying, and you are still close by. It's not like you've abandoned them."

As Hannah talked, Davis relaxed, thinking of how, inside, everything really was okay, Kate sleeping off her cramps, Tyler taking care of the kitchen. After all, hadn't he given them money, talked about school, brought them a pizza, answered questions? He was here, at his house, taking care of things, and Hannah needed him, too. He could be at both places this way, share himself, make everyone happy. Nothing was wrong, anyway. He'd just seen them both, both his girls, women almost, and nothing was wrong at all. Kate was old enough to take care of Tyler; she could take care of them both.

"I guess you're right," said Davis, looking up and breathing in the smell of her perfume, Calyx, an orange/melon smell, a smell of Florida and exotic drinks and spring.

"I think so. I really mean it," said Hannah, looking at her watch. "Oh, we better get the boys out of day care. It's almost six."

Davis looked in his rearview mirror. "Okay. Let's go. You're right. I don't know what was bothering me anyway," said Davis, taking his foot off the gas, and then pushing his garage door remote, the metal curling closed, his house safe for the night as he drove away to pick up Hannah's boys.

{a}

After Kate had finally told her she was pregnant, Tyler realized she already knew something, not just because of Kate's rushes to the bathroom, the too-clean smell of 409 disinfectant hovering over the vomity air in the morning bathroom, the long, dead naps Kate took in the afternoon. Tyler would pass by her bedroom and push her foot through the door just enough to see Kate asleep on her bed, her mouth open, her closed eyes still. And there were the quickly closed doors, the angry "Why don't you ever knock?" and the "This is my room" when Tyler walked in unexpectedly, Kate pulling down her sweater over her stomach. What Tyler really noticed, though, was what wasn't said. They sat flopped on the couch, watching MTV at night, Tyler looking anxiously at her sister, knowing there was an invisible conversation over their heads. She wanted to reach up and grab the words, stuff them in her mouth and ears and know what was going on and why Kate wouldn't share when she always had before.

Finally, Kate called her to the dining room one evening after their father had left with Hannah for the night, empty Kentucky Fried Chicken boxes still on the table.

"What?" said Tyler, irritable, a mud mask on her face, cotton balls between her toenails. "I'm in the middle here, you know?"

"I have to tell you something," said Kate, insistent, her brown eyes hot and dark and full of tears.

"Okay," said Tyler, thinking, *I don't like how she looks. I don't know if I want to know. There are things I don't want to hear. Things about death and sickness. Things about Dad.* "Okay. What? What is it?"

Kate swallowed, crossing her arms. "Well . . ."

"What, Kate! Jeez."

As Kate looked at her, Tyler wished she could shape the words that would come from her sister's mouth, something like, "You know, Dad just called and he's coming home, for good;" or, "Aunt Gwen's coming for a visit;" or even better but impossible, "We were wrong about Mom. She's still alive." Tyler couldn't imagine how anything anyone said could be good, though, and she realized how long she had been waiting for something wonderful and clean and happy.

Tyler sighed. "Are you going to tell me or not?"

"I'm pregnant."

"What? What did you say, Kate?"

"I'm pregnant."

Tyler felt the mud mask pulling away from her face. She opened her mouth wide and silent, cracking the dried clay. She sat down, careful still with her toes. "I knew something was going on. Who? Whose is it?"

Kate shook her head. "I can't. I promised. Well, it would be really bad if anyone knew. Seriously. He doesn't even know."

Tyler picked nervously at the mask, dried chunks dropping on the table. "Why? I mean, don't you think you should tell him? Is it someone from school? That Teddy guy? What's going to happen? What are you going to do?"

"I don't really know. I'm three months pregnant, so I'm not going to have an abortion. I already decided that," she said, laying her palms flat on the table, then slowly curling her fingers into fists. "So, I just have to have it. But he can't know, and Dad can't know."

Tyler felt the urge to rub the mask off her face and lie on the table. She wanted to crawl to Kate and hit her and hug her. Why was it always like this? Tyler wondered, holding her ribs tight with her arms. Why did these things just fall on her even though she knew there was nothing she could do about them, no way she could change anything? Tyler remembered when her mom had said, "Honey, I need to talk to you," and then, at that second, her mother's sad smile before her, Tyler knew there was something terribly wrong that would change everything and that there was not one damn thing she could do to stop it.

And later, as her mother's hair fell out from the chemo and her bones seemed to almost pop up through her skin, Tyler could only watch, bring her cool washcloths and close the bedroom curtains, and hope despite everything that her mother would be all right. And now, here it was again, but it was Kate asking her to watch something, something that could only end badly, like it always did. Tyler looked down at her arms and saw goose bumps, her almost invisible blond hairs on end, and felt a sick convoluted feeling clanking up her spine into her neck and head. She now knew some of what Kate had been hiding from her, but Tyler knew that Kate was keeping things from her still, the most important things, the things that mattered.

"Why can't you tell Dad, at least? I mean, what is going to happen to us? Where will you have it? How will we take care of it after it's born?" said Tyler.

"We'll get lots of books. There's this movie I saw on PBS. We can do it."

"Oh, sure. Right! You don't learn to deliver a baby from TV! People go to medical school to do that. God!" said Tyler, standing up and slapping her hand against the wall.

"Think of all the people in the world, Tyler, who don't have babies in a hospital," said Kate quietly.

"But we're here! We don't live in some hut on a river's edge. You aren't going back to the fields the next minute to pick corn." Tyler glared at her. "I don't want any part of this."

"You are the only one I can trust, Tyler. I don't want anyone to know. Not Mom's friends, not Rachael. Not Aunt Gwen. They'd tell Dad."

"For God's sake, why can't you tell Dad?" Tyler asked angrily. "He's our father."

"Because. He'll make me . . . Well, I don't know what he'll do."

Tyler sat back in her chair. "Kate? What are you thinking? How can we *do* this? You don't just *do* a baby. There's all this stuff, medical things, tests. I'm not going to do anything. We're going to have to call Dad."

Kate sat up straight and shook her head. "We can't. I can't. I'm not going to have an abortion, and I can't go to a doctor. It has to be like this. And listen, where has he been all this time anyway? He would never understand."

"You have got to be crazy! Are you serious?" Tyler pushed back her chair, stood up, and walked into the kitchen. It seemed strange to her that this room could look the same, the dim lights hitting the browns and creams and reds of the tile, the refrigerator humming its same hum, the ordinary outside sounds of the neighbor boys and passing cars sliding through the open window. She turned to face the dining room, shouting, "Just tell me how we can do it? People *die* in childbirth, Kate. Sometimes the baby gets stuck and they have to pull it out and everyone dies. I read about it last year in freshman health. I read about this woman who pushed so hard all her insides came out, her uterus and stuff. They had to surgically replace it all or she would have died! What then?"

Tyler wiped her eyes, brown mud tears on her hand, and walked back into the dining room. Kate was still, straight, and pale, her top lip firmly on her lower. Tyler shivered because this was how Kate looked the time she and her friends Erin and Brittany decided to sneak out of Kate's window at night and meet up with a group of friends at Oak Creek's public pool to skinny-dip under the moon—just like she did the time when she was fifteen and decided to sneak the BMW out of the garage and drive to the Monte Veda movie theater for a special twelve o'clock showing of *The Rocky Horror Picture Show*. This was how Kate looked the first night their dad didn't come home, calling from Hannah's in Oak Creek instead, asking her to heat up some crusty old casserole for dinner, promising fun on the weekend, a picnic at Tilden Park, a movie that never materialized.

"Are you thinking of anyone but yourself, Kate? This is so selfish. What about me and Dad?" said Tyler, holding on tight to the back of a chair.

Kate looked at her, her eyes dark and sharp. "I'm thinking of the baby. I'm thinking of all of us."

"Really," said Tyler, sitting down tiredly, her face dripping brown and wet. She ripped the cotton angrily from between her toenails. "That's kind of hard to believe by the way you're talking. You're not the only one who has to go through it all. God! This is so crazy."

Kate took a breath, deep and long, and nodded. "I guess it seems so now. But just trust me. I know what I'm doing."

For the first few nights after Kate told her about the baby, Tyler refused to look at or talk to her sister, slamming out the door in the morning without breakfast, and then coming home later after cheerleading practice, sitting silently at the kitchen counter eating Top Ramen or a bowl of SpaghettiOs. At first Kate tried to talk, rubbing her hand across Tyler's rigid back, saying, "Come on, Tyler. You can't stay silent forever."

But Tyler shrugged off her sister's hand and thought she actually might be able to keep all her words inside, the ones that said, "You are going to die bloody on the floor. The baby is going to die. It can never work. And what about me? I can't take this. So, I'm going to call Rachael and Meera and Aunt Gwen. I'm going to call Dad."

When her father came home early one evening, Tyler felt the bowl of words on her tongue, heavy like clay, and she watched Kate's face, pale and red around her nostrils, as she talked to their father in a high, bright voice, one she saved for adults she wanted to please or placate—teachers, neighbors, friends' parents.

"Oh, Tyler's been doing great at cheerleading. You should see her, Dad. Better than ever. Right, Tyler?"

Tyler felt as weighty as the truths inside her, her shoulder and head like monstrous boulders, her legs stone heavy against the slats of the chair. "Yeah, great."

Davis smiled at her absently, pulled out his wallet, and counted some cash, talking about groceries and phone bills, not looking, Tyler realized, at either of them. How long would it be, she wondered, before he just disappeared altogether? Tyler stared at him while he piled twenties on the counter, wondering if he already knew about the baby and was just pretending. How could he not notice? How could he not see that something was wrong? Why wasn't he looking?

Tyler gritted her teeth silently, imagining something worse than just a pregnancy, imagining that her father could have slipped into Kate's room one night, one sad lonely night in this house, and forced himself on her. Tyler knew about these things, read books with her friends in the bathroom, tales of sick and twisted love, abuse, and all things gone bad in the world. She watched Jerry Springer and Jenny Jones, listening to mothers and fathers and sisters and brothers all tell how someone did it to them, how bad it was, how much it hurt, story after story about betrayal and despair and anger.

Tyler watched her father and wondered if he was still the same father, the father who placed Kate and her on the sturdy oak limb at Heather Farms Park, saying, "Hold on, girls. Let me take the picture. Smile!" Was he the father who drove them to swim practice at Meadow Lane Pool and watched her practice cheerleading moves in eighth grade? When had he disappeared, exactly? What was the precise time he slipped into some other shape, and how much had he changed? Was it when her mother died? Or when she was sick? Or later yet, not until he met Hannah and traded them in for her? How much more could things shift and morph until absolutely nothing was recognizable? All Tyler could say for certain was that he had been leaving them, slowly, trying to stay connected by visits like these, and it didn't make sense that he would want either of them in that other, deeper, sicker way. It didn't make sense, but nothing did anymore. Nothing at all.

Davis felt Tyler's eyes on him and looked up at her. "Well. I'm glad you're doing so well at school and cheerleading. I suppose if you weren't, the principal would be calling me, huh? Keep it up." Silent, Tyler watched him walk out of the kitchen and into the garage. Kate made sounds of conversation, starting off in the same bright tone she had used with their father, but Tyler slid off the counter and went to her room, closing and locking the door. *I don't need them,* she thought. *I don't need either of them anymore.*

Tyler stayed in her room all evening and into the night, studying for her graded frog dissection the next day, all parts needing to be identified and diagrammed while Mr. Musante watched, his eyes on them and his watch. When the house seemed silent and still, she slipped out for some Froot Loops, but as she walked past the living room, she found Kate asleep on the couch, her mouth open, her hand by a book. Tyler walked over and looked at it, picking it up and reading the title, *What You Should Know Now You're Pregnant.* She sat down on the floor, her back against the couch, and opened the book in the middle. Tyler saw pictures of stomachs rounded like

sand dunes, breasts with darkened nipples, a color photo of a fetus
in the womb, all red and blue veins and black bulging eyes, almost
like the frog she would take in her hand tomorrow and slice open,
looking for heart and stomach.

Tyler looked up at Kate, sleeping still, her breaths low and
smooth, and she imagined the tiny thing living inside her sister, a tad-
pole, a fish, a doll, growing, its bean-sized heart pumping blood, its
stumpy arms and legs fluttering in the amniotic pool. *God, that is so
nasty,* she thought, but then, as Tyler stared at the pictures and read
captions, she realized that she should not be thinking about a frog of
some kind, but a baby, a human, her niece or nephew. Here she was,
in her living room, sitting next to two people, not just one but two,
and they were both her family, and they were both alive, needing her.

The next morning, Tyler walked into the kitchen, banging a bowl
to the counter, pouring Froot Loops into a rainbow pile. Kate was already eating, the morning paper in front of her. "Okay," said Tyler.
"This is crazy, but okay. Fine. I'll help. How are we going to do it?"

Even now, the days long and hard because of all the lying and the
fear of exposure, even after she had to quit cheerleading and ignore
her friends, giving up on dances and basketball games and the hope
of running for class president, none of it mattered as much, and Tyler
mostly remembered her sister's face, the sudden tears and sharp wail;
she remembered Kate's body as Tyler held her, hugging those bones
she has long known, whispering, "Yes. I mean it. I'll do it. I'll help
till the end."

When Kate began to show, her stomach rounded, her butt wide
under her loose sweatshirts, Tyler would take the 950 bus downtown to
shop for things on the list she and Kate wrote out after consulting books.
They had first read the baby books their mother had kept for both of
them, running their fingers over the lists of *First Gifts, First Visitors.*

"Your list is longer," said Tyler.

"Well, they didn't need as much by the time you came. They already had the main stuff," said Kate.

Tyler shrugged, flipping through the pages in her baby book, the
pages only partially filled out. "That's always what happens to the
youngest. No one cares anymore."

"That's not true," said Kate.

"Doesn't matter now anyway. . . . What is a trundle bundle? A stretchy?"

"She wrote that down here, too. And lots of undershirts. But, I don't know."

Tyler imagined her mother writing out these words and names: *Rose Tranby, zip quilt; Zel Rice, receiving blanket; Peggy Hillman, infant seat.* Tyler didn't remember any of these people, her mother's college and Oakland friends, women from before they moved to Monte Veda, names from infrequent calls and yearly Christmas cards and old memories, her mother talking on the phone, asking about children and schools and new jobs. *Where,* thought Tyler, *are these women now? They need to tell us what to buy and what to do when the baby is born and how to put baby arms through tiny sleeves.*

Tyler didn't know who else she would call, knowing that the secret was too big for the neighbors, imagining Meera Chaturvedi's raised eyebrows and stern mouth. And even though she craved her Aunt Gwen's lap and arms and quiet words, there was no way Kate would let Tyler call or write, knowing that Gwen would tell their father.

There was no one left. Her mother's friends had called for months after she died. Rachael Norton came by in the mornings with croissants and juice, knocking as their father poured dry cereal into bowls, his eyes bleary and unconcerned about what anyone ate.

"Hey, Davis," Rachael would say. "I got a few extra at the bakery and thought you and the girls might like some." In the days and years before her mother's death, Rachael wouldn't have even knocked, sliding into the house like family, sitting sometimes at the counter with her mother when Tyler and Kate came down for breakfast, both drinking coffee and talking about children, though Rachael's were older and one already had his driver's license. In the afternoons, especially when it was warm, the two women would be out on the deck, the wind blowing eucalyptus leaves on the lawn, her mother laughing and drinking a glass of white wine. Sometimes, they all went to Rachael and Bob's house for dinner, Kate and Tyler trying not to act stupid around the Norton boys. The sixteen-year-old, Peter, would grunt hello as they walked into the family room, not bothering to stop playing his video game, killing every evil soldier that turned a corner. Steve, the eighteen-year-old with recently cleared-up skin and a sexy, mysterious silence, would look at the two girls and say, "I'm outta here," hopping in his Jeep and driving away before his mother even knew he had gone. Now, Tyler secretly hoped that he was the baby's father because then Rachael would be related and she could take care of all of them.

For a few weeks her father took the rolls or doughnuts and the hurried words of consolation and advice, but soon he'd answer the knocks slowly, listless in his responses to Rachael's questions, so obviously wanting her to be gone. One day Rachael pulled up to Tyler and Kate as they walked to school, stopping her Land Rover and unrolling the window.

"Girls," she said. "How are you? How are things going? I haven't heard anything from your father."

"Oh, things are okay, I guess," Kate said, looking at the slick silver rims, the large black tires of Rachael's car. "You know."

Rachael nodded. "Yeah. I know. Listen, if you need anything, anything at all, call me. I mean it. You don't have to tell your dad you're calling me. Just do it."

They nodded, and Rachael left them with a look they never talked about, but it was one they both recognized, one their mother might have given two other unfortunate, almost tragic girls—girls who were sad and alone and needing help but couldn't ask for it. Girls who didn't know how.

Rachael had tried and so had the women from the cancer support group—skinny women in hats and perfect wigs—but at every call, Tyler heard her father say, "Everything's fine. . . . Oh, no. We don't need anything. The girls are doing okay." Even when her mother's college friend Nancy showed up on the doorstep one evening with a plate of cookies and a potted ivy, her father was clear and cold, the same message given to everyone. "Really, we're doing all right." Tyler had wanted to reach out from behind his back as he stood at the wide front door, hold out her hand, but she couldn't, couldn't let them know that her father was wrong and that they were really not all right at all.

Finally, the phone stopped ringing, hamburger casseroles with flowered notes tucked under them stopped magically appearing on

ep. Tyler imagined the old life she once knew—car pools
...cks and cocktail parties where she and Kate sat at the top
of t.. stairs listening to the laughter and clinking glass—going on
without them, someone else, some other woman moving into Tyler
mother's place.

Tyler closed her scrapbook. "This isn't any help, Kate. This is old.
Things have changed since we were born. There are new baby things
now. There are just things we don't know about," she said.

So Tyler went downtown or, better yet, traveled on BART to Oak
Creek where she knew she'd find better bargains. At first she stood
behind racks of Carter's sleepers at Roxie's Baby or the bins at the
Goodwill, listening to other shoppers, mothers and sisters, aunts and
grandmothers. "Oh, look at this, Sue! What a cute shirt. See how it
buttons at the neck. . . . This doesn't have snaps for diaper
changes. . . . Do you have fire-retardant sleepwear? . . . What about
those new bottle nipples?" Tyler watched and listened, wandering
through aisles of flowered sheets, blankets, and stuffed animals and
studying her list, marking changes and additions. Finally, Tyler
pulled sheets and baby washcloths from the bins, slid teething rings
and diapers from the shelves and brought them to cash registers, trying to smile and ignore the mild questions. "Are you going to a
shower?" . . . "Do you want an extra receipt so the mother can return this if it doesn't work for her?"

But eventually, Tyler would almost rush to salesladies in the baby
departments, telling them about her much older sister and her surprise first pregnancy, and they gushed as she picked out T-shirts and
undershirts. Tyler sometimes made up elaborate scenarios, moving
Kate to another country where she was unable to find this one thing
that this particular store carried, a baby food grinder, a special bottle
nipple. And as she left the stores, the women behind the counters—
fully versed on her CIA operative or writer or engineer sister—often
called after her, "Come back and let me know what she had—boy or
girl." Tyler always nodded and waved, holding her package to her
chest, smiling, imagining she was riding home on BART in order to
wrap up a gift for her exotic sister who lived in London or Paris or
Rome.

But Tyler also knew that if Kate had her way, it would be Tyler who held the wet, bloody baby first, who cut the umbilical cord, who made sure nobody died.

§●

Kate expected the cramping. Since seventh grade she'd had knockdown, face-paling menstrual cramps. Her mother once had to pick her up from her third-period French class, where Kate had curled up on a back table, unable to move, her teacher Mademoiselle Barbour wringing her hands, whispering, *"Mon Dieu"* while the class worked on dittos.

Kate wasn't afraid of blood either, bleeding so heavily during her periods that one morning she realized blood had seeped through her sheets, mattress pad, and even the mattress. "Goodness," her mother had said after changing the bed and calling the gynecologist. "How can you still be alive?"

So when, one evening, she started to feel rhythmic pulsing over her abdomen, culminating in a sharp but short pull somewhere deep in her womb, she thought, no biggie. Anyway, these were probably just Braxton-Hicks contractions, she believed, those fake ones that are kind of a rehearsal. Kate didn't even bother to tell Tyler right away. They sat watching game shows for an hour, and Kate just counted, slightly grimacing for a second, then continuing to watch the adults spinning wheels and buying vowels.

There was a part of her that wanted to call her dad, tell him to come get her, now. She wished she were little again, and she could run to him, press against his legs, and hold her hands up. "I want uppie. Uppie!" she used to say, and he would pick her up under her arms and throw her up over his head, catching her as she fell. But Kate couldn't do that now. There was too much wrong this time, so much that he might just shake his head and slam the door behind him as he left, leaving this time for good.

"What should we watch now?" asked Tyler when the shows were over. "What? What's wrong?"

Kate wanted to say that nothing was wrong; she wanted to tell Tyler to flip the channel to *Say What?* on MTV. Maybe, she thought, if she could hide these contractions, which were clearly part of the real show, it wouldn't happen yet or now or at all. Kate breathed in, pulling the beginnings of tears into her lungs with the air. She wasn't ready; it was too soon. And she knew, as Tyler had said over and over, that something, everything, could go very, very wrong.

"Oh," Kate said finally, looking into Tyler's eyes. "I guess I'm in labor. Just a little bit. It just started."

Tyler jumped up, her nerves jangling so much Kate could almost see her shake. "It's time? Damn, you were supposed to tell me as soon as it started. What should we do? . . . Okay, I've got to time this. Let me go get the stopwatch."

Kate lay down on the couch, feeling her abdomen go hard, breathing in briefly like the books and videos described, gently, smoothly, trying not to tense. She tried to picture what was happening inside her body, or what she prayed was happening: her cervix opening and thinning, a little each time; maybe, she thought, a lot, so this would be over fast, and she would have a baby. What Kate couldn't bear to think about were all the ways labor and delivery could go wrong, the baby in the wrong position, its head trapped on her cervix's lip, the umbilical cord wound around its body like a deadly necklace.

Tyler ran back into the family room, the stopwatch hanging from a red cord around her neck. "I think we should go into the room, right? Or stay here. But what if it happens fast? What about the mess?"

"Okay," said Kate. "Let's go into my room." Tyler took her hand and they went into Kate's room. Tyler had pulled the mattress on the floor and covered it with a plastic and then a regular sheet, just like the home-birthing book had suggested. Kate noticed the scissors, twine, latex gloves, and towels on the dresser.

"Here, let me get the pillows. Or do you want to walk around for a while? The books said that, too. Remember? What do you think?"

"Maybe," said Kate. "I don't know."

"Did your water break?"

"I don't think so. No dramatic gush, or anything."

"Jeez, Kate, you're supposed to keep track," said Tyler. "That's a really important thing for us to know."

"Well, I don't know, Tyler. It's just the pains now. What do you want me to say?" said Kate, sitting on the chair, her face tightening as she felt another contraction.

Tyler stared at her, her hands rubbing the stopwatch cord, her face pale. "I don't know. I guess . . . I guess I can't believe it's happening. I mean, do we really have to do this? Seriously, can't we just go to the hospital? I'll drive. I can do it. It's just a few minutes away."

Kate put her face in her hands, her back shaking. "No," she said, the word muffled in her palms.

Tyler started walking back and forth in the small room, her shoes slipping on the carpet. "I said I'd do this but, Kate, this is real. This is it. I mean, if something goes wrong, it's my fault, goddamn it. It will have been me who did it wrong, who hurt you or the baby, who killed both of you somehow. It'll be my fault."

Kate breathed in, her abdomen tight. Tyler stood silent in the room, her face wet, her hands in fists. *What do I say to my sister?* thought Kate. *What can I tell her that will make her stay here, in this room, with me, and not bolt out the door?* Kate remembered how she felt when her father came home after her mother's first operation. His face was full of something she had never seen before, something that she had never wanted to know. That night, at that moment, as she sat on the living room couch with Tyler, she felt her legs want to pull her away and outside. If she moved fast enough, Kate thought, the truth could never find her.

"Please. Please stay with me. You know how to do it. We watched the movies. Oh, please," said Kate, holding her belly. "Don't leave me."

Tyler stopped and stared at Kate, her hands unclenching. "I won't. I won't leave you, I promise. I'm just scared."

"I'm scared, too. I can't do this . . ." said Kate, stopping her words as her body tightened and the contraction struck like a knife.

"What? What is it?" asked Tyler.

"It just hurts. It really hurts. Could you read to me? Read something to me," said Kate, her face pale and wet.

"Okay, okay. Here," said Tyler, running her hands through her hair as she went to the bookcase. "What about this, *The Secret Garden?* Do you remember that?"

Kate nodded. "Oh, please, Tyler. Read the end. The best part. Start with the chapter called 'Magic.' "

Kate groaned, her hair wet with sweat, her face red from push-ing. Blood poured out of her vagina, and Tyler prayed it was just from the placenta, and cupped her fingers around the curved top of the baby's head. This birth—seeming to go on forever and full of pain and messy fluids—was not turning out at all like the one they had both watched sixteen times in *The Miracle of Birth* on the VCR. On the video, the woman grimaced and breathed hard, but there were no screams and no blood gushing down her legs. The father whispered words of encouragement, soft sounds, really, only his tat-tooed arm flexing as the baby crowned and emerged. The baby cried exactly how Tyler expected babies to cry when they were born. A high-pitched *wah, wah, wah,* and then the baby was lulled into silence by soft lights and warm blankets. It looked, they both thought, so easy.

In fact, the whole video birth seemed to take the course of twenty or so minutes, the first forty minutes being egg meets sperm, the re-mainder of the hour-long show ending with the birth and then the happy parents beaming over the wrapped and wide-eyed baby, no pain, no tears.

No, it was nothing like this real version, Kate exhausted from pushing, after each grimacing, strained push falling to the bed, ex-hausted, sore, sweat wetting her hair and face. When Tyler allowed herself to rise up into the panic that threatened to spill out of her and flood the room, she could feel each nerve in her body like electricity, her hands shaking as she pushed Kate's legs open to try to see what she didn't know how to look for. Even though she and Kate had studied charts that diagrammed the stages of labor and the thinning and stretching of a cervix, she didn't really know how to check to see how far Kate was dilated; she didn't know when to tell Kate to breathe or when to push and when to wait. Sometimes, she slid her ear against Kate's pulsing, warm stomach and tried to listen for a sound, imagining she could hear the baby's heartbeat. Finally, she yanked a glove on her hand and reached inside her sister, gasping when she felt the baby's head hanging hot and slick in Kate's vagina. Then she knew she could say, "Push" and know she was right, and now Kate was pushing, the baby inching downward, Kate stretched thin and red and the baby's dark hair exposed to the light.

"Okay. Okay. Push. Push, Kate," Tyler said, feeling the baby's slick head slide under her fingers.

"Oh, God! Shit!" said Kate. "It hurts. Take it out. Take it out!"

"Slow down. It's coming out. Oh, there," said Tyler. "One more. Really."

Kate pushed again, and Tyler saw the baby's eyes, then nose. She knew that only the rest of the head and the shoulders were left—the shoulders were as hard as the head—and then the rest was easy. The books said easy. "Okay. Really, Kate. It's almost over," she said, carefully sucking out some clear liquid with the blue thing she had bought earlier that month, knowing from Dr. Spock that it was called an aspirator. Kate closed her eyes, and Tyler imagined suddenly that her sister would never open them again, like her mother at Mt. Diablo Hospital that last day when they all went to say good-bye. Tyler remembered almost holding her breath, imagining that in one second, no, the next, maybe the next, her mother would shake back to life, open her eyes, defy the doctors who told them, "She is basically dead. There's nothing going on in her brain." As she stood at the bed, the mattress at her belly, Tyler imagined that if she concentrated hard enough, her mother's hand would lift off the cold sheet and touch her. The machines would twitch to life, squiggles bounding off the screen, showing the doctors that there was life in her mother's brain and blood. Then her mother would get well, come home, the house sliding back into order as if nothing had ever happened.

Kate panted, trying not to scream, pulling a pillow to her mouth as some huge force seemed to bear down in her body. "Oh, my God, Tyler. Get it out, pull it out."

"Okay. Okay. Just push. Just push another time." Tyler lifted her sister's legs higher, held them steady, fumbling for and then finding the aspirator, suctioning the baby's nose again so it could breathe its first clean breath on earth.

"What's happening?" panted Kate. "Don't forget the mouth."

"I can't yet. I got the nose. Push again, slowly," said Tyler, and Kate pushed. Tyler saw the baby's mouth, the little lips ready to cry, and she stuck in the aspirator, slurping up more liquid, and then did it again, and again. The third time the baby began to cry. "Okay. Now we've got to do the shoulders. It's all over after we get these."

"Should I push? Oh, I've got to push," said Kate, her voice, uneven with pain, turning to a scream as Tyler found a small round shoulder, held it, and steadied the baby out of the birth canal, her hand like a chair as the baby poured into her arms, the wet, white cord with and behind her.

"Oh, my God," said Tyler, looking at the little girl baby in her lap, her eyes open and searching. "Oh, my God," said Tyler, breathing out in surprise and relief.

"What? What's wrong? Is something wrong?" said Kate, unable to lift her head from the mattress.

Tyler swallowed back a lump of tears and sadness and joy, her throat tight with new feelings and words she could not say. Here she was, finally. The baby they'd been waiting for. "No," she said, putting an arm on her sister's thigh. "She's fine. Oh, Kate, it's a girl. A perfect little girl. Oh, my God," Tyler said, taking in a deep breath and reaching behind her for a blanket and wrapping up the baby despite the cord still attached to her, carefully covering her small reddish feet. "I'll clean her later. Here," she said, placing the tight warm bundle on Kate's stomach.

Tyler watched her sister struggle to lift her head, and Tyler walked to the bed and put some pillows under Kate's neck. Together they touched the baby as Kate held her in the crook of her arm.

"She's amazing. Oh, Tyler. Oh, Tyler," said Kate, relaxing, her eyes wet and exhausted. "I can't believe you did it. Thank you. Thank you."

Tyler slumped to the carpet and looked around the room she wished she'd been able to run away from last night, wanting to leave Kate's withheld screams and tense body. But here it all was, almost finished except for cutting the cord and getting the placenta out. Here was this most perfect baby, more beautiful than all the other ones they'd seen in the books and movies, soft and dusky. Tyler shook her head, almost disbelieving that it had worked out, that she had done it, that she had held a baby's head in her hand and pulled it out in one smooth piece. *How is anyone ever born?* thought Tyler, suddenly falling back to her own skin, bones, and muscles, feeling her sharp, tense shoulders, her empty stomach, her full bladder.

Tyler watched Kate stroke the baby's head, then fumble at her breast, holding her nipple for the baby, who actually took it.

Tyler got back on her knees and leaned over the bed. "Is she?" said Tyler. "Is she doing it?"

"She is. She can suck." The baby made swift clicking sounds, and then seemed to find what she was looking for, closing her eyes and pulling hard on Kate's nipple. "I'm so tired, Tyler," said Kate. Kate sighed and laid her head back. Tyler wanted to lie down, too, to rest, to sleep, to have someone comfort and hold her and tell her she had done good, done right. She wanted her father to come in and be amazed at the live little girl she'd managed to pull out of Kate. She imagined the hugs and the congratulations; she imagined her bed, clean sheets, the comforter cleaned and fluffy. She imagined it all, but then she looked at her exhausted sister and the baby who sucked at Kate's swollen breast and realized it was up to her. Everything was up to her.

❧

After it was over, Kate couldn't exactly remember the pain, but at the time she was certain she would never, ever forget it, the edges of it hard like a dozen knives, and long like knotted ropes tied to her body pulled ever so slowly. There were the minutes, seconds sometimes, between the contractions, when she would open her eyes, see the ceiling, look at Tyler's face, know that it was almost over. But then the pain came again, first the knives, then the ropes, and it went on so long Kate felt herself slip inside her own body, the dark, wet purpleness of her slick insides, slide next to the baby, feel the giant round muscles of her uterus, cervix, and vagina squeeze and pull them both to someplace new. In pain and with her eyes closed, Kate wrapped her mind around the wet, white body of her baby, felt its shiny black head, ran her fingers across its tight closed eyes, telling it, telling her, *Time to come out, now, please, time to come home.*

❧

Later, days later, it seemed, but really only twenty-six hours, Kate and her brand-new baby girl were asleep. It was only nine in the morning, but it felt like twelve midnight, the ache under her eyes like two pulsing moons. Tyler had taken all the bloody sheets to the washer, pouring in half a jug of Clorox as the swirling hot water turned pink, then red, and now she was in the backyard burying the placenta that just an hour before had spilled from her sister's body.

As she dug in the soft dirt by the dead lemon tree, she eyed the plastic garbage bag she had slid the placenta in. To her the fleshy thing looked like a bumpy liver, full of knobby, viny white veins, the umbilical cord hanging from it like a shriveled dying thing. Tyler thought it was awful to have to deliver a placenta after delivering a perfect baby girl.

Kate had opened her eyes after passing out, it seemed to Tyler, for a few minutes, the baby still sucking at her breast. Kate looked for Tyler, sweaty and tired, and she'd said, "You've got to cut the cord."

Tyler stared at the connection from baby to bloody mess. "What if. . . ? I mean, doesn't the baby need that blood? We read about that, cord blood, you know? I've got to tip it in."

Kate dropped her head to the mattress, holding the baby to her stomach. "Just do it, Tyler. Just cut it. Take the scissors and cut it. Then use the twine."

Tyler began to shake, her hands at her sides. She wanted to say, "Do it yourself. Haven't I done enough just about now? Here . . . here are the scissors," but Tyler knew this was her job, even though she dreaded one more thing, picking up the sterilized scissors and cutting that damn ugly sausage-thick vein. But Kate was still breathing, the baby was breathing. There was blood, but it wasn't killing anyone. "Okay, okay," Tyler whispered, holding the sticky cord in her palm and scissoring through it, feeling each vein, all the flesh.

And now she had to look at it again. Tyler picked up the bag and then poured it into the hole, the blob falling on the wet dirt, reminding her of a poison jellyfish on the beach. One book had said that in some Native American tribes they ate this thing for good luck; other people buried it like she was doing, honoring it for serving the baby well. One book said that hippies in the seventies used to fry it up like steak—onions and mushrooms and everything—and eat it. Tyler, almost shivering as she covered it up with shovelfuls of dirt, thought that she would have flushed it down the toilet if she could have gotten away with it. But she didn't want to call Roto-Rooter, telling the guy, "Well, everything was fine until we flushed the placenta down the toilet."

Before she spilled the dirt over the flesh, she looked around her yard and up, toward the Andersons', then the Chaturvedis', and then the Chans' behind her. It was her same neighborhood, the sounds of the morning commuters turning out onto Wildwood Drive and heading west to Oakland or San Francisco, KFOG or KCBS alerting them to pile-ups on the 880 or 680 freeways. People stopped at Starbucks quickly for their lattes, rushing back to their cars for long drives, her father in his truck, a double decaf latte in the cup holder. No one was looking out a back bedroom or family room window at her, pointing, the phone dialed to 911. No one. Even the kids were already at school or preschool, teachers telling them to open books and take out pencils or crayons. At Las Palomas High, her gym teacher, Ms. Winters, was probably well into warm-ups—knee bends, cherrypickers, jumping jacks. Everything was going along as if it were just another day in Monte Veda, no one knowing that, in this house, nothing would ever be the same. No one knew, Tyler thought, that her life and Kate's life and maybe the baby's were probably ruined, forever. She didn't know exactly what would happen, but she knew some adults would eventually take care of this mess, no matter what Kate thought. Adults would find out and know that neither of them should do this, alone, without parents, without a father or mother or friend. It was wrong, and Tyler felt herself holding her breath somewhere deep in her lungs, holding it for the time when she could breathe and know that it was not just she who knew the truth held in these four walls.

In the kitchen, Tyler washed her hands, breathing in steam and the smell of Clorox. She could barely keep her eyes open, having slept only minutes during the night, falling asleep between Kate's contractions, waking up to hold her hand, then begging Kate to breathe slowly, smoothly. Tyler looked at her hands, dirt and blood, her long metallic fingernails cut short to the red quick earlier in the morning because she was scared she'd scratch the baby as she tried to pull it out. She turned off the water and walked into the laundry room, pulling out a clean dry shirt and pair of shorts from the dryer, changing right there, stuffing her wet and stained jeans and top in the hamper. She hoped she'd remember to do another load of wash as soon as the sheets were done so she could get rid of all the evidence.

Kate and the baby were still asleep. Tyler sat down on the floor and watched them, the baby a dark little thing with perfect, cinnamon-colored skin and a tuft of black hair. Her little girl lips were pursed in a perfect flower. *Just a day ago, hours ago, she wasn't with us,* Tyler thought, *but now, here she is, a whole new person.* Tyler leaned next to the baby, breathing in her cleaned skin, and wondered, *Who are you?*

⁂

Kate had nursed the baby twice, falling asleep with the tiny girl after each feeding, and now she lay awake in bed, the three o'clock afternoon gray showing through the window. She shifted to her side, feeling an ache in the tendons in her neck and in her belly from pushing, wincing from what she imagined was a gaping open hole leading to her uterus. Kate didn't know how anything could pull back into place after that.

Tyler was asleep on the floor, a pillow under her head, a baby blanket on her shoulders. After Tyler had washed all the linens and towels, fed Kate, and changed the baby, she had knelt and then curled up on the floor, her breaths steady and deep in a second.

Kate stroked the baby's head, feeling the thin black hair between her fingers, stroking the soft cheeks, wondering if she would relax now. The baby was here. No one had died; Tyler hadn't had to call 911. All the terrible problems Kate had read about—preeclampsia, ruptured uterus, breach birth—hadn't happened. Kate's labor had followed all the predicted stages; the baby was positioned just right; the placenta followed the baby with one swift contraction; Kate wasn't bleeding to death; the baby was drinking the yellow colostrum that was coming from her breasts. And throughout it all, Tyler had taken care of everything, talking low and sweet the whole time.

Kate looked at her sleeping sister, wondering how Tyler's hands had known how to hold a baby's head, then shoulders, and finally body. How had Tyler learned to do something no one—not Kate, not their father, not their mother—had taught her?

Now there are just so many different things to worry about, thought Kate, bending her head down to the baby's forehead, breathing in and kissing the soft skin. She wondered if Tyler had noticed the baby's skin and hair, so much darker than Kate's, so much like the baby's father's. But there hadn't been time for Tyler to think, everything so rushed after the delivery, everything needing to be picked up and cleaned, just in case their father came home. *But later,* thought Kate, *later she's going to ask . . . she's going to want to know.*

Kate shifted the baby in her arms, and thought of her father, probably still at work, sitting at a computer terminal, reading numbers and watching the stock market climb. What would he do if he came home and found her? By the time he came by, though, probably tomorrow afternoon, she would be in the closet with the baby, hiding, listening to Tyler lie about her whereabouts.

"Oh, she's at the library. Erin took her. She's got this big test in English coming up. . . . She's fine. . . . Of course. I'll tell her what you said."

Kate held her baby tight, knowing that she understood her father less now, thinking, *He has let us loose like old party balloons, and we are soaring and shrinking over land and sea. How could he just watch us float away?*

Kate began to turn her mind to the baby's father. She held the tiny body to her own, and remembered him saying, "What would you say if I asked if I could kiss you here?" Kate hadn't said anything, but let him pull her hand to his lips and press on the upturned flesh of her palm. He'd closed his eyes, breathing in, she imagined, something of her smell: perfume, summer sweat, chlorine from the pool. He'd asked her again, kissing this time the crook of her elbow, and then again, this time her rounded shoulder. Kate closed her eyes and breathed in the memory, the thrill of her body as his lips traveled it, some special blood seeming to rise to her skin, making it an alive thing, not just her protection from the world. And later, his hands did what his lips did before them, and she felt something slipping out of her—fear, worry, embarrassment—and something new take its place. Joy, maybe. Or hope. Or recognition of something she re-membered or knew about but had long ago forgotten.

Kate opened her eyes wide, stopping herself, trying to catch her thoughts before they turned into the dreams of late last summer. But even as she pressed against the memory, she heard him say, "So lovely. You are so lovely." Kate didn't want to need to pretend that it would ever be different from what it was now, but sometimes she couldn't help it, the old lie of true love aching in her chest like a sad animal. She turned her head to her baby, their baby, and knew that the baby was all that was left—she was their best thing, even if he would never, ever know about it. Because if he found out, she would lose the baby and all she had left of him and the summer when her body turned into something Kate had only imagined. Now, she knew, she had to concentrate. It was simply enough, she thought, to get strong, feed the baby, somehow try to go on with her life, try to go on with the rest of all their lives.

                    ❧

While she was in labor, Kate let herself think about the baby's name, even though she wondered if that was bad luck, deciding too soon that everything would be okay and that there would be a baby to name and talk to. As her body stretched and pulled, she thought: Cody, Marshall, Tucker, Julien, Mitchell, Stephan; Amelia, Daphne, Sofia, Rose, Jayna, Michela. Over and over, she rolled those names as her body rolled with muscle waves. Kate wondered if your name made you something you weren't supposed to be; for instance, if you were plain and square, would a name like Sofia make you beautiful, willowy, and graceful? If you were weak and scrawny, would Tucker make you strong and brave? What name, then, would give her baby the best chance of being perfect; what name would keep it safe?

And then, between contractions, Kate knew what she needed to give her baby: all the goodness that a name could bring. "Tyler," she had whispered, her sister sitting up against the wall almost asleep.

"What? What is it?" said Tyler, opening her eyes wide and mov-ing toward Kate. "Is it another?"

"No. No. Listen, if it's a girl, I know what I want to name her."

"What?"

"Deirdre. I want to name her Deirdre."

❦

Until they were married and had moved into their own studio apartment on Bancroft Avenue—Deirdre's mother and Davis's father waving from the Oak Creek courthouse, his older sister Gwen holding the small sunflower bouquet—it didn't matter where Davis and Deirdre were; it was about bringing Deirdre's body to his own. While watching *Ordinary People* or *Raging Bull* at the Elmwood Theater or sitting at the Chez Panisse Café over a dish of fettuccine with tomatoes, he held her hands, stroked her knees, wished he could press his head against her breasts, pulling away at the fabric until there was just her skin.

Now, sometimes in the shower, Davis would remember their first apartment, the small stall shower, his hands curving around Deirdre's rings, smoothing aside soap as he gathered her flesh into soft, so soft handfuls. But the water would wake him from this dream, and he'd find the Finesse shampoo in his eyes, and he'd shut off the water just to stop his memory from going on. But he could never really stop the pictures, the scenes of their life, one after the other springing to his mind again and again and again because their life was full. Before he knew it, they had Kate, graduated, had Tyler, and then they were working, buying cars, toys, moving toward this suburban life as if that were what they had been training for all these years. When Deirdre's mother died of breast cancer, they inherited the house—the house Deirdre grew up in, the perfect place to raise children, buttressed against the Berkeley hills, protected from crime and violence by landscape and wealth, the green valley that held Monte Veda, Lafayette, Oak Creek, sliding green and wooded for miles up to the base of Mt. Diablo, the devil mountain.

"Do you really want to move back there?" Davis asked her, leaning against the wall of their rented Oakland house. "Won't you miss it here?"

Deirdre looked at him, her head cocked, and he knew she was thinking he was crazy. While they were close to everything, San Francisco and his job at York and Prescott Brokerage, theaters, restaurants, and people, so many different people, he knew she was also remembering the three times their car was broken into and the day the neighbor kids mangled the garage door trying to get into the house.

"No. I won't miss it. I want to go home," she said. And as soon as the will was settled, Deirdre and Davis and their two small girls moved to Monte Veda, slipped into a life that seemed as charmed as the town itself. At night, he heard bats and crickets in the swirl of bay and oak leaves. Davis began to breathe. He began to believe that it really would be all right.

When his own father died, leaving them alone except for Davis's sister Gwen and her family, leaving them suddenly official adults, suddenly with additional inherited money, Davis realized that childhood, school, college, marriage, and death had pushed them to this very certain life, the lawns, the neighbors, the light, warm summer days and then nights under deck lights and stars.

Davis remembered one of the last summer barbecues when Deirdre had been well, the cancer gone, briefly, her breast and body put back together with a saline-filled bag and stitches. The next-door neighbors to the left, the Chaturvedis, were over, spooning spicy food next to the grilled chicken, laughing at Davis's jokes, ignoring Deirdre's thinness and small, white arms. Next door, Jill and Tom Anderson were barbecuing, too, Tom sticking his head over the fence, asking, "Hey, man, any more mesquite?" as Jill chided him about letting their own burn out. Davis could hear the Chan kids taking an evening swim at the house directly behind theirs, water amplified like music in the warm still air. Laughter from all around him moved across the yards like waves.

For a moment, Davis had stopped talking and listened, breathing in new spices and familiar sounds. Tyler and Kate played with the Chaturvedis' two toddling boys on the lawn, throwing soft colored balls just to watch their laughing, diapered runs. Meera Chaturvedi's voice was round in his ear, clipped but soft, excited as she and Deirdre talked of fall bulbs, daffodils, freesia, and allium. Meera's husband Sanjay watched the women, something contented in his eyes, and then he looked at Davis with a smile that brought them all together, four adults, on this patch of ground that was theirs, this neighborhood worked into their lifestyles and needs, this particular sky hung, it seemed, just for them.

Davis didn't know when it all had stopped working. When Deirdre got sick? Or even before then, Davis leaving for his then new job at York and Prescott earlier and coming home later, missing out on school recitals and Girl Scout ceremonies, his body almost an apparition at dinnertime, present but vaporous?

"Davis," said Deirdre, bringing him a plate of food and sitting by him at the counter. "What were you doing so late?"

Davis had turned to her as he took the plate from her hands, thinking he might see recrimination, or a sarcastic smile, or serious eyes looking for a detailed explanation. But that's not what he saw. Not at all.

"I think I might have to fly to New York. It's the CompuLink account. The Human Resources people . . ." He went on, but he saw Deirdre was smiling, not listening. She didn't care. She really didn't care that he wasn't home all the time, and he could hardly chew as he thought about what that meant.

"I'm sorry," he said. "I'll try not to be so late."

Deirdre touched his shoulder, pressed down, her bones against his skin, muscle, and flesh. "We're fine, Davis. Everything's fine. Don't worry." And with that touch Davis thought she was telling him he didn't have to feel guilty, and he didn't have to worry. Because Deirdre was home even if he wasn't. She was magic. She was home when he was far away, and he could think of her and remember her there like a stable center around which he could swing.

❦

"I have nothing to wear," said Kate, throwing down her jeans on the twisted pile of pants and skirts at her feet. "I can't wear these, Tyler. I can't wear anything. I'm too damn fat."

Tyler was in the bathroom. "What? What did you say?"

"Oh, never mind. I'll find something," said Kate, knowing that she had to find something eventually, even if it did yank at her crotch or pull across her breasts. When she was pregnant, Kate didn't mind not wearing her favorite clothes, almost forgetting about her short skirts and flared pants hanging in the closet. But now, she thought, clothes spilling from her drawers in waves, she wondered what she had become, what strange body she was living in.

Tyler walked into the room, looking to Kate like something perfect someone might want to grab from a tree. "Jeez, where did you get that top? It looks good."

"Well, like, yesterday, when I went to Oak Creek to get diapers, I found this at Target. Looks good, huh?"

Kate looked at her sister, her round curved body so unlike Kate's usually long lanky one. Ever since she had turned twelve and puberty struck, Tyler had looked just like a little woman. "Coke bottle," her mother would say, admiring Tyler at a swim meet or gymnastics tournament. "Tyler has a classic figure."

And in this bright pink top, the polyester bands fitting her like second skin, Tyler looked like Kate knew she would never look: Tyler's breasts round and contained in her bra, her butt and thighs slinging from the valley of her waist like smooth beige foothills. Now, Kate's breasts were the size of cantaloupes, all blue veins and sore red nipples, her butt, it seemed to her, flat and sad in her baggy jeans, her stomach a crosshatch of reddish stretch marks. The only thing Kate had ever had were legs, and now she wasn't even sure they were any good, especially hidden under loose pants and long shirts.

"Yeah. It looks good," said Kate. "What am I going to wear so I don't look so bad?"

Tyler walked over to Kate's closet, peeking into the crib at the baby. "She went to sleep pretty fast."

Kate sat down on the bed. "Yeah. What am I going to wear?"

"Okay. What about these? . . . And this?" said Tyler, handing Kate a pair of big black jeans and a long-sleeved T-shirt. "This won't show anything if you leak. And these will button and feel loose. And you know, black's the color if you are bleeding."

Kate took the clothes. "I'm glad we found those breast pads."

Tyler laughed. "I think they're like maxipads for boobs."

Tyler sat down by the crib as Kate got dressed. "So," she said, pulling up Deirdre's blanket, running her finger over the little hands curled up by the baby's head. "How are we going to do this today?"

Kate looked at her sister, wanting suddenly to weep. "Well . . . I guess we both have to go. But there is only about one hour that we'll be gone. I'll go to English, you go to English. Then we'll come home. Will that work?"

"But what if she cries? Or gets sick? One of us has to stay home," said Tyler.

"It'll only be an hour. Or a little more. We've got to take our tests or someone will find out for sure."

"But we're going to have to do this a lot. Finals will be coming up," said Tyler. "I don't like it. It makes me nervous. I'll stay home."

Kate shook her head. "You've got a test. You've got to go. You've missed too much school already. Do you want them to call Dad? They've already been calling for me."

"I don't care if they call Dad! Who gives a shit about that? What about the baby, Kate? What's more important here? This is like so wrong." Tyler scowled at Kate, putting her hands on her hips. "You're acting crazy."

Kate stood over her sister, watching Tyler watch baby Deirdre. Kate knew that Tyler was right, but so was she. What could she do? If they left Deirdre alone, even though asleep, she could die. She could choke and turn blue and strangle in her own spit-up. The thought stopped Kate's breath, but she forced herself to think on. She knew they could both go to jail. And then their father would know, and Deirdre's father, too. They would all know. They would all know her failure. But, chances were, she thought, Deirdre would sleep, even longer than the time they would be in class. Every morning she slept for three, sometimes four hours, hours when Kate fell on her bed and slept, too. So she and Tyler would get home and everything would be fine. They would take their tests and pass their classes, and no one would call their father or the authorities and no one would ever find out what she had done. No one would take Deirdre from her.

"Just trust me, Tyler. We have to do it this way," said Kate, putting a hand on Tyler's shoulder.

"Shit," said Tyler, shrugging off her sister's hand and standing up. "Okay. Fine. But if anything happens to her, I'll never forgive you. It'll be your fault. Not mine."

Kate watched Tyler walk out of the room and she knew her sister was right. It would be her fault. And no one would ever forgive her.

The girls didn't speak in the closed air of the BMW as they drove down Moraga Way toward the high school. It was raining again, like it seemed to every day, the eucalyptus and pine trees heavy with water and spring growth. The taillights of the cars in front of her flashed and blared in constant warning. Kate drove carefully. Nothing could happen to them because they were the only ones who knew about Deirdre. They had to be careful. They had to come home, alive. Tyler put her backpack on the floor and turned to Kate. "Okay. Let's just keep to a schedule. One class, then home. No talking, to Erin or anyone."

Kate nodded, relieved. "Okay."

Tyler was quiet for a second, then said, "Why can't we tell Erin? Why can't we trust someone to help us when we have to go to school?"

Kate shook her head. She couldn't tell Tyler what Erin, her best friend, had known eleven, ten, nine months ago, about the baby's father, how she had described his face, his looks, his words to her friend. Without giving names or being too specific, she had told Erin what had happened and when; and then Kate wouldn't know how to tell Erin what she hadn't told her, about the months of pregnancy and fear. Erin, Kate knew, once she came to the house and saw the baby, would be smart enough to know who the father was. And Kate knew with a story that good, Erin would have trouble keeping it to herself. She thought about all the lies she had told Erin: she had told Erin she was bloated, had mono; that her new boyfriend had dumped her; that her father was thinking of home schooling. Kate thought about all the lies she had told everyone. But she hadn't had a choice.

And she knew she couldn't reassure Tyler or even herself. But, she thought, Deirdre was fed, and changed, and comfortable, and warm. Kate sighed. "We just have to do it, okay?"

"Okay. But let's remember the schedule. Let's make sure we get home on time, okay?"

"Okay," said Kate, turning right into Las Palomas High's parking lot. "No talking."

*   *   *

Kate sat in the front row of Mr. Edgar's fifth-period English class thinking: Rose of Sharon, Hester Prynne, Daisy Buchanan; Rose of Sharon, Hester Prynne, Daisy Buchanan. The names spun in her head like a sea chanty, and as she sat, her pencil in her hand like a spear, she wanted an idea more than anything, wanted to write a thesis that brought these three characters together brilliantly, but all she had were the names and the clock and an image of Deirdre—alternatively choking and sleeping, fitful and quiet—none of which, she knew, would help her.

Mr. Edgar sat in front of the class. He was too young for Kate to think of him as a mister, but that is what they all called him except behind his back.

"What a prick," Erin had said the night after he'd assigned *Macbeth* and an interpretive essay. "This isn't Berkeley or Harvard or something. Shit."

At the time Kate was focused on terms like *placenta previa* and *toxoplasmosis;* she hadn't really felt much about the assignment and, in fact, hadn't even done it. She'd just nodded at her friend's words and pulled her shirt down over her stomach nervously.

Just two days ago, Mr. Edgar had asked her to stay after class. "I'm worried about your work," he said. "I wonder what you've been doing lately. I did call your house, but I got your sister, or someone. What's going on?"

Kate sat there like a toad, her body lumpy, her swollen breasts secretly dripping under her long-sleeved Nike shirt. She wondered how she could say, "Well, I've been creating new life in my bedroom. I was in labor for twenty-six hours, and my sister almost had a nervous breakdown." But Kate just stared at him, tugging on her shirt and pants, anxious that her maxipad was leaking, that her bra was wet, that at home, Tyler was waiting impatiently for her turn to go to school, that Deirdre was hungry, crying, her mouth opening like some desperate baby bird.

"I haven't been feeling too good," she said. "I'm going to be here for the test, though. I've read all the books."

Mr. Edgar coughed and rustled essays on his desk, finally pushing his chair back on its two back legs, leaning comfortably. "Why hasn't anyone been calling the school when you are gone? I left about three messages for your dad. I think a couple of other teachers did, too."

"My dad works nights, mostly. He is really busy. He sleeps during the day, so the answering machine is on. I know he's gotten all the messages, but it is really hard for him to keep up with everything in the house. . . ."

"I'm sure, I'm sure. I didn't mean to imply—well, I know about your mother . . . of course, it is hard. Yes. Well. I'm glad you will be here for the test. Bring extra pencils and paper."

"I will. Bye, Mr. Edgar," said Kate, spinning off the wood seat and leaving the classroom. Kate held the doorknob as the door closed, trying not to make a sound.

After English, Kate turned her locker combination, the edges under her index finger and thumb. Left to twenty? Right to sixteen? She couldn't remember, realizing she hadn't been at her locker in weeks, usually flinging all her books into her bag and then into the BMW. Finally, leaning her forehead on the cool, sticky metal, she remembered, twenty, sixteen, five. Kate stared into the steel emptiness, pulling out an old lunch bag and putting away *The Scarlet Letter, The Grapes of Wrath,* and *The Great Gatsby,* knowing as much as she wanted to about those books and the sad women, not caring anymore what grade she got in Mr. Edgar's class. *God,* she thought, banging her locker shut and walking down the hall toward the parking lot. *I probably flunked the test. And Mr. Edgar probably knows,* Kate thought as she passed talking groups of kids. She lowered her eyes, nervously holding her sweater against her chest. Did all the teachers know there was something wrong with her family? Were she and Tyler as obviously messed up as those kids who wore black, ripped T-shirts and pierced every piece of soft flesh? Or the kids who wore tie-dye and sailed into class on wafts of weed? Or those silent, geeky ones who hid out during lunch in the library, accessing pornographic Web sites on the computers or playing with yo-yos in the stacks? But who was she fooling? Kate thought. Those kids weren't in as much trouble as she was, all their pain on the outside for everyone to see, hurt written in tattoos and dyed hair and Marilyn Manson posters. Something must show, and Kate imagined her teachers in the faculty dining room, shaking their heads over sad sandwiches and thermoses of coffee, saying, "Oh, those Phillips kids. Well, something is definitely wrong there. We need to do something about it."

"Kate? Kate Phillips?"

Kate shook herself out of her thoughts, turned her head, and stopped. There was one of those concerned faces she had just been dreaming of. "Oh, hi, Mrs. Kessler."

"Wait," said the art teacher. "When did you drop my class? I haven't seen you for . . . what is it? Weeks?"

"Yeah. I wanted to take keyboarding instead," said Kate, thinking about the clay pots she had thrown on the wheel before her stomach made it uncomfortable to sit on the stool, the gravity of the high perch making her want to give birth right there in the art room. Probably everything she had made was unfired and crumbling in some dirty corner.

"Well, that's practical. It's good experience for later. Well, you have some work still in the room. I actually glazed and fired it because there was some space in the kiln. Can you come by and get it?"

Kate flushed red, blood rising to her neck, her breasts aching and sore. Mrs. Kessler looked at her, questioning. "Um, not now," Kate said finally. "But later. Tomorrow, okay?" Kate moved her lips into a smile and turned away from her teacher.

"Wait. Kate? Is everything okay?"

Kate closed her eyes and then turned, opening her lids to another lie. "Yeah. Why wouldn't it be?"

Mrs. Kessler smiled. "I don't know. Okay, Kate. I'll see you tomorrow."

As Kate walked down the hall away from her teacher, she remembered the first and last time that her family went to Queen of Heaven cemetery in Pleasant Hill after her mother was buried. The dirt was still unplanted, but someone had smoothed it down, and the headstone, *Deirdre Phillips, 1961 to 1996, Beloved Mother,* stood cold and erect at the head of the grave site. Both she and Tyler had left flowers picked from her mother's garden—freesia, daffodils, the first late winter roses—by the marker, and then turned to leave. Her father and Tyler had walked straight back to the car, cutting across grave sites, walking over what Kate knew were bodies, skeletons, bits of flesh, pieces of people who had died. So, Kate walked the rows instead, cutting sharp angles to miss the mounds, the six-foot spaces she gave for each body, making it to the car a full five minutes later than her father and sister. *Now,* Kate thought, *this place, this school, is just like the cemetery. Everywhere I go, there is danger. I need to walk much more carefully.*

"My eyebrow is killing me," said Erin. "God, I don't know what I was thinking." She rubbed the skin around her newly pierced eyebrow, a ring of red around the shiny silver stud that matched the one already in her tongue. "I think it's fucking infected."

Kate looked behind her but kept walking toward the parking lot. She had managed to miss all of her friends by ducking behind tall boys and behind lockers, smoothly continuing to walk on, or by pretending to study her notes, writing nonsense on her pad as they passed by, their waves ignored. She had almost made it to the cafeteria when Erin ran across the grass quad and pulled on her shoulder, refusing to stop. It was only a few more yards to the car, and she saw that Tyler was waiting, her books and bag slung on the hood.

"Jeez, Kate. Slow down."

"I've got to get home. My dad has stuff for me to do."

Erin stopped, watching her friend walk to her car. "Did I tell you about the rave I went to last weekend? In San Francisco? SoMa."

Kate slowed and turned slightly. She remembered when Erin tried to convince her to go to these parties, telling her stories of all-night dancing, drugs being passed out like party favors, and wild sweaty kisses with boys and, sometimes, girls. Kate used to listen, giggling on the other end of the phone or with Erin in her bedroom, the music on loud so Erin's mother wouldn't hear them. She'd gone twice to raves, one down in an abandoned storefront on Shattuck Avenue in Berkeley, and the other at someone's father's warehouse in Emeryville. Both times she sat drinking a beer while everyone all around her took Ecstasy and some strange blue-colored concoction called Blue Nitro and pulsed to music beyond the music of the band, something internal and wild and frightening to Kate. Kids bashed into each other, some sucking pacifiers.

"Why are they doing that?" she asked Erin.

"What?"

"Sucking on pacifiers. That is so weird," said Kate.

"Don't you know? They do it so they won't chew off their own tongues. While on E," said Erin, moving and swaying away to the beat of the music.

And despite her fear of their let-loose feelings, Kate had been mesmerized, watching the sweat and skin and kisses of the kids like a vivid, amazing dream.

Kate slowed and then stopped walking and looked at Erin. "Really? What happened?"

Erin walked toward Kate, hitching up her backpack. "I met this guy who used to be a roadie for Smashing Pumpkins. Really! And he had all these tattoos on his stomach."

Kate smiled, thinking of the little she knew about Erin's boyfriends of the past year: Damon, the junior college student who played bass in an alternative rock band; Jeffrey, the poet who hung out in coffee shops and skipped school; and Tran, a boy who worked with Erin at the yogurt store. "Well, how does he rate on the boyfriend scale? One to ten."

"Hah! I'm not going there again this year. I tell you, I still have nightmares that Jeffrey is going to stalk me or, worse, read me his poetry all day and night."

Kate laughed. "So?"

Erin sighed. "I'm just going to meet people. I can't get tied down. I mean, next year is senior year."

"What do you mean?"

"Well," said Erin. "Don't you want to have a really cool date for the prom, someone you really like? I mean, you know. Spending the night at the hotel in the city."

Kate shook her head, slowly thinking, *Prom, prom.* The word sounded strange, like a steel instrument, a fork, a spear. Kate was about to ask Erin who she thought was cool when she realized that Tyler had walked away from the car and was calling to her. "Kate. Come on!"

Kate almost let out a moan and looked at her watch. "Oh, my God. I've got to go."

Erin yelled after her, "Can't I get a ride?"

Kate didn't answer. She ran to the car, let Tyler in, and drove off, not seeing Erin wave, not noticing anything at all.

❧

Tyler felt her palms on the cool surface of the BMW's hood, the blue metallic shine barely reflecting back her face. She could see her mouth, somewhat wavery, but as still and serious as she felt. Deirdre had been alone one hour and three minutes, now four, and Tyler knew that they had to get home. Kate had promised, had said they would race back, but there Kate was, her backpack hung over her shoulder, talking to Erin as if this were just some ordinary Monday, nothing different, dates and grades, and someone's ugly pants to talk about.

Tyler blew air quickly out her mouth and looked around the parking lot. For all she knew, the baby's father could be walking to his car right now, too, sauntering past Kate without a nod, forgetting what had happened nine months ago, not realizing that his own flesh and blood was in Kate's closet, crying. He would get in his car and drive to his job at the Monte Veda theater or Nation's hamburgers or to the public library to study his calculus, not knowing that at home, his baby slept or screamed. *But who is he?* Tyler thought. *Who could it be?*

Tyler moved away from the car, moving slowly toward Kate and Erin. She watched a group of boys, their pants so low and baggy, she could barely see their shoes. The father would be dark, maybe Latino, maybe Asian, thought Tyler, thinking of baby Deirdre's brown skin and straight black hair. She remembered the boy Teddy who called the house a couple of times, Kate running into her room to use her own extension, soft laughter coming from behind the door for hours. But that hadn't lasted long and then there was the conversation in the dining room when everything had changed. And maybe, Tyler thought, it wasn't even a boy from school. Kate and Erin had gone through the Caldecott Tunnel a couple of weekend nights, dancing at raves, talking low and quiet after they came home, Tyler finally able to relax and sleep because she wasn't alone anymore.

As Kate listened to Erin, Tyler felt blood slipping up from her belly and into her throat. Why was she the worried one, wanting to go home and see Deirdre? Why wasn't she the one talking to her friends, putting on her practice clothes, and choreographing a new cheerleading routine? Why was she the one thinking of the baby while Kate just stood there and talked and talked to stupid Erin.

Tyler wanted to scream, "The baby could be dying! The baby is choking! The baby needs us!" But she didn't, keeping her dark imaginings inside. "Kate, come on!" she said instead, gratified that Kate moved immediately, ran to the car, and let her in. Once they drove out of the parking lot, Kate staring straight ahead, leaning slightly toward the windshield, Tyler shook her head. "Goddamn it! What's wrong with you? Why were you talking so long?"

"I don't know. For a second, I guess, I forgot," said Kate.

"Oh, great. You forgot? How could you forget? I didn't forget," said Tyler, biting down on her lip.

"I said I don't know!" yelled Kate, tears coming from her eyes, the idea of her old life falling as far behind her as Erin standing on the edge of the parking lot. "I don't. Just stop it, Tyler. Let's just go home," said Kate, pressing her foot to the gas pedal.

"Okay, fine! Just remember that I was ready. I'm the one who re-membered," Tyler said, turning her head away from Kate and toward the window, wondering how this could be happening, how they were headed home to a baby that no one knew about. She wondered about Deirdre's father, who gave her those short round legs, tiny lips, the hair and the skin. She wondered who bent his body over Kate's and murmured the words, the right words that made her open up and let him into her.

"I can't believe you won't even tell me who the father is. Even after all I've done. It's not fair, Kate."

"I can't," said Kate.

"You can. You do everything you want to," said Tyler. Kate said nothing, and Tyler stared at her, felt the breeze from the open win-dow, and wondered about the silence between them.

Kate ran in the house from the garage, leaving her car door open, her purse on the floor by the gearshift. Tyler stayed behind, closing the doors, hitting the garage door button, watching light slide outward into the afternoon. She held everything to her chest—Kate's purse, her own books, a brown bag full of snacks no one ate—as if trying to protect herself from a cry, a scream, a moan that would tell the whole horrible story. They hadn't taken care of Deirdre—that was for sure. *We left her alone and she died,* thought Tyler. *No one will care what happens to us when they find out. Everyone will want us gone.*

Tyler stepped into the kitchen, holding her breath, waiting, but then there was no sound. She breathed out and dropped her armful on the counter, slowly following Kate's path into the bedroom. As she peeked around the corner, into the room, there they were. There they both were, Kate bent over the box, pulling a blanket over the baby's shoulders, Deirdre asleep. Alive. This time.

⁊ఆ

"Davis? Davis!" said Rachael, rolling down her window and leaning out over the passenger's seat. Davis stood in front of the open garage door, staring out at the five o'clock street, watching the pattern of departures and returns he remembered, the Howards' squeaky Lexus, the Garcias' old tabby curled up at the edge of the road despite traffic, deaf to everything but fatigue.

"Oh, hi, Rachael. How are you?" he said, not moving, not even really looking at her car, trying to avoid the swinging of her arms, her smile, her eyes behind her Anne Klein sunglasses.

"It's good to see you, Davis. Good to see you. How are the girls?" Rachael turned off her car and moved her whole body to the passenger's seat.

Davis rubbed his forehead. "Good. Good. Everything's fine."

Rachael opened the door and swung her legs out, looking at him almost as if to ask permission to come closer and, not finding it in Davis's eyes or face, slowly stepped forward anyway. "I haven't seen you lately. I've seen the girls. But . . . I just wanted to make sure everything was okay. With them."

"Why wouldn't it be? Why are you asking?" asked Davis, his skin flaring. "Do you think something is wrong?"

Rachael took off her sunglasses, her green eyes squinting against the sun. "I really don't know. How could I? You don't call. You don't come over. I just don't know."

"Great. That's great. I'm so sick of people asking me how things are all the time. Does the house look like it's falling apart? Are there parties here on the weekends? Does it look like I'm not doing my job?"

Rachael didn't look away, so he did, not wanting to watch her eyes anymore, remembering them from across Deirdre's hospital bed and at the funeral. "I just think . . . I just know that Deirdre would want me to check in," said Rachael. "I was her friend, Davis. I was her very best friend. And I haven't been able to get close to you or the girls for months. It's like you're all hiding."

Davis flinched as the sprinklers turned on, the water first spitting out like snakes, then fanning to plumes along the edges of the lawn, drenching Deirdre's careful plantings, flowers and shrubs now trimmed weekly by a gardener. "We're fine, Rachael. I know you were her friend. But we're all fine."

"I'm your friend, too. Remember? Remember all those times? Re-member our life, Davis?"

Davis looked at Rachael, her eyes slick with memory. "Of course. Of course I remember. It's just that things are different now. You know that. I don't need to tell you that."

"But can I help? I've been trying."

Davis shook his head. "It's okay. Really. Listen, I'm going inside right now. But we can talk. Later."

Rachael put on her glasses. "All right," she said. "Okay, Davis." Rachael walked to her car, getting in the way she got out, finally rolling up the window and driving away. For a long, panicked sec-ond, Davis imagined he could chase her down, beat on the rear win-dow, and beg. He thought he could say, "Please. Take them. Take them home. I can't do it." But instead he went inside, filled with guilt and fear, wanting to know what Rachael saw. What he did not.

"What's going on, Tyler?" asked Davis, standing with his hands on his hips, the door to the garage and the afternoon open behind him.

Tyler started, and in that movement he could still see her child self under her new woman flesh. "What?" asked Tyler, pale, turning from the kitchen counter. "What?"

Davis turned back to the driveway behind him, the smell of Rachael's exhaust and displeasure still in his nose. "I just want to know . . . You need to . . . Is . . . What's wrong?"

After asking the question, Davis wished he could suck it back in his mouth, the sudden pain and fear on Tyler's face enough to make him jump in his truck and leave without saying good-bye, leave before he could see or hear one more thing.

"What?" she asked, a broken vowel, a sigh, a yell in her mouth, with more to follow, more to say. But then the sound was swallowed and the fear evaporated—maybe it wasn't there anyway—and it was just Tyler, washing a few dishes, her homework on the counter, the house as it always had been.

"Everything's fine," she said, breathing, watching him with her calm eyes. "Why?"

"I just wanted to know. That's all. You can tell me," said Davis, wishing that he were telling the truth. "You can tell me anything."

Tyler put a towel down and turned off the faucet. Davis wondered if her hands were shaking or if it was the tears in his eyes making the scene quiver. "Okay, Daddy. I know." She walked to him, curling her hands around him, her hug still a little girl's hug, needy and tight. The hug she used to give him at night when he came home from work. The hug he used to expect from Tyler and Kate, Deirdre standing in the hallway, smiling.

❧

All the books that Kate and Tyler had read said that the umbilical cord would fall off in one to two weeks. The cord stump, probably longer than it should be—Tyler, almost irrational by the time she cut the cord and scared it would somehow kill or damage the baby, clipped as far away as possible—was now as brown and wrinkled as a small prune.

Supplied with alcohol and cotton swabs, they cleaned the umbilical cord or what was left of it each time they bathed and changed Deirdre, folding the disposable diapers down so the top would not rub the healing cord.

"This is really nasty," said Tyler. "Look at how white it is where the belly button is. Like you could just push into her stomach." Deirdre stopped fussing as Tyler spoke, staring up with dark eyes.

"Stop it," said Kate, taping up the diapers and putting Deirdre's small, chubby arms through a tiny T-shirt.

"I wish it would heal. I hate looking at it. It just reminds me of that thing. Jeez."

"Okay, okay. But, Tyler, you did it," said Kate, picking up the baby. "You delivered her. And the placenta. It wasn't a thing."

Tyler smiled at Deirdre and took her from Kate. "I did. I pulled you out," she said, kissing Deirdre's soft face and laughing. She stopped quickly when the doorbell rang. "Shit! Who is that?"

Kate stood still, a tube of Desitin in her hand. "How would I know?"

"What if it's Dad?" asked Tyler.

"Well, he would come in the garage door. And he was just here yesterday afternoon."

"Well, you get it, Kate. I don't want to."

"Let's not get it at all. We shouldn't even be home today. Let's just pretend that we aren't here." Every time the doorbell rang, she imagined everyone it could be—Rachael, her Aunt Gwen, the police, a social worker, or even worse, the baby's father. Each time, while she waited for Tyler to get the door or as she walked onto the cool marble of the entryway, she could almost feel someone taking Deirdre out of her arms, wresting her baby from her forever.

Tyler pushed Kate with one arm. "Just get it. Act normal. Pretend that you're home sick. Everything's fine. And anyway, it's probably just some Jehovah's Witness or salesman or something."

"Look," said Kate, her stomach seeming to be full of small bees. "The Witness people only come on Saturdays, and besides, let me finish with Deirdre."

"Okay, fine," said Tyler, leaving the room and talking as she walked down the hall. "I have to do everything, I guess."

Kate picked up Deirdre and rubbed her hands on the baby's back, the skin so fine and soft, tiny hairs under Kate's hands like feathers. *It is amazing,* thought Kate, blocking out the sound of the door opening and Tyler's voice, *that this body was inside me, living, and here she is breathing and eating and crying.* Kate sat down on the chair and laid Deirdre on top of her belly, knowing Deirdre had already changed and become part of the world.

Tyler ran down the hall and into Kate's room. "He knows about the baby! You got to get rid of him. He's on the porch," she hissed through her teeth.

"Who?" said Kate, knowing it didn't really matter who it was. Someone knew. Someone who could come in and change things. She rocked the baby in the chair, feeling her soft skin, thinking about the right words to say to someone, anyone, even the baby's father. She needed time, much more time.

"Sanjay. He's talking about all the crying. He's heard her at night or something."

Every word in that sentence stabbed at Kate, so she paled at them all, standing up stiffly and handing the baby to Tyler. She felt her face harden into lies.

"Jesus, Kate! What? Kate?" asked Tyler.

"Nothing. Close the door. Lock it. I'll be right back."

Kate walked down the hall toward the door, and then looked through the peephole and saw her next-door neighbor, Sanjay Chaturvedi, standing on the porch in the khakis and white button-down shirt he always wore—winter adding a vest or sweater, summer unbuttoning his shirt two buttons instead of one. Kate watched him for a second. He didn't move, staring straight ahead of him, as if he knew her right eye was behind the glass. His hands were in his pockets, the thumbs hanging out and aligned with his hips. It was drizzling again, and Kate saw Sanjay's footprints on the wood, perfect penny-loafer feet.

Kate breathed deeply, and then held the air inside her, holding the silence of the house in her lungs, thinking, *Deirdre just can't cry. Not now.* She wished it were anyone but Sanjay at the door, even Sanjay's wife, Meera. Meera had a quick, brusque way of doing everything: grocery bags militarized into the house, the lawn charged and contained, the children regimented and scrutinized before and after play. Kate knew she could get rid of Meera by saying, "I'm doing homework and I've got to get it done" or "My father is expecting me to have the house cleaned by dinner." Sometimes when she used to baby-sit the Chaturvedi boys, she would come home, scan her house, and see everything through Meera's critical eye: laundry—clean and dirty—piled high on the couch, dishes on the coffee table, counters, bathroom sink, dust bunnies the size of genetic mutations.

Kate unlocked the door, testing out her smile—pull this muscle up, higher, lower, stop there—and then opened the door to Sanjay's fixed gaze.

"Hi, Sanjay."

"Oh, hello."

She thought he was blushing, but it was hard to tell, his skin the color of honey. "Hi."

Sanjay coughed. "I am wondering when your father will be home."

"Oh. Well, tonight. He's . . . working. And then, at his girlfriend's house. Why?"

"Well, I was wondering if I could be of help."

Kate scratched her arm, noticing how pale she was, how pale in comparison to Sanjay. How pale and fat, like a grub worm exposed to the light by a garden shovel. "What do you mean?"

"I have heard the baby at night. And during the daytime as well when I come home with the boys from day care. I suspect that your father has more than he can handle at this time. We would like to baby-sit. Both you and Tyler have been very good to the boys." Sanjay stopped, looking down at his loafers.

Kate swallowed, having never thought that the crying, which went on and on, it seemed, all night, every night, was bothering anyone but Tyler and her. She was glad that her father stayed every night at Hannah's, glad that her two boys seemed to need the comfort of their own house more than her father did.

"Oh, the baby. Right. Well, it's one of my Aunt Gwen's kids. She's down here visiting from Santa Rosa. Um, she's out, you know, shopping. Gosh, I'm sorry. We didn't mean to disturb you, really."

Sanjay cleared his throat, still looking down. He did not say anything for a while, and Kate was suspended in his silence. If he were anyone else, she suspected, anyone other than this quiet, polite man, who always asked permission, he would come in, wheedle for lemonade, talk about the weather or the six-foot fence the Dickinsons built on the corner lot while furtively looking for clues.

"Well, I just wanted to offer assistance. We have missed you at the house, Kate. The boys ask for you all the time."

Kate began to shut the door. "Tell them I said hi. Okay? Okay. Bye."

Kate closed the door, holding on to the handle, feeling the latch click into the lock, brass on brass, wood scraping wood, her feet hitting the weather stripping as she stood still facing the door, head bent down. She thought about looking out the peephole, but decided to just listen for his steps, and after she breathed three times, long inhales and exhales, he was gone, his steps slow on wood, then faster, hard clacks on the wet brick.

Kate was unsure what she was feeling, some strand of sadness pulling like elastic from Sanjay's retreating body to her own, and then, at the same time, such powerful relief that she wanted to exhale the past, letting it go and go and go. Kate knew that she could open the door, call to him, use any word to bring him back here, to her, this house, this hallway, this room, this baby. His baby.

Sanjay wouldn't make a scene, and suddenly everything would make sense. There would be plans, discussions, and phone calls. There would be bitter discussions in his house, but Kate would never hear them, and she would be gone by then, sent somewhere by someone. If she stopped him, maybe Kate would never have to see Meera's horrible black eyes, full of disgust and hatred; she would never have to watch anyone's pain but her own and her family's. And that was enough.

"How did you get rid of him? Is he gone?" called Tyler from the room.

"Yeah. I told him it was Aunt Gwen's baby."

"Really? Do you think he believed that?"

"I don't know," said Kate, walking into the living room and sitting down on the couch, suddenly breathing in Sanjay's skin, his olive oil soap, his short, straight hair. She remembered the day he reached for her, his brown hand small—smaller than her father's—but firm at the thumb and wrist, something she could really hold on to.

There was that second, half a second, that she felt him before she touched his fingers, something crackling in the space between them, something pulling her forward, like static electricity. Kate had never really felt the need for a stranger, someone other than her mother or father or Tyler until recently, that summer, maybe when she watched people dancing at the parties she went to with Erin. At night in bed, Kate would think about how it felt to leave your own space and have someone welcome you into theirs, take you in, cherish the smells and movements that were personal and embarrassing and so deeply intimate Kate could barely understand how it was done. So when Sanjay asked if she would mind if he kissed her, she said no she didn't mind and yes to everything else, even when all he did at first was lightly brush his lips against her palm. She said yes with her eyes and yes to his body, even though it was not a body she could claim or ask for later.

That summer afternoon she felt ripe under her skin, her bones and muscles and nerves leaning her into Sanjay's body as if she needed this other flesh to survive into the next minute.

"Are you frightened?" he had asked her, his body dark over her, his eyes the color of water pebbles.

"No. No," she said, unsure, frightened only that it was not what she had expected. No tribal instinct was telling her how to move, which way to bend, how to accommodate another person on top of her. She wanted to blend with him as she had seen couples do in the movies, but this felt stiff and uncomfortable. They lay on his bed—his and Meera's—the curtains drawn, the summer sun shooting out rays from the sides and bottom. Kate's skin looked dusky, her arms almost tan as she held his body against hers, waiting for what would happen, and then she felt him go into her, stop, push through, a stab and then a rush of warmth, first from her, and then him.

"I am so sorry. I could not keep . . . I could not make it last any longer."

Kate wondered how long it was supposed to last, what the averages were, and if she was supposed to be disappointed. She had not learned much from Karl, her eighth-grade boyfriend, the last real boyfriend she'd had since before her mother got sick. With Karl, there had been sweaty dances, his hands all over her clothed body, one night an insistent finger in her flowered underwear, quick scared lips on her breasts. Nothing he did or touched or kissed looked like the diagrams she had been shown by Mrs. Kilmartin during her family life classes in fifth grade, strange cow head–shaped uteruses and fallopian tube horns, ovaries stuck like decorative doughnut holes on the tips. Kate and her classmates had stared up at the pictures, huddled on the floor, legs crossed, watching the egg burst from its follicle, make its determined but tremulous journey down the tube, and wait for the swimming sperm, a raindrop with a tail, to somehow find it and bury its head into the egg as if it were so much sand.

Later, in the untitled picture books Erin had found under her mother's bed—men and women, men and men, women and women, went on and on—some kind of gymnastics interrupting and then becoming the lovemaking, twistings of bodies and strange maneuvers, heads on crotches, crotches on heads, legs on backs, backs against walls. "Do people really do that stuff?" Kate had asked Erin.

"Some, I guess. But, like, it's usually much simpler. Just in and out. Penis and vagina. Or rubbing, lots of it. This has got to be all hype. But let me read you page 354."

Kate, remembering page 354, almost laughed. She turned toward Sanjay, stroking his shoulder awkwardly. "That's okay," she said.

Sanjay had pulled himself from her, lying next to her on the bed, stroking her right nipple, running his hands over the bowl of her stomach from hipbone to hipbone. "It really is not okay. I would like to try again."

Kate smiled and turned her head to the pillow. Sanjay moved up on her body, kissing her, holding her shoulders, his thumbs rubbing up toward her neck. He pushed her dark hair away from her forehead, watching her eyes, wanting her to watch him as he moved, shaped her waist and breasts and thighs with his hands. And without her thinking, their bodies seemed to become words, sentences, whole paragraphs of stories about what they were doing and how, punctuated with the thick air, smells of sweat and Cloroxed sheets. This time, this second dance, was more what she imagined, and soon she forgot that she was expecting anything at all, letting herself slowly fall into the rhythm of their skin and breaths and hearts.

Now, sitting here on the couch, Sanjay's body so distant from her own, she wished she could translate those movements, articulate a turn of wrist, thrust of pelvis, arch of neck so she'd remember the things she knew she was forgetting. She knew she had already forgotten the feeling of someone's naked skin, the rush of gooseflesh and breath as he rubbed her waist and thighs, the notion that they were so close they breathed the same air, and at least for a while, for this hour on a stolen mattress, their bodies joined by sweat and muscle and words, they lived together in the same moment.

Later, after that first time together, though, home with Tyler and their Burger King dinner, Kate knew that he was home with Meera, everything as it should be, the boys listening to stories, Sanjay's arm pulling all three close as they laughed over nursery rhymes. Looking out her window, she could see yellow light coming from the Chaturvedis' family room, and she knew she wished she were as far from home as possible, someplace where she could forget what had happened in the bedroom. That first night Kate knew she could forget, too, knew that if Sanjay left her alone, and the minutes and hours turned into days and weeks, she would not remember his flesh or hers or even the way they both came together.

But the next time, Meera on-call and sleeping at the hospital, Jagdish and Ardashir asleep for the night, Kate held Sanjay, pulled him to her.

"This time I want to try it again," she said, lifting Sanjay's head from his hands with her own.

She learned that his body was softest on his lower back, that his toenails and fingernails were clipped so that no white showed at all. She felt his hairless chest, the V of his rib cage, his small nipples hard under her fingertips. She listened to her body open under him, joints, tendons, and ligaments softening, unknown muscles hardening and flexing. Kate knew when Sanjay was ready to come, his breaths fast, his voice a small worried sound, and then breathing, and then silence.

By the time their affair was over, she felt she could meet him without questions, take off her clothes without fear, lie next to him as a woman and take and give, take and give, language passing between them through fingers, arms, hair, and heat.

"I know this is unreasonable on my part, Kate," Sanjay had begun one day in the beginning of August. The sun held Monte Veda and

northern California in its hot hands, and Wildwood Drive hummed
with electricity, air conditioners running morning and night. Outside
on the Chaturvedis' patio, Meera's pansies folded in on their stems
liked broken, withered umbrellas. Sanjay sat next to her on the
couch, holding her hands in his, kissing them as if they were alive on
their own, creatures he was begging forgiveness from.

Kate said nothing, a small field of energy gathering force in her
chest.

Sanjay sighed. "I should have thought this out better. I should
have known that I could not continue. I want to . . . but then Meera
comes home from the hospital, and the boys look at me during meal-
times, and I think, I am betraying them all."

The energy, white flecked and dancing, had spread to her stomach, making Kate sure she would vomit. But she also knew she could
not get up, her legs tingling, too. She was reminded of how she felt
in the hospital waiting room as the doctors took the breathing tube
out of her mother's lungs. Once they were done, they motioned the
family in, and Kate had felt herself clinging to the stiff plastic chair,
then the doorway, finally the curtain by her mother's bed, certain she
could not live into the next moment, wanting everything to freeze
right there. Now.

Kate looked at Sanjay, forcing herself to hold his gaze, even
though she was about to cry, her mouth pulling down at the corners,
making it impossible to talk. He had no idea what he was asking her
to give up. Not just him and the afternoon bed, but something that
made her feel different, better than she had in a long, long time.

"What did you think was going to happen with us, Kate?" asked
Sanjay, still holding her hands. "How did you imagine this would end?"

Kate could not tell him that before she fell asleep at night, she
imagined him packing his suitcase, khaki pants, white shirts,
sweaters, vests, and leaving his house, locking it behind him. She
could not tell him that each night he liberated her from her twin bed,
and her sad, empty house, taking her and her own packed suitcase to
his car, pulling silently out of the driveway, the cul-de-sac they lived
on, and out to Highway 24, where they drove and drove, away from
the Bay Area, down Highway 5. Maybe she could tell him that they
only stopped in seedy central California motels, The Bar-S Homtel,

Gateway to Yosemite Inn, registering under false names, and never found rest, driving and driving down a long highway, as if they were in some bad road movie.

It would be impossible to admit that those fantasies were the tales she put herself to sleep with, that what she became more familiar with was not his body, but her own life in motion, something moving, something exciting.

She would also never tell him that sometimes, her story drifting into dream, she saw the two of them back at Sanjay's house, in front of Meera, her mouth moving to a hundred frightening truths: "You have ruined us all, you have disappointed everyone, you are both terrible people, no one will love you after this. No one at all." In this dream, when she went back home, no one was there, not Tyler, not her father.

Sanjay put his lips to her hands. "You are so young," he whispered to her palms. "I have behaved badly."

Much later, Kate would think an appropriate response would have been anger or, if possible, truth. She should have asked, "How did *you* think this would end? What did you think you were doing?" and waited for a reply. Even as she sat by him, feeling Sanjay's warm body next to hers on the couch, she thought she could feel her right hand tingling from cracking against his cheek. Kate almost brought her palm to her nose to breathe in his cologne and shaving lotion, knowing the smell and even wanting it as she imagined the blood under his skin after her strike. But really, it made more sense to walk back into the lonely, alone, bodyless place of the last two years, the last months really just as imaginary as her fantasies before sleep, something else she could not hold on to for keeps. Kate stood up, found her legs under her body, and walked to the door over perfectly white carpet, vacuum cleaner marks leading her to the door.

As she walked out the door, into the slap of afternoon heat, Kate felt tears in her chest and face and the sudden urge to lie down, now, on a bed or floor or couch and let the tears jerk out of her like knives. But she swallowed and breathed them away, realizing again that it was just easier to pretend that things didn't hurt, that when people left, she could be fine all by herself. Kate thought that if she didn't believe anything too much, they might all come back.

"What are we going to do? We've got to do something. He'll

probably be back," said Tyler, holding Deirdre, who was dressed and asleep in her arms. "Why are you just sitting here?"

"I got really tired suddenly," said Kate, standing up, holding out her arms for the baby. She kissed Deirdre's forehead, cheeks, hands, and feet, knowing with her lips she was searching, desperate for the smells of the father, desperate for herself, the one who, for a small time last summer, breathed and laughed, and felt the skin of a whole new life.

His Everyday Wife

At first he thought he was imagining the noise. As Sanjay lay awake night after night, trying to lull his guilt and despair with thoughts of work or his two boys, he began to believe the noise sounded like kittens. And as Sanjay lay in his bed, Meera asleep beside him, he thought, *It is spring, and the animals are reproducing.* He thought to look under the house or in the woodpile for a stray litter, wondering what he would do with them once he found them: keep them or take them to the brand-new SPCA in downtown Oak Creek. The boys undoubtedly would want one or all if he showed them, and Sanjay knew what Meera would say, "Animals are dirty. They belong outside, but not in this yard and not with us."

When they were in college, Meera at UCSF and he at Berkeley, Sanjay had brought home a small black cocker spaniel that a friend of his couldn't keep because he was going home to New Delhi for the summer. Sanjay was hesitant, knowing Meera well even then, but the dog was all large, wet eyes and soft fur, winding round and round his legs as Swapan convinced him.

"Look, Sanjay. He likes you already. You will be the best of friends."

"But, Swapan, Meera does not like animals at all. Not even kittens," said Sanjay.

"How could she resist such a face? Look," said Swapan, picking up the dog and turning toward Sanjay. "My goodness, what a face!"

So Sanjay brought the dog, named Cocoa by Swapan's English

girlfriend, back to his student apartment, hiding Cocoa under his jacket as he walked through the rain. He liked the feeling of the warm dog body next to his, the way the dog just allowed such a thing, this taking over of its body by a larger one, this claustrophobia of jacket and weather.

But Meera didn't even let him in the door. He stood at the jamb, wet, the lump of the dog at his chest, Cocoa's sad eyes peering at Meera over the V of his coat as she calmly told him to take it back.

"But, Meera, I told Swapan I would take the dog for him. He is going home to visit his family for the summer. It will just be for a couple months."

Meera opened the door wider, but still did not let him in. "Sanju. Do you not see this apartment?"

Sanjay nodded, taking in the stacks of papers and books—his engineering, her medical—the austere glass tables, and red rugs, the three computers, two printers, fax machine, and Xerox.

"Do you think this apartment is a place for an animal, Sanju? Do you think it would be acceptable for it to run around here? Am I supposed to come home from a weekend at the hospital and take care of that creature?"

Sanjay wanted to shrug but didn't. He wanted to say, "But what about when I am home and you are at the hospital?" But he didn't. Instead, he said, "I did promise Swapan. He is my good friend."

Meera sighed, then walked up to him, running her hand on his shoulder. "Sanju, you will just have to take it back and say that it won't work out. He will find somebody else who has more room."

Meera started to close the door. "Take it back before it gets used to you."

"Now? You want me to return to Swapan's apartment now?"

Meera pushed her long black hair behind her shoulder, her black eyes—so black Sanjay could never see the irises—widening. "Of course. We don't want the wet dog here. As it is, we are going to have to get your coat cleaned. I will call ahead to Swapan's to tell him you will be arriving."

So Sanjay returned the dog, silently handing Swapan the animal and returning home. Meera let him in, took off his coat, placing it in a large plastic bag, and made him dinner. Later that night she massaged his back, running her thin fingers over his whole body until he finally wanted to make love to her, letting go of the sad feeling that had covered him like dog hair. And it wasn't so much to let go of, really, not with her slim legs and curved body that smelled of pomegranates and raisins; not with her hair in his face, not with the dark, spicy Bengali words she learned from her mother seeping into his ear, her mouth the shape of the moon as she came.

Later, as he fell asleep, he tried to figure out what she had said, but he was never sure, certain it was mysterious, a secret message, code telling him what would make her want dogs, wet coats, him on the weekends.

So now, ten years later, Sanjay knew it was impossible to suggest cats; the children, first one boy and then a year later another, were all the animals Meera could handle. But after a long week of small night cries, Sanjay got up, covering Meera's shoulder as he left the bed, and then walked out of the room, down the hall, into the living room filled with strips of harsh streetlight. Sanjay found his Cal sweatshirt on the couch and went outside to the deck, the spring night dense with suspended water, the light from the pool—Meera would never let him turn it off, always wanting it as a warning beacon for unsuspecting swimmers—a drowned blue glow from beneath the pool cover. He walked to the edge of the backyard and stepped up on the fence runner, listening with his ears and heart for sound. Out in the open, the cries seemed louder, and Sanjay realized they were not kitten or cat at all, but baby, small baby, new baby. Sanjay covered his eyes, taking in a sharp deep breath, realizing he had known it was a baby from the start, even as he lay in his bed next to Meera imagining animals. In his own way, Sanjay had been waiting and listening for the cries for nine long months.

Later, Sanjay tried to remember what he had felt at that moment, and could best decide that it was a sinking, first of heart to stomach, stomach to gut, and then to groin, his legs wanting to bend him off the fence, and yet there was a lifting also, something being pulled up and over him; and he went with it, watching his body, still and stiff, stuck in place, unable to move or think or run; unable to hop the fence that separated the yards and peer in the window, watch Kate with the baby that was his, and he knew it, right then, clinging to the fence on that spring night in the fog, the pool and the street casting ugly light all around him.

Sanjay had known he was going to sleep with Kate the afternoon he watched her pull his son Jagdish's T-shirt over the boy's head and onto his body, fluffing his straight black hair and rubbing his cheek after she had tucked it in. Her hands were smooth birds, he thought, small white birds, the nails pale white—not the dull metallic colors her sister wore or Meera's smooth glossy-red—and short, filed into safe, perfect half-moons.

"There you go, Jaggu. Now, get into your bed for your nap," said Kate, running her hands over his back and chest, giggling into his shoulder, the boy curling into her breasts.

"I'm too big for a nap, Kate. Da! You tell her. I'm big now," said Jagdish, holding on to the stuffed bear named Peri that he brought everywhere, the sad thing thin and bare from nights of heavy dreams.

"Now, Jaggu," said Sanjay. "We have talked about this before. You don't have to sleep as long as Ardashir, but you must sleep some. Do you remember?" said Sanjay.

"Yes," said Jagdish.

"Well? Then get your fine self into your room!" said Kate. "I'll be there in a sec. Before I go."

"Okay. You promise?" said Jagdish.

"Of course. Now, go." Kate stood up, putting her sweater on top of her purse. She stretched, and Sanjay watched her torso thin and tighten under her white T-shirt, her long body like a foreign road, so straight and lean and undiscovered.

"I am sure I don't know how much I owe you for today," said Sanjay, standing up to take out his wallet.

"Well, Meera didn't leave until eleven. After I got back from swim team. So it's four now. Five hours," said Kate.

"It is a price well paid," said Sanjay, handing her thirty dollars, his hand running across hers as he handed her the bills. He felt his body still, and he breathed in her scent: chlorine, tanning lotion, the heat of the day. "Meera won't be back until the weekend. So tomorrow is acceptable?"

"Yeah. We worked it all out. I'll see you in the morning. Look, I've got to tuck in Jaggu. Then I'll go, okay?"

"Of course," said Sanjay, watching her walk down the hall toward his son's room, knowing she would kneel on the floor by his bed, tickle him on the chest, pull the covers up and tuck them in, watch until Jagdish closed his eyes, smoothing his black hair off his eyes. He had watched her do the same with Ardashir, talking both boys to sleep with silly stories he imagined Deirdre must have told her when she was little and a soft roll in the mouth that only mothers must know, a sound passed down the generations, a *hum, hum, hum, sleep, hum, hum, hum, sleep.*

Sanjay sat back down on the couch, unbuttoning the top two buttons of his shirt. The four o'clock sun pulsed through the room, hot enough today to cut through the swirl of air-conditioned air, and he closed his eyes, letting the arms of heat hold him. Sanjay thought he knew why Jagdish clutched the bear, the creature was always body temperature and giving what was asked—*Let's play, move over here, come with me!* He wondered how it felt to be the bear, willing to do what was asked in return for being loved in a way that Sanjay found unimaginable. He thought he could remember a blanket from when he was a child of about five, but there was also a memory of his *nani* taking it from him, and burning it over the ash can in the yard, saying, "Now it is gone. You are a big boy now, Sanju. Time to grow up."

When Kate held his boys, like today, he knew he wanted to be Jagdish or Ardashir, held in her arms, talked to in that foreign mother tongue, that lulling sound that had no verbs or order, just the beat of a steady open heart.

"I am most pathetic," Sanjay said, opening his eyes, seeing Kate standing over him.

"What?" asked Kate.

Sanjay stood up, hoping she did not see his face flaring. "Oh, I was thinking about my employment."

Kate picked up her purse. "What is it that you do, exactly?"

"I am a chemical engineer. I work with petroleum products. Light gases, heavy gases."

"Oh. At the refinery in Martinez, right?"

Sanjay nodded, feeling free to look into her eyes, the same dark eyes of her mother, round and full and lit from inside. He remembered Deirdre looking at him just like this, but then he pushed the thought away, pushed her back and down into his mind so deep that finally all he saw was her daughter, Kate. "Yes, I am afraid that it is not a politically correct line of work these days, but we must all drive."

"I didn't mean that," she said, putting on her sweater. "I just didn't know what you did exactly . . . Well, I've got to go."

"You know, Meera will not be home until very late. Why don't you ask Tyler and your father if they would like to eat here tonight? We could all go swimming. The boys would be very happy to see you when they wake up."

Kate looked at Sanjay. "Well, Tyler is at cheerleading camp in San Diego this week. And my dad is . . . He has a girlfriend now. You know. Hannah. She has got these two little boys, about the age of Jaggu and Ari. Her husband left them. Anyway, it's complicated. He's just not home much anymore. Not tonight, anyways."

Sanjay would later wonder why it happened the way it did, how he managed to move his arm and open his hand, and how Kate seemed to understand, reach into his palm, pull herself to him as if his arm were a rope. Then he asked her. Sanjay would always remember that. He asked her first. And then he had her next to him, her face against his shirt, his face against his hair.

❦

As Sanjay watched Kate shut the door, he imagined the odors of baby he well knew: powder on soft skin, milk on cotton, ointments and liniments and urine. He stood still, as if Kate had not just locked her front door in his face, and tried to figure a way into this house. His lies had not worked, and now he wanted to batter the door down, but was unsure how to do it. Would he kick or hit? Fists or feet? Could he push himself into this house as he had pushed himself into this girl who, last summer, lay under him like a river, quivering and moving him to somewhere unexpected?

He turned, walking slowly over the planks of the porch, redwood painted two years ago by Deirdre just months before she died from cancer. Everything had been fine back then, just fine: barbecues in the summer, Meera introducing both Davis and Deirdre to lamb and cous-cous and curry, both families spending Fourth of Julys in the backyard of this house, the colored explosions glimmering over the neighbor-hood, while his small boys ate hot dogs, Fritos, and watermelon.

The steady Pacific drizzle had turned to sprinkles, and then to hard rain. He could hear the steady rush and shudder of water in the gutters, wondering if downtown would flood again as it did at least once a year, cars and shoppers moving in sad exaggerated steps down Monte Veda Avenue, everything slow and wet and gray. He felt like that now, as if he were stuck underwater, and he pulled his hands out of his pockets and looked at them, flipping them palm-up, palm-down, wondering how he had let them slip over Kate's body like thieves, taking and taking, not only from Kate but also from his wife and, he thought now, himself. He had no right to run in, find the baby, boy or girl, and ask, "Is its skin like mine?" He could never pick it up, bury his face between its head and shoulder, and reclaim his flesh. He knew he could not reclaim what he had not owned in the first place.

The distance to his own house—brick path, concrete sidewalk, his own driveway—was not long enough, he thought, not long enough to forget what he knew he had to do.

It was eleven in the morning. Meera stood at the kitchen window, watching spring wind push the pool cover in thick rubber ripples. The fifty-five bulbs she'd planted last fall were blooming in neat con-tainers on the edge of the deck, ruffled yellows, oranges, and whites against the gray sky. As she washed the dishes, she thought, *I must get gladiola bulbs, and some dahlias. I will send Sanjay for them today. He can take the boys to the nursery. It will be good for them to see growing things.*

Meera put down the last wet cup, wiping her hands, looking for her briefcase and bag even as she took off her apron. The boys were at day care—Sanjay had driven them there early this morning—and Sanjay was home, taking a sick day, his face pale, his voice soft.

"Let me look in your throat, Sanju," Meera had asked earlier in the morning.

"I am not a three-year-old, Meera," said Sanjay, pulling away and turning his face from her.

Meera almost flinched, but then put her palm on his shoulder, feeling the warm bone and muscle under her skin. "Do you not think that many diseases are the same for every age. You might have streptococcus. Or an ear infection. Just let me look."

Sanjay shrugged her off and sat on the chair beside their bed. "I just feel fatigued. That is all. I will stay home and do some work around the house."

Sanjay sat in the chair as Meera showered and dressed, moving only when she told him his soft-boiled eggs were done, sitting silently at the table, spooning wobbly egg into his mouth. When he was finished, he didn't look at her, but left the house. Meera went to the living room window, watched him walk down the sidewalk and up the Phillipses' driveway.

Meera watched the space where Sanjay's body had last been, the asphalt of the Phillipses' driveway empty, just black and shiny with rain, the same color as his hair. Sanjay's hair was the same as Meera's mother's had been, straight, black, and thick. When Meera was small and her mother stood over her talking, Meera imagined the shiny strands running down the back of her silk sari to be little ropes she could climb to reach her mother's arm. "Amma! Amma!" she'd want to cry, imagining pulling on the soft fabric and being lifted to her mother's neck, breathing in the fragrance of the delicate green sampungi flower her mother often tucked behind her left ear.

But Meera had never made that cry, at least that she could remember. She made do with the folds of her mother's sari, the perfect red disks of her toenails, the soft *shif, shif* of her mother's sandals on tile. Mostly, even now as she thought of Delhi and her mother, Meera saw her mother sitting, laughing, talking to her father at night, putting a perfectly brown hand on his white-clothed arm. Meera could feel herself in the corner of the hallway—her brothers asleep, her *nani* talking to the servants—watching and listening, waiting for any word to let Meera know that she mattered.

*   *   *

Meera found her leather briefcase and opened it, scanning her appointment book. Not too many today. She could get home by five-thirty, five if she was lucky, and they could all have a late dinner together, something Sanjay really liked, maybe puri sabjee and dal makhani. If she had time, Meera thought, she could even make kheer for dessert. She wondered how she would have time to get to Sangam Grocery in Pleasant Hill. Maybe she could write a list—okra, lentils, pistachio nuts—and ask Sanjay to pick everything up, but she shook her head, unable, she realized, to ask him anything today. Meera closed her eyes, and then thought of calling her friend Momta from work. She had met Momta, a woman the same age as Meera's mother, at temple her first year in the Bay Area. As she and Sanjay stood awkwardly in front of the temple door, Momta had turned from her seat with some other women and stood up, greeting them with palmed hands and the language of her family, her people. After that day, brought as she was to the group of women, their silks mingling together on the smooth floor, their voices mixed with incense and bells, she had someone to call, even as, year by year, Meera forgot what Delhi and her old life were like. She always knew Momta would help her in the old ways of home.

Meera packed up her briefcase and breathed in slowly, realizing she had a feeling in her body she could not diagnose, a lightness in her stomach, a slight ache behind her eyes. Neither of them had been sleeping well lately, and Meera wondered if she and Sanjay were getting a late case of the influenza.

Sanjay came in the front door, silently taking off his shoes, standing frozen in the foyer.

"Why did you go to the Phillipses'? What has been going on over there? Something is just waiting to happen," said Meera, moving to the coat closet for her raincoat and umbrella. "Davis should stay with those girls more often. Last time I saw him, I said so, of course. Deirdre would be so disappointed."

"Meera," said Sanjay, grabbing her arm as she slipped it into her coat sleeve.

"Yes?"

"You need to cancel your appointments for today. We need to sit and talk and then there will be much to do."

"What are you talking about, Sanju? I can't just cancel my appointments on a whim, suddenly. Whatever it is, we can talk about it when I get home. I have a short day. I have plans for an excellent dinner."

Meera tightened the strap on her umbrella, making sure the fabric folded in on itself perfectly before closing the snap with her thumb and forefinger, liking the feel of slight metal under her fingers.

"Meera," said Sanjay. "You cannot go to work today."

"Don't be ridiculous. We can talk later. I have patients to see, Sanju," she said impatiently, tapping the metal tip of the umbrella on the smooth Spanish tile.

"Meera, I am not being ridiculous! You must stay home," Sanjay said, his face flushed, his eyes wide and brilliant.

Meera looked up, dropping the umbrella to the floor. Sanjay was not avoiding her gaze anymore, and she wanted to rip the sorrow and fear and anger she saw in his face and turn it into yesterday, when it didn't exist, when all of the hugeness that just walked in the front door with him wasn't there.

Meera stared at her husband, the pain in her eyes growing to a headache, a pool of tears she had never shed glimmering inside her. Meera remembered her mother's feet, the soft *shif, shif* of leather that always meant she was leaving Meera behind.

"There is a baby, Meera," said Sanjay.

"A baby? What are you talking about, Sanju?"

"Yes . . . Well," said Sanjay, wishing those were the only words he had to say, the echo of them still on his tongue. "Yes. A baby. At the Phillipses'."

"Well, whose is it? Davis's?"

"I think it is Kate's."

Meera opened her mouth and breathed in. "Oh, no. It cannot be! How terrible. How did this happen?"

Sanjay kept his eyes on the floor, working words in his mouth.

"Well? Do you think Davis knows? Of course not. How could he? He's never there, and if he'd known even he wouldn't have let it go this far. They've probably never taken the child to a doctor."

"I am not sure," said Sanjay. "I don't know."

Sanjay closed his eyes, and Meera picked up her briefcase. "I should go over there immediately. Someone needs to give the child an examination."

"Wait. Wait. We must talk before we go over there, Meera."

Meera put her briefcase down and looked at her husband. *Why, of course,* thought Meera, *there is the ill feeling incubating inside me all day.* Meera stood still, and she could hear it, too, the cries of a baby not her own. At night, they had been almost dreamlike, simply a work dream, she had thought, turning in her bed and pulling the blankets over her head, images from the hospital, something that kept her from knowing whether she was asleep or awake. But all along the cries had been from next door, the windows of their houses like faces looking over the fence that parted them, cries that should have pulled Meera up and out of bed.

"Let's sit down," said Sanjay, walking toward the dining room.

"For goodness' sake, Sanju. Let's go over to the Phillipses' and take care of this infant," said Meera, her hand on the doorknob. "You must realize the girls could not have taken proper care of the child."

Sanjay stopped and turned back toward Meera, his shoulders slumped and low. "No. Meera. No. Wait. There is more, and you must listen to me," said Sanjay. "The baby is mine."

❧

"Why? Why?" asked Meera, sitting across from her husband at the dining room table

"I am not certain."

"Please. You must have some idea, Sanjay," said Meera. Sanjay wondered if she was imagining naked legs and hurried kisses that did not belong to her. "You must know why."

Sanjay sat with his hands at his sides. "I think . . . I am not certain. Maybe because I felt some sense of loneliness."

Meera flicked her hair behind her shoulders, and then grabbed the smooth rounded edge of the table. For a second Sanjay thought she might lift and tip the table over, tensing her biceps a bit, feeling the wood move in her hands. Meera was strong enough, lifting her children and other people's every day from beds and examining tables. Her shoulders and back were firm from digging the earth outside. When he held her at night, he could feel her defined muscles. How easy it would be for her, he thought, knowing that she could stop the conversation now, glass and china and linen flying to the ground, his face falling from wasted effort, the day going on as it should have, these imagined bodies stopping, disappearing, moving off and over her bed, disappearing into ugly memory.

"What loneliness?" Meera said finally. "How could you have felt lonely in this house? What are you saying? You have Jaggu and Ari and me. We have our friends and colleagues. You and I sleep in the same bed each night. Tell me, Sanjay, is this a definition of loneliness? If so, I have never heard it put this way."

Sanjay looked down, knowing he could never tell his wife that what she said was true, and he still felt lonely. Sanjay couldn't say there was a place that Meera never touched, couldn't enter, even with her beautiful face, and slim legs, and smooth hands. Finally, Kate had, somehow, moved into the emptiness with him for a while, not taking it away exactly, but making it bearable, sometimes beautiful. He knew if he said that, she would get up, and this conversation might never be completed. "I don't know. But I did it, and now . . . We need to go in and find out about the baby."

Meera was silent, a vacant look crossing her face, and Sanjay knew she must have heard the cries as well, that all those hours he had sat up in bed, awake, listening to the tiny cat sounds, Meera had been listening, too, waiting for someone to make it disappear. And, of course, Meera would have known that sound, hearing it daily at Mt. Diablo Hospital as she made her nursery rounds, listening to those sharp, high cries for mother and milk; Meera would have known all along that next door, one of the girls had a baby.

"Oh, Sanjay," she said. "What could you have been thinking?"

Sanjay looked down, knowing the answer was that he had not, that if he had been, he had been thinking only of himself and Kate. Maybe not even Kate, even as he held her against his body, feeling the joy of her flesh and his, together, even as Kate had looked at him with those open brown eyes.

"This is too much," continued Meera. "What do you expect me to do? You want me to go in and examine this child now? This . . . this child? After what you just told me? How can you ask me such a thing?" Meera pushed back her chair and stood up. She was wearing her raincoat, the belt still slashed around her middle.

"You are the only one I can ask."

"I should go. I should, but it is too much to ask, Sanjay. You are going too far."

"I know," said Sanjay.

"You know? You know this now?"

"Maybe I do not know anything. But we must find out."

"How can you be certain it is your child, Sanjay? What if it is Tyler's? Who knows what has been going on over there this past year?"

Sanjay looked at his wife, who now had tears on her face. He had seen her cry only once, her first year of medical school during an oncology rotation at UCSF. She took care of a twenty-year-old man with testicular cancer, his genitals swollen to the size of balloons. He was unable to move for fear of pain, and when Meera came into his room to take his blood pressure to listen to his heart, she would sit and hold his freckled hand, the skin underneath the freckles yellow and dry.

When she came back to the apartment after seeing him, she would slip into bed with her clothes and white doctor's coat still on, weeping. Sanjay could only sit at her side just as she sat at the young man's, waiting, just waiting. When he died, she sat with his parents and his young wife at his bedside, listening to their tears, finding her doctor's voice, the same soothing sound he heard Kate use with the boys; but it was not a sound Meera used at home, saving it, he thought, for those she thought really needed it.

"We don't have to be the ones to go over," said Meera, wiping her eyes with her sleeve. "If we call the police, they will take care of it. We don't have to go over there at all!" Meera cried. "But even then, Sanjay, it won't matter, will it? You know what will happen to you and to us, Sanjay, don't you? I have seen these cases before."

Sanjay nodded, slightly, his hair in front of his eyes. "Yes," he said, thinking how when he had first held Kate's hand, he had remembered the ads on the billboards and bus sides down by the Martinez refinery that read: SLEEPING WITH A MINOR IS A CRIME. Over the caption was a photograph of a young man, usually black, behind bars. "So it will be better this way. If we got to them first. If we take them to Mt. Diablo, where people know you. Will you come with me to the house? Will you help me find out what is going on?" asked Sanjay, reaching for her hand, slowly.

"Where they know me?" said Meera with a hiss.

"Please," said Sanjay. "Please help me."

Meera stared at Sanjay for a long time, enough, he thought, for their entire marriage to replay in her mind. Somehow, the marriage must have won out, he and the children tipping the scales against revenge, aloneness, and divorce, because Meera nodded and went for her bag. But before she left the room, she stopped and turned to him, her black eyes slit in the shape of anger. She walked to the table and picked up a jar of mango chutney, the one Momta had purchased for her just last week, the slices of mango and onion slick and orange in the sweet brown sauce. Her eyes wet, she fingered the glass jar, the steel top, and then hurled it over his head and against the kitchen wall. He closed his eyes as he heard the jar break, felt the spattering of liquid on his neck, and he turned, watching jagged streaks of chutney stain the white wall. Meera wasn't watching with him. She was staring outside, looking toward the Phillips house. Finally, she said, "You will have to live a long time in the same room with me before I will forgive you."

Sanjay nodded, expecting this, at least.

❧

Before they left the house, Meera opened her bag, realizing that she didn't have much in it besides her stethoscope, odoscope, and some antibiotic samples given to her by a Merck pharmaceutical representative. What good was she outside the hospital? she wondered, remembering the late-night knocks on her family's door, the hushed voices of the servants, and then the calm, deep voice of her father, talking to the neighbors who were worried over a sick child or aunt or grandparent. Sometimes, she would walk into his study and sneak a caramel from the yellow glass candy jar. As she chewed and sucked on the sweet, Meera would walk around the study, finger vials of fluid, the hard stiff spines of medical books, and the rubber of syringes and stethoscope. Everywhere he went, her father, Manjit, was a doctor. Even when her brother Nikhil almost died from the measles, even when her mother miscarried her last pregnancy, a second baby girl.

Everywhere he went, Meera heard the same strong voice, saw him make the same deft, sure movements, as if nothing could change the flesh under the office, the degree, the knowledge.

Meera wondered if she could be that dispassionate, her heart beating almost through her raincoat, her stomach alive with fear. She sighed and closed her bag. "How old do you think this baby is, Sanjay?"

"I am not certain. I have only heard the cries for a few days, I think."

Meera grabbed his arm, her face stern. "When did you last sleep with Kate, Sanjay? This would be a better way to determine the age of this baby."

"What does it matter?"

"You fool!" said Meera, closing her eyes, impatient, angry. "Of course it matters! I need to know what questions to ask." Meera yanked and wrested herself from the fact of the baby being Sanjay's to the realities of a newborn baby's skin, soft and papery, fragile bones just under the skin. She knew that in a week, or even two, the baby should be eating well, maybe eight times a day, the skin under her hands would have fullness to it, not rolls of loose skin. If it was two, three months old, it would need inoculations. "Also, this baby will likely need a vitamin K shot, erythromycin ointment in the eyes, a newborn blood screening. These are extremely important things, Sanjay."

Sanjay let go of the doorknob. "You are right. Of course. The last time was August. It is May. So maybe days, or a week. Maybe two."

Meera listened and wondered, What was August? What happened that month? She reopened her bag and absently organized her tools, tongue depressors, and medicines, feeling plastic and metal and wood under her fingertips. August. Meera remembered unusual, constant heat, maybe ninety-five, one hundred, the boys, Kate, Tyler, and Sanjay in the pool and she dug up gladiolas and spent nasturtiums and trimmed wilted alyssum, sweating under her white hat. Even now Meera remembered Jaggu's and Ari's laughter as Tyler and Kate threw them into the air, catching them as they fell toward the water. In her memory, she looked for Sanjay and found him on a chaise longue, drying, watching the children playing, smiling, drinking a tall glass of orange juice. Meera also remembered the late August vacation to Sea Ranch, just south of Gualala. Their rented house was cool in the afternoon with Pacific wind and fog, the ocean sliding into the thin beaches in smooth slopes, she and Sanjay sitting together on the couch with binoculars watching black oystercatchers and brown pelicans on the barnacled rocks just off the shore. Together they listened to terns, gulls, and the sea as their two boys slept the sleep of afternoon heat in the next room.

Meera felt there was a fist in her throat, clenching up tight, choking off air, but she said, "All right. Let's go." She thought to put on her coat, but then realized she still had it on as if nothing had happened at all; as if she could still get in her Volvo, drive to work, and take care of other people's children.

Sanjay knocked on the door and rang the bell, rolling his fingers through the change in his pocket. Meera stood still, facing the door, following the grain of the wood, noticing its shine, the clean brass of the knocker and door handle. The cocoa mat read WELCOME. The rain had stopped, and the air was warm and wet.

Meera heard footsteps and turned to Sanjay, wanting to move into him, wanting him to protect her from what was coming, but then changed her mind, too angry to touch him, knowing she needed to be protected from him. Meera folded her arms over her chest, lifted her head, and held her breath as Tyler opened the door and wedged her body in the open space. Tyler didn't say anything, blinking into the daylight, Meera thought, as if she had been closeted for months, some underground animal exposed and vulnerable to the light, or the truth.

"We have come to see the baby, Tyler," said Sanjay.

Later, Meera would think about Tyler's face when Sanjay said the word *baby*. At the time Meera thought it was fear that made the girl's hands shake and her body go soft. But Meera realized it was pure relief because the next thing Tyler did was stop and stare at both Sanjay and her for what seemed like minutes. Meera could almost see the life the girl had lived for the last few months find expression on her face: the sadness, the grief, the fear illustrated on her lips, cheeks, and forehead. Then she opened the door wide, wordlessly, and let them in, following them silently down the hall, into the bedroom where Kate sat by a cardboard crib, humming invisible words to a baby.

"When the baby first emerged from the birth canal, did it cry?" asked Meera, holding the baby's chest between her shaking hands, feeling the firm, round chest, flesh around the ribs, noticing that the baby's skin was the exact shade of Jagdish's, creamy brown, like coffee heavy with half and half.

Tyler nodded. "I took that aspirator thing and did her nose, and then I cleaned her mouth three times. Then she started to cry. Hard. Her face was all red."

"What is her name?" asked Meera, looking into the infant's dark eyes.

"Her name is Deirdre," said Kate, still sitting by the closet. She hadn't moved since Meera reached down and pulled the baby to her shoulder, ignoring Kate's face.

Meera swallowed, looking at no one but Deirdre, named for her friend who dug in the soil and who died, leaving only plants and two children for Meera to remember her by. But while the plants bloomed, spring and summer bulbs, flowering perennials in fall and summer, the girls disappeared and holed up in this house in order to bring their mother back to life. But they needed Sanjay to do this, needed a man to cast the spell, plant the seed, and pull Deirdre back to the living.

The baby squirmed under Meera's hand, yawning and letting out a tiny squeak. Deirdre.

Meera blew on the top of her stethoscope, warming it with her breath before she placed it on the baby's chest. These were her rote moves, the questions, the procedures, the measurements, yet her legs wanted to buckle; she wanted to rip the fabric of her husband's shirt; she wanted to wrap her arms around Tyler, comfort this fifteen-year-old who had brought this tiny girl into the world. Meera remembered the first birth she observed during medical school, her shock at the woman's pain, somehow believing that in a hospital, suffering could be avoided. She had read about it in books and heard about it during lectures, but Meera was shocked into silence by all the fluid and blood pouring to the ground, the incredible stretched size of the woman's shiny vagina and labia. And then there was the grayish baby, squeezing into the hospital room, its face wizened and prunish, eyes and mouth scrunched until the doctor stabbed it with rubber, slipping gloved fingers in its mouth, wresting it from the body of its mother. As Meera looked at this baby, Sanjay's baby, she was amazed that it had made the journey with only these two girls, one pushing, one pulling it into the light.

Meera clenched her stomach muscles tight and envisioned her office, took notice of her ordinary moves, her hands whisking over the tape measure. She measured the baby's chest and head, writing notes on a yellow pad she'd pulled out of her bag. She weighed the baby on Deirdre's old scale that Tyler brought in from the bathroom, wishing instead that she'd brought her own scale, the old one she took from the office years ago to weigh the boys in between well-child checkups. Meera found herself nodding her head. Nine pounds, almost ten. It was hard to say. But a girl. *Sanjay finally has a girl. A fine healthy girl. Deirdre.*

Meera rubbed her hand over Deirdre's silky head, knowing this was not a doctor move but a mother's, knowing that behind her Kate sat like a dark stone. Maybe, Meera thought, she could accept this baby, slash some space open in her heart for this child, but what of Kate? Ugly English words she had learned at boarding school almost slipped through her teeth like snakes, words she had practiced with her friends at night: *slut, bitch, whore.* Meera looked at Sanjay, knowing he had broken the relationship off before he had known about the pregnancy, but what brought him to that point of pulling Kate to their marriage bed, what brought them all here now, to this room? Meera almost whipped her head around, wanting to find who was at fault, who she could blame for this mess, whose hands she could lay the baby in and say, "Well, there you go. How do you like that?" Her hands wished for another jar of chutney, something to throw and break, something to leave an angry mark.

Instead, she breathed in and watched Deirdre's eyes open wide, searching for her mother, her mother's nipple. "How often is she eating?" asked Meera, stroking the instep of the baby's foot with her finger.

"All the time. About every three hours," said Kate.

"Maybe less," added Tyler. "She's up, like, all night it seems sometimes."

Sanjay looked down at his feet. Meera imagined he was remembering the night cries. She imagined Kate feeding the baby, the suckling, the quieting while Sanjay was outside, standing in their backyard, unable to move.

"And the stool? What color is it?" asked Meera, looking at Tyler.

"Stool? Oh, God, this yellow stuff. All over. The first day. On the second, there was this black blob, but then, yellow."

"Like mustard?" asked Meera, pulling off her stethoscope.

"Yeah, like mustard," said Kate quietly, moving toward Deirdre.

"Did you ever think to go to a clinic for a prenatal visit?" Meera asked, finally turning to Kate. "You are very, very lucky. Your baby is wonderfully healthy. We will have to run some blood tests and administer some medication, but considering what she has been through, it is a miracle things turned out this well."

Meera wanted to say that if she'd had Jagdish and Ardashir at home, she and the babies would be dead, both catching on the lip of her cervix despite hours of pushing, the attending doctors finally getting Meera to sign the cesarean release forms. Her births were hazy dreams, the deadness of her lower body, the strange zigzag sawing motion of the scalpel, and then the pulling and tugging of hands in her body. Meera remembered her hand in Sanjay's, his words, each time: "Oh, Meera. Look, such a fabulously big boy." And then there was sleep, and later pain, her swollen and tender abdomen and then swollen and tender breasts making the first week almost impossible to survive.

"We read a lot of books and watched films," said Kate quietly. "We knew what to buy and what to do. If something really bad was happening, we were going to call 911."

Meera had always imagined herself like a wood figure at the prow of some old warship, sailing head on into ignorance, picking up all the children who needed her as she blasted through waves of bad habits, poverty, abuse, and cruelty. At work, in her smooth doctor coat, her full name in brown embroidery on her left breast pocket, she could nod and listen but then call the right authorities, hand an adult the correct pamphlet, make decided referrals to therapists and social workers. And she was like that figure at home because she was above it all, her own children well fed, happy, Jagdish singing his ABCs in the bathtub. Now, if she knew how, she would topple herself off the prow, rip her coat from her shoulders, and wail, her hair blown by sea wind that all the time had been meant for her. She had just never known it. She had never seen it coming.

What would a slap sound like in this room? thought Meera, biting the side of her cheek until blood ran on her tongue. But here they all were, all those complicit, pulling closer to her as if she could answer the hardest questions, not about the baby and her health and weight and size, but about why they, any of them, were here. It was as if they expected her to make everything okay just by her walking in the room with her bag and measuring a small, perfect head and chest. Meera wanted to shake them all and say, "Just let me alone. I don't know anything. This is all your doing," but instead she bit down harder, studied the baby, moved Deirdre's legs, circling the small bones in their sockets.

"For goodness' sake, why didn't you tell anyone?" asked Meera finally, and then she wished she could take it back, swallow up the air that carried the words.

As Kate stared at her, Meera wished she could get inside Kate's head for a minute and take in the sideshow of the last nine months, even earlier, watch the affair, the lies, the sad birth in this very room. For an instant Kate seemed full of words, but her mouth stayed still, air swallowed down and silenced. Meera almost nodded and then turned away, realizing the answer was that no one wanted to know about this baby. Meera didn't even want to know now.

"Listen, we did everything we should've," said Tyler, her face red. "We didn't *need* anybody else. We were fine all by ourselves."

Meera turned away, her body flinching, and put a clean diaper on Deirdre and picked her up and handed her to Sanjay. "Here. Here is your daughter."

Tyler, still red from her anger, made a sound like a whistle and a sob, harsh air coming from between her teeth, her face visibly draining down to a shocked, pasty white. She looked at Meera, her hand at her temple. "What are you saying?"

Meera looked at Tyler, considering the girl's empty white face. There was no time for this, Meera found herself thinking, wanting to yank Tyler out of her surprise by the scruff of her neck. How could the girl have been here, with this child, pulling this baby out of her sister without seeing Jaggu and Ari, boys she had bathed and fed and diapered? Why was no one seeing anything? "Oh, please, Tyler. Surely you knew Sanjay was the baby's father?"

Tyler shook her head, her mouth filled with unsayable words. She grabbed Kate's arm and said finally, "All this time and you didn't tell me?"

The sisters hung like a still life in the middle of the room, their hands touching, Kate looking away from Tyler. The only noise in the room was the *shhh, shhh* of Sanjay's smooth hand rubbing Deirdre's back. Meera turned to the wall, fighting an urge to vomit, tasting bile and the blood from her cheek in her throat and stomach.

"Foolish," Meera whispered while bending down to her bag. "Foolish," she said louder, standing up. "But that makes at least two of us who have had this unlucky surprise today. . . . Now. We will all need to go to Mt. Diablo Hospital." She turned toward Kate. "You must give me your father's work phone number or his girlfriend's. I will call him right away."

Both Kate and Tyler looked up at Meera, this new shock pulling them away from the last, their faces young moons, pale and open. "Now?" asked Kate. "Do you have to call him now? Can't we go to the hospital first?"

Meera found the groove she had sawed in her cheek and bit down again, flicking her hair behind her shoulder, first one side and then the other, staring at the girls, who suddenly looked as young as they had when she and Sanjay first moved in, when Deirdre was still alive, when she and Meera would talk over the fence about salvias, buddleias, and potato vines.

Meera turned to Sanjay, who still held Deirdre against his right shoulder, his eyes closed. "All right. But we will call him from the hospital. People will want to ask him questions. He will need to be with us," she said, then adding, "And people will want to talk to Sanjay, too."

Kate and Tyler stood up together, ready to follow the Chaturvedis. Sanjay opened his eyes and said, "Let's put something back on the baby. At least a blanket."

Kate went to the closet and pulled a pink stretchy sleeper from a bag, and took the baby from Sanjay, their hands, Meera noticed, touching so slightly as they passed their newborn child between them.

❧

Kate had only had one pelvic exam before, when she turned sixteen, and the clicking of the metal speculum still surprised her. As she lay on her back, watching the ceiling, feeling the cold tool inside her, she imagined an old-fashioned car crank, the ones in the cartoons, characters turning and turning them before the engine would start.

"Now, I'm not going to do much here. I'm barely opening this. I just want to look around a little with my light," said the doctor. Kate could see only the top of his head, sparkly silvery hairs smoothed over a pink scalp. "Okay. Looks good. I'll give you a Pap smear because we're in here already. There we go." The doctor stood up, sliding out the speculum. Kate grimaced, looking at the silent nurse standing in the corner of the room.

"Are you still bleeding much?"

"A pad a day, maybe. I had some big clots. Sort of like the end of a period or something."

The doctor nodded. "Any fever? Pain? Any strange discharge or odor?"

"Nothing I've noticed."

"All right, then. I'm going to press on your abdomen. Let me know if anything hurts. There? There? There? Nothing? Okay, good." The doctor pulled off his rubber gloves and threw them away, sitting down to write on her chart. "You had a little tear during the birth, and I need to stitch it up. One stitch. Nothing drastic. I'll give you a shot, and you won't feel a thing. I want you and Nurse Randall to talk about birth control later, and she can give you some pamphlets about breast-feeding. You need to make a follow-up appointment with the nurse at the desk, too."

Kate sat up, covering her legs with the papery gown. Her feet looked purple and skinny in this light, and she wished she were dressed and out of this room.

"When do we do this stitch thing?"

"I want to do it now. It isn't quite healed, so we can still mend it."

"Oh."

Nurse Randall walked over to Kate and held her hand. "Don't worry. I'll be here the whole time. Just lie down. We've got to clean you up, then give you the shot first."

Kate looked at Nurse Randall and tried to smile, liking her reassuring voice, even as the doctor walked over to her with the needle. She wondered what they both thought of her, here with her legs splayed and her body unhealed, a baby in another room, a baby she left alone sometimes, people already lined up to talk to her. How many girls did this doctor see like her, hurt, alone, still ripped open from all that had gone in and through her? She wished the needle could cure her, fix everything—her home, her life, her family—even as she felt the shot, moving up, it seemed, into her spine.

§.

Later, Kate sat uncomfortably on a rough tweed couch in Mt. Diablo Hospital's administration meeting room, thinking she'd been doing just fine with the tear—she never even felt it happen—and now, with it mended, she was shifting side to side, pulling at the crotch of her pants, wishing she could sit in a cold bath. As she waited, she watched people walk back and forth in front of the window, all at a fast pace, women in suits and nylons, men in ties and hard shoes, going somewhere crucial, important. She also watched doctors, usually walking with their heads down, writing on pads, or talking to other doctors, hands moving, fingers pointing. This world was so different from the last months of her life, the rhythms of her body taking over anything else, her thoughts only on what she should eat, what the baby would need, where she should hide when her father came home. And then, after the baby was born, it was the hours Kate counted, the hours of sleep, the hours between feedings, the hours before Tyler would come home from school and talk to her. She forgot that during all that time, all those days and hours and minutes, there were active, noisy places like this.

"Kate? I'm Mrs. De Lucca. You can call me Cynthia."

Kate looked up, not having heard the woman walk in the door. "Oh," she said quietly.

"I'm a social worker. I'm here to talk with you about your baby."

"Okay. All right."

"Do you need some water? A soda?"

"No . . . thanks."

Cynthia sat down and adjusted herself on the plastic aqua chair, trying to cross her chubby legs under her wool suit, finally giving up and sitting straight-legged, both feet on the floor and tucked under the chair.

Kate watched as Cynthia got comfortable, thinking it had been a long time since she'd fed Deirdre. She plucked her shirt from her breasts, both engorged and starting to leak. She felt a tingling ache behind her eyes. "Where is Deirdre?"

"Now, Kate. Your baby is being checked and given shots. They're taking some blood. Mr. Chaturvedi has signed all the consent papers."

"Why can't I do that? It's my baby." Kate thought that if she didn't see Deirdre soon, she might explode from tears and milk. She imagined throwing herself down on the floor like she used to do when she was three, kicking her shoes and banging her fists against the linoleum.

Cynthia wrote something down on her notepad. "Kate, you aren't an adult yet. We need someone over eighteen to sign."

"What about my father? Has he come yet? Did anyone call him?"

Cynthia took off her glasses. "Yes. Dr. Chaturvedi called him. He's . . . Well, when he gets here he'll be talking to someone, just like you're talking to me. We need to figure this story out."

"Where's Tyler?" asked Kate, unused to being without her, wishing she'd gone over the story with Tyler before they were separated. *What if she says something different than I do?* Kate thought, anxiously pulling at her shirt again.

"Tyler's in another room. People need to talk to her, too. You'll see her soon," said Cynthia in a clipped tone, anxious to move on.

"How long will we be here? I need to feed Deirdre," said Kate, looking toward the window.

"If you can just tell me your story, how this happened, then I'll go and see about Deirdre. But we need to talk first," said Cynthia, impatience flickering across her face and then hiding under a practiced smile.

"Oh," said Kate, slumping a bit. "Fine. What do you want to know?"

Cynthia raised her eyebrows and put her glasses back on. "All right. Can you tell me when your father stopped living at your house?"

"He met Hannah about a year and a half ago. I guess my mom had been gone . . . dead six months, seven months. I don't know. Something like that. A couple months later he started spending the nights there. He'd come home and all. I mean, he still lives there," said Kate, but she remembered how she and Tyler would wander through his room and the garage after he and Hannah left, listing aloud what was gone this time: razor blades, work ties, fishing pole, gas can, Steely Dan records. Sitting in the living room after their search, Kate wondered which missing thing would signify her father's final visit. She wanted to know what exact item she should hide in order to keep him coming back again and again.

"So would you say he was there one or two nights a week?" asked Cynthia, writing on her pad, the pencil squeak echoing in the bare room.

Kate wanted to nod, but then realized that the last months of her pregnancy, he had been there only in the afternoons for visits, a couple hours to fix the water heater, check the cupboards or fill them, adjust the sprinkler system. Then, as her stomach had gotten harder to hide, she had been relieved, thankful for the quiet nights, the safety of his absence. "Well, maybe one night. But why are you asking me about this? I thought you wanted to know about the baby."

Cynthia looked up at Kate. "This is about your baby. We want to know why no adult knew you were pregnant. Why your father didn't notice."

"But I hid it from him. I hid it from everybody but Tyler. No one knew, not my friends, not the school! I made sure no one knew. I did! I did! It's not his fault he didn't see! Sanjay didn't see either!"

As Kate yelled, her full breasts let down, her T-shirt blackening with milk. "Oh, I want my baby. Give me my baby. I need to feed her."

"We've really got to finish talking, Kate, before I can go get Deirdre," said Cynthia, her pencil scribbling fast on the yellow pad.

"I won't talk any more until I see her. I won't! I've got to feed her! Can't you see? Are you blind?" Kate bent her head to her knees, tears and milk, just as she had imagined, wetting her shirt and pants.

Cynthia stood up stiffly. "I'll give you a minute to calm down. I'll see what I can do." As she left the room, Kate brought her hands to her face and wondered what else would happen, what other answers would come from her, what lies she might have to tell to get Deirdre back in her arms.

Kate stopped crying just as Cynthia returned, bringing Deirdre, who was making a sucking noise that Kate could hear across the room. Suddenly, Kate could almost forgive Cynthia her questions about her father because she had brought Deirdre back.

"She certainly is hungry," said Cynthia. "What a nice big girl."

Kate took Deirdre from her and lifted up her wet shirt, Deirdre latching on to her nipple despite the swollen breast around it. "My milk just came in four days ago. At first there's that yellow stuff, you know. Now I'm just like a cow or something."

Cynthia smiled. "I remember those days. Any baby would cry, and boom! there I'd be with a wet shirt. But don't worry, your body will figure it out."

Kate leaned back, settling her body into the chair, wishing Cynthia would leave Deirdre and her alone. "How many more questions do you have?"

"Not too many. Are you feeling like you can answer them now?"

"Yeah, I guess."

Cynthia sat down, readying her pencil. "Thank you. Okay. Can you tell me about the delivery?"

"Well, Tyler and I read up on everything. We had all the supplies. There was this great home birthing book at the used baby-supply store. So, when I went into labor, Tyler and I just followed along. Tyler was great, though—she delivered her all by herself. And everything was fine. Nothing was wrong with Deirdre."

Cynthia had stopped writing, looking at Kate. "Were you scared? Did you wish you'd told somebody?"

Kate looked up at the social worker, wondering what she expected Kate to say. No? No, she wasn't scared? That she thought, the whole time, that things would be just perfect? How could this woman think that Kate never worried about birth trauma and bleeding and unimaginable suffering? Did she assume this was just some stay-at-home birth project, some kind of extra-credit science experiment? "Of course," she snorted, adjusting her arm as Deirdre stretched. "Of course I was scared. But I knew that if something bad started to happen, we would call 911. We aren't that far from the hospital, you know."

Cynthia waited for more, and then asked again, "Well, then, if you were so afraid, why didn't you tell anyone?"

Kate stopped breathing for a moment, and then sighed into the memory of the time she stared at Sanjay's bedroom window from her backyard, deciding that if she thought hard enough, he would hear her message: "I am pregnant. Please come here to help me." But even then she worried that Meera would intercept, storm over to the house, overturn everything with strong words. More than anything else, she was scared of Meera's eyes. She knew what they looked like even when she was happy, as when Kate played nicely with Ardashir, or cleaned the kitchen before Meera came home—expressionless except for the fact that her smile would pull them upward, crinkle the skin under her lower lids, lessen the darkness Kate did not want to fall into. She knew that when Meera and Sanjay fought, there were silences for days, the whole house falling into despair, sad dinners of Boboli pizzas and microwave meals, Kate silently sliding through the house in her socks as she tended to the boys, as if the Chaturvedis' relationship were a fine crystal glass she carried on her nose.

Just hours ago, Tyler had leaned over in the back of the Chaturvedis' Volvo, leaned over Deirdre in the car seat, and whispered, really almost mouthed, "Do you love him?" Kate pulled herself to the window, ignoring the question and her sister's eyes, asking herself the same question. Kate thought that she had loved him initially, thought that love began with a bringing together of bodies, just what happened in the romance novels she read. Somehow, even if the couple didn't love each other at first, sometime after they made love, they found each other again, and again, and lived happily ever after.

Kate looked at Cynthia, wondering how she could tell her that by not saying anything to anyone, not to her father or Sanjay or Meera, she could keep alive longer the hope that it was love; she could protect them all from the truth that it was really nothing more than three beautiful, sad times in bed. Kate could imagine that all their lives were now ruined for something bigger and more important than kisses and fluids. But things weren't totally ruined—that's what made it confusing. Here she was, with a beautiful baby, and the love she felt for Sanjay and his body was transformed into milk running from her breast to Deirdre.

"I didn't want Meera to know. I didn't want their relationship . . . I didn't want Sanjay . . . It just seemed better to keep quiet."

"Were you scared to upset Sanjay? Did he threaten you in any way? Did you ever feel forced to have sex with him?"

"Oh, no! Never. He is so kind, he . . ." Kate stopped when she saw Cynthia's forehead crinkling, her eyebrows beginning to rise. "He never threatened me."

"Did he know you were under eighteen?"

"He knew how old I was."

"All right. When you were first pregnant, did you think about having an abortion?"

Kate nodded. "Sort of. Not really. I mean, I had the money from all the baby-sitting I'd been doing."

"At the Chaturvedis'?" asked Cynthia.

"Yes, mostly. Some other families. But, like, I'm for it. Really. I've had some friends who've had them. I just couldn't. I kept thinking about those pro-lifers and their poster of someone holding those tiny feet. Not like I agree with that or anything."

Cynthia nodded. "So did you go to a clinic? The Oak Creek Clinic?"

"No. But Tyler did. Tyler got some stuff, asked some questions."

"Okay," said Cynthia.

Kate took Deirdre off her left breast and shifted her to the right, the baby's eyes closed, her mouth moving even as she searched for the new nipple. "Are you done?"

"There's just a bit more. Did you ever leave the baby alone? Even just for a hour or so?"

Kate bent her head down toward Deirdre, thinking about the cardboard crib, and how she and Tyler had stared at the baby before they both had to leave. When they finally made it back home, she realized she never should have left because not for one minute did she stop thinking about Deirdre. Through each day, even those when Tyler got home before her or even those when she knew Tyler was home, through all the writing, geometry, historical periods, basketball hoops, and economic crises, Kate wondered what way the baby's head was turned, if she was wet, imaging a sodden diaper stuck to Deirdre's smooth skin. And sometimes, on her way back from school, driving fast in her mother's old BMW, she imagined Deirdre dead, on her stomach, drowned in milky vomit, or tied up in her sleeper somehow, choked, blue, stiff.

"Yes," she whispered.

"For how long?" asked Cynthia.

"Three times. One and a half hours each. To school and back and a fifty-minute class," she said, then louder, "Tyler and I planned it out as best we could. There were just these three days we couldn't figure out. I had some tests!"

"Okay. Okay. I just needed to know. I guess that's all for now. I'll be back in about fifteen minutes for the baby."

"What do you mean, for the baby?" Kate asked.

Cynthia put her glasses in her pocket. "They didn't finish everything they needed to do."

Kate unconsciously pulled Deirdre tighter to her. "They're not going to take her away from me, are they? You're not, right?"

Cynthia stopped and looked at her. "I can't promise anything, Kate. It's just not up to me."

"But why? I did a good job. She's healthy, right?"

Cynthia eyed the door and then sighed, sitting down again. "Look. We have to talk to everyone—the detectives and doctors and your family—and then we'll figure it out."

"But how long would they take her? Where would she go? How soon would she come home?"

"Listen, let's just take it one step at a time. I can't answer any of your questions, Kate. Now isn't the time to start worrying. It's too late for that," she said, standing up and walking out of the room, her heels clacking on the floor like bullets.

Kate hung in the empty silence of the room after Cynthia left, shaking her head. She never imagined that this would really happen. Her mind hadn't reeled out the story this far. Each day since Deirdre's birth was its own logistical nightmare, a worry of feedings and diapers, tests and reports, and daily discussions about her father's schedule. She had never thought about this stark room with its stiff chairs and brilliant, harsh light, Deirdre's eyes closed to everything but her milk.

Kate jerked as the door opened and a nurse walked in. "Hi. I'm Raylene. I'm going to sit here with you and the baby. If you have any questions about the baby, go ahead and ask," she said, but instead of sitting across from her like Cynthia did, she grabbed a *People* magazine from the table and sat on a threadbare couch by the door, curling her legs up under her.

Kate nursed her baby, thinking, *If I'd wanted to escape, I should have left long ago. Now it's too late. I'm never going to see Deirdre again. They are going to take her from me and give her to someone else because I did the wrong thing.*

Kate knew she shouldn't have let Sanjay and Meera bring her here. Or, she should have gotten out of the car with Deirdre, jumped into a taxi, and taken that long road she'd imagined she'd take with Sanjay, the one that never ended.

❧

When Cynthia De Lucca asked, "How often was your father home each week?" Tyler wanted to say, "Oh, every night. He came home really early, like, maybe three or four each day and didn't leave in the mornings until nine. He helped us with homework and took us to movies. You know, like any dad."

But instead she said, "Once every, like, two weeks," surprised those were the words that came, almost grimacing at the way the ugly sentence hung in the air.

When Cynthia said, "Were you ever scared about having to deliver a baby?" Tyler wanted to say, "Never. I always knew everything was going to be fine." Instead, she told Cynthia that she was scared almost every day, wondering how she was going to pull the baby out of Kate. Tyler told her how she had nightmares of the baby half hanging from Kate's body, lifeless, blue, the cord around its throat. She told Cynthia how she prayed that the baby had turned head down and how she sometimes felt her sister's stomach for clear signs of rear end and kneecaps. She told Cynthia about all the lies: how she lied to her father, and to the school, and to her friends. She told Cynthia that she missed all sorts of homework and tests, and that she had to quit the cheerleading squad because she had to go home to make sure Kate wasn't in labor or, worse, had delivered, the baby white and dead on the bedroom carpet. Tyler told Cynthia that despite the daily, constant worry, her father hadn't come home, discovered them, and gone crazy, knocking glass and books and papers to the floor. Tyler told Cynthia about all the blood and the Clorox; she told her about how she dug the hole for the placenta. And finally, she told Cynthia how she hated Kate sometimes for her pure selfishness, for doing this without thinking about anyone else. Tyler told Cynthia how she wished her life could go on as normal, how she didn't know then that Sanjay was the father, how she thought about calling her own father, late at night, when Kate was asleep, whispering, "Come home, come home. I can't stand it anymore. Take care of this yourself."

"Of course. Of course you felt that way, Tyler," said Cynthia, shaking her head. "But has anyone told you how brave you were? Delivering a baby. That's not something everyone does often or ever."

Tyler looked up, her brown eyes full of the last six and a half months. "No one's said that. Kate has thanked me. But no one said I was brave. Like, I've never been brave. I'm afraid of daddy longlegs and spiders."

"Well, in my book, you acted very bravely."

"Thanks," said Tyler, wiping her nose, wishing she had a Kleenex, and rubbing her hand on her jeans.

"I want to ask you a couple more things," said Cynthia. "You didn't know about Sanjay, did you? Okay. But did you ever hear Kate talking about him or notice anything peculiar about their relationship."

Tyler shook her head. "You know, I just found out today. At first I thought it was this guy who used to call her about a year ago, Teddy! I don't know . . . I think I knew it wasn't Teddy. I wondered why Kate didn't want me to baby-sit over at the Chaturvedis' anymore, but I was so busy with school it didn't really matter. I guess I really must have known, from when she was born. But not really."

Cynthia smiled at Tyler and patted her arm. "That's okay. That's all for now. In a bit, I'll come back, and we'll talk again."

"But, Cynthia, what's going to happen? What's going to happen to us?" asked Tyler.

Cynthia looked at her, her face tightening in a way that made Tyler nervous. The social worker stared at her and shut something down, her gaze full of truths that were going on above and beyond her. "I don't know yet. But don't worry."

Tyler watched Cynthia leave the room and sighed, trying to believe what she said. She slid down in her chair, almost happy. She put her feet up on the chair across from her and, for the first time in months, closed her eyes without flinching at every sound, without thinking, *Where's Kate? How is the baby? Does anyone need anything?* In just two minutes, her head on her shoulder, Tyler was deep in a dream.

※

What was waiting for him inside wasn't what kept Davis Phillips from barreling through the hospital doors, grabbing his daughters, and taking them and the new baby home. It was the smell: something he imagined was colored the sickly green of hospital garb, something with the tang of overcleaned floors, ammonia, sterile bandages, the forced air pumped into someone's lungs. It was the memory of walking down the eighth-floor walkway toward Deirdre's room, the bank of windows facing Mt. Diablo, bay fog creeping over the hills, spreading around the mountain like cold hands, his two girls at his sides. It was his wife's face, pasty, bloated, the tubes in her mouth pulling her lips raw and red, her eyes shut, her hands limp. It was the smell of her breath, full of metal, the chemotherapy still in her system. It was the clicks and whirs of the wheezy respirator, the buzz of the EKG, the slow drip from the IV. And there were the bags full of Deirdre's fluids hanging on the side of the bed. At least when they were full, he knew Deirdre's body was still working, that she was still alive. That day he noticed someone had braided her hair during the night, a nurse, he thought, but as he felt Deirdre's leg under the thin sheet, he felt a week's growth of hair, something that would have made her laugh. She might have kidded, "I'm going native on you," rubbing him under the sheets with her legs. But here, in the hospital, her unshaved legs meant that Deirdre couldn't take care of herself, that she wasn't able to feel her own body growing away and apart from him, the girls, and everything.

There were more visits like this, until the last one, the tubes removed, her still hands folded on her stomach, only a tremor of breath under her ribs, and then nothing, no monitor sounds, no air pumping, no busy nurse and doctor voices asking questions. Just Davis, his two girls, his sister Gwen, and the nun, who pushed him toward his wife's bed, saying, "It is good to see this. This is something you must see." Davis tried to believe her. He remembered the cross hanging next to her bed, the bronze Jesus hanging over them all.

"Right this way," said the police detective, taking Davis through the door, the smells hitting him all at once, but there was no stopping this parade of blue and white, doctors and social workers and police detectives leading him to a room where they sat him down and gave him a Dixie cup of water.

"No. I'm okay," he said, then almost recoiled at his lie, realizing that he was not okay, that he hadn't been okay for a long time. "Listen, I want to see my daughters."

The police detective who seemed to be in charge sat down with him at the table, taking out a slim notebook and a black pen. The man didn't look at Davis as he spoke. "This is very complicated. We've got a number of things to deal with."

"You can't keep me from seeing my daughters. I'm not under arrest, am I?"

"No. Not at this point. But you are just going to have to wait," said the detective.

"What do you mean? Why can't I see them?"

The police detective shook his head. "First, let's you and me talk. My name's Johnson. You and I have got to figure out what went on with your girls."

"You now, I have a right to see my children. I want to see that they are all right. I want to know if Kate is okay," said Davis, gripping the paper cup. "And the baby."

Johnson looked up at him, his blue eyes full of contempt. "Look, everyone's fine. This isn't the place where they need to be checked up on. That was a lot earlier. Right now your daughter Kate and the baby are being seen by medical personnel and social workers. Your other daughter has talked to the social worker. We just need to get some information from you before we can proceed."

Davis swallowed some water, gritting his teeth as it went down his throat. He stood up, knowing he was a big man, a tall man, and he knew he could walk out the door. No one had arrested him, but there were rules, he knew that, had known that since they kept his wife away from him just after her surgeries or while she was in the ICU. "You can't come in right now, Mr. Phillips," the nurses would say. "The doctors are with her. We'll let you know."

Then, like now, he'd wanted to beat down doors and throw tables. He looked at the wobbly Formica table at which Detective Johnson sat, and realized he could flip it easily, with one hand, stall the man who looked at him with such disgust, and run out of here, up to pediatrics, where the children must be—or maternity. Davis didn't know, exactly, but he could find Meera, and she'd show him where to go. She was the one who called him. She must still be here for them, as she was when Deirdre was sick, making sure the staff was taking care of her, checking her chart, reading books to Deirdre even as she slept in a chemoed dream.

But Davis was too late. That's what Detective Johnson meant. This wasn't the place to worry about his daughters. He should have been worrying about this the day Rachael cornered him in the driveway, the day Meera told him to stay home more. He should have been in the house, waiting for all the things that obviously went wrong. But he was here instead. This was the place they were taken when all the trouble had been had. Davis shook his head. He had not kept his wife or his daughters safe, so why would he be allowed to go to the dark, private places that were theirs alone?

"Sit down, please, Mr. Phillips," said the detective, who had pushed his chair back from the table, ready, it seemed, to jump up and grab him if necessary.

Davis felt like a fake. Someone who blusters and roars, when inside, there is nothing but dead air. "All right," he said, sitting down, his big bones awkward on the plastic chair. "I'll answer your questions. But I want to see my daughters."

Detective Johnson coughed. "I'll see what I can do about that after we're done."

"Fine," said Davis, folding his hands on his lap, waiting for the questions.

"Now, you say you never knew your daughter was pregnant? How is that possible?"

Davis felt his face grow red, anger bloom hot in his throat like a queue of swear words, but he sat silent for a minute. Detective Johnson continued. "Nine months pregnant, Mr. Phillips. Surely you must have seen something."

"I didn't. She wore really baggy clothes, and she's grown so tall. I guess she really tried to hide it. Or . . ."

"Or you weren't paying attention. How long has it been since you lived in the house?"

"I still live in my house."

"That's not what your daughters told the social worker. One said you were there once a week, the other said maybe once every other week. Both said you came by in the afternoons to check on them, but they weren't often home when you showed up, just finding notes on the table and the like."

Davis flashed to Hannah, her tidy little cottage downtown, Sam and Max in matching bunk beds, her cozy double bed that left no room for thought. "I have been spending a lot of time with my girlfriend, Hannah. At her house downtown. She's got little kids."

"Um-hum. So what was it? Once a week or once every other week?"

"Why does this matter? Am I on trial here, or something? What, exactly, are you trying to determine?"

"Well, to be frank, Mr. Phillips, how you acted as a parent. I suppose we assume parents will notice when their daughters are nine months pregnant and ready to give birth in the house."

Johnson was right, of course, but Davis wished he could crush him as he had the empty water cup, the waxed paper crumpled in his palm. "Once every other week. Sometimes not even that."

The detective looked up at him, scratching his cheek with his pen, then inked out more words. Davis asked, "Do I need my lawyer?"

Johnson coughed again, a nervous habit, thought Davis, something to keep sound in a painful room, where the words were too ugly to hang alone. "We're not going to arrest you, if that's what you mean. We've got to figure out if we need to call CPS."

"CPS," said Davis, rolling the letters on his tongue like bad medicine.

"Child Protective Services."

"Why do they need to be called?"

"Mr. Phillips, let me try to give it to you straight, as you don't seem to be getting this at all. You have two girls, both underage, living at your house basically alone. One somehow gets pregnant and stays pregnant for nine months without anyone noticing. Not the school, not the neighbors—obviously—and not you. Then, come labor time, the younger one has to deliver a baby. And then the three of them are living at your house alone until the neighbor finally hears the cries and brings them all in, the mother and child both needing medical attention. We call this child endangerment, Mr. Phillips, and we need to ask some questions and do some looking around."

"I love my daughters," said Davis.

"Maybe you do. But we're not talking about love here. You'll need a lawyer, though not for keeping you out of jail. Probably for keeping custody of both your girls, but that is for the social workers and the judge to decide. They'll figure out what to do with the baby, too. For now, you tell me what I need to know, and I can talk to the social worker, and we can figure this out."

"What about the baby? What do you mean?" asked Davis.

"They have to decide who will get custody. Your daughter, you, the state. There'll be an extensive investigation," said Johnson, leaning back in his chair. "It's not going to be easy."

Davis put his arms on the table, staring down at the strange dotted Formica, breathing in his own stale breath, his sudden sweat, the heat from his face and hair. They were all his responsibility—Deirdre, Kate, Tyler, and this new baby—and he could not move his mind to imagine how he could take care of them.

How had he ever taken care of any of them? Life had just happened until the day Deirdre found the lump. He remembered her anxiety as she said, "Here, press here. Do you feel it? Do you feel anything?"

Davis had wanted to say no, he felt nothing, and hold her breasts as he had done so many times, kissing away this thing he did feel, this grainy pellet under his fingertips.

He thought of Tyler the last time he had come home to check on the girls, furiously cleaning dishes as he grilled her, the clank of glass after glass, her mother's apron tied around her small woman's body. Now he could see her lies, her mouth lurching over her words, "Nothing's wrong. Everything is fine." And he wondered where Kate was that day, slipped behind a door, crouched in the closet, hidden under her bed or in her closet with her baby that she soothed into silence.

"Listen," Detective Johnson said, putting down his pen. "Just take it as it comes. We've got this one other thing. About pressing charges against the father."

Davis looked up. "You mean me? I thought you said I wouldn't need a lawyer."

"No. Against the father of the baby."

Davis realized that in the flurry of bad news this morning, he hadn't really thought about the father. When Meera called, she'd just said, "Davis. I'm with the girls down at Mt. Diablo Hospital. Kate has had a baby."

"Excuse me? Meera, what did you say?"

He heard her clear her throat. "Kate has had a baby. You need to come to the hospital. There will be . . . there will be people waiting to talk to you."

Davis hadn't even bothered to talk to Steve, his boss, or his coworker Roger, who stared at him as he left his desk without a word, or even to call Hannah. He just pushed back from his desk, leaving his suit jacket hanging on his chair, and rushed out the door, finding his truck and driving to Mt. Diablo Hospital almost as if he were in a coma, following a path he felt he knew by heart, the turns, the lights, the bumps on Ygnacio Valley Boulevard. But he hadn't bothered to ask, "Who? Who did it?"

Johnson coughed again, running his hand through his hair. "The father of the baby is your neighbor, Sanjay Chaturvedi."

"What? What?" said Davis. "Sanjay? My neighbor?"

Detective Johnson looked at Davis a minute before answering. "Yes. Sanjay Chaturvedi."

Davis dropped his head and closed his eyes. Sanjay! His friend. A friend who had betrayed him. But wasn't he just as bad? Davis knew the detective really wanted to arrest him, even though it had been he and Kate who had been betrayed, by Sanjay, by life, even by Deirdre, who left them, left them to this horrid thing. "She isn't . . . isn't even eighteen."

"Dr. Chaturvedi alerted us to this fact when she called," said Detective Johnson.

"Meera told you that? Meera called you?" asked Davis.

"Yes, she did, Mr. Phillips."

"I don't believe this. I just don't fucking believe this," said Davis, standing up again, turning to the slit of light coming from a tiny strip of windows just below the ceiling. "Shit," he said, knowing this wasn't possible, bringing his palms to his face, feeling his stubble and sweat, making sure he was really still here, in this room, with the vision of two mismatched, illegal bodies, his daughter, his neighbor, together in a bed, maybe his own. His stomach rushed to his mouth, and he leaned over, holding on to the chair, swallowing stiffly.

Detective Johnson stood up and pushed in his chair. "Hey. Hey. We're going to take care of it. And the last thing we need is for you to go acting up now when it's too late. We're taking good care of your daughters and baby Deirdre. Listen, stay here, and I'll be back to talk to you some more."

"Wait!" said Davis, looking up surprised. "Wait. What did you say the baby's name was?"

"Well, I thought it was . . ." Detective Johnson looked at his notebook, flipping through pages. "Yeah, just what I said. Says here they're calling her Deirdre."

❧

After Sanjay signed the papers and handed his baby girl to the nurse, a plainclothes policeman and a detective whose name was Johnson took him to a waiting room.

"Mr. Chaturvedi, did you know that Kate Phillips was under eighteen?"

"Do not answer him!" Meera hissed, pressing his arm with her fingers.

Sanjay closed his eyes, feeling the "yes" on his tongue heavy as guilt.

"Yes."

"Well, then, Mr. Chaturvedi, I am placing you under arrest for the statutory rape of a minor. You have the right to remain silent. Anything you say can and will be used against you. You have the right to have an attorney present during questioning. If you cannot afford one, the court will appoint one. Do you understand? Are you in need of a Hindi translator?"

Sanjay looked at Meera. He wondered, for a second, if she would turn, stare with angry eyes and a repressed sneer, and state, "We have both been schooled in British and American Standard English dialects," as she had to preschool teachers, grocery store clerks, and real estate agents. But instead she turned from him, leaning her shoulder against the wall. He looked at the officers, wanting to tell them about his own grandmother, who married at thirteen, had her first baby at fifteen. He wanted to say that Kate never seemed underage, that she spoke wisdom through her body and her touch. Sanjay wanted to say that he would take back all his kisses and soft words and pleasure now, take back the passion and the mistakes if he could, but instead he said quietly, in clipped, perfect English, "Yes, I understand. I do not need a translator."

"Okay. We are going to take you downtown, where you will be able to place a call to your lawyer."

As they led him out of the hospital, Meera turned to him, following the three as they walked. "I will call the lawyer, Sanjay. Do not say anything until he arrives. Do not say a word more to anyone."

For the first time since they had walked down the Phillipses' hallway and into Kate's bedroom, Sanjay looked at Meera. There were tender wrinkles under her eyes, smudges of time and weariness. He was slung back into the memory of the first time he saw her at his friend Swapan's apartment, drinking a glass of red wine, her small body wrapped in deep purple fabric. When they were introduced, she looked at him with these same eyes, but then they were open and unlined with no idea of what was inside him, all that would later lead them to this dark moment in the hospital. Yet here she still was, this same woman, watching him, knowing him better than she ever had before, knowing the longing and sadness and fear he had kept to himself all this time. And that was when Sanjay began to weep because in her way, without touching him but by calling the lawyer, by facing him with her fierce eyes, Meera was saying, *I am still here, Sanju.*

❧

When Meera hung up the phone after talking to the lawyer, the world began to move at a slow fluorescent hum, the nurses sliding by her as she leaned against the counter, the busy voices on the intercom, the whirs of monitors, the swift rings of the telephones merging into one mass of noise and light that pulsed around her like a migraine. For the first time, her agreeing to bring everyone to this hospital, her hospital where she had privileges, seemed insane, something she would always wonder about. Earlier, Meera thought bringing them all to Mt. Diablo would mean she could oversee the case herself, determine who knew what and how much, but the moment she walked inside, Sanjay, the girls, and the baby were sucked from her hands, and she was as ignorant and alone as she would be anywhere else.

Meera wasn't sure she could look up, scared to see a face, a smile, feel a pat on her shoulder, take in any of the pity that was already stinging her like nasty grammar school pinches.

"Dr. Chaturvedi?" said a nurse sitting behind the counter.

Meera looked up, recognizing the woman, an LPN, a woman who baked bourbon bundt cakes during the holidays and wore cat pins on her uniform. Phyllis. Her name was Phyllis. "Yes?"

"Um, can I do anything? Should I call your office and tell them you won't be in?"

Meera shook her head. "I have already called them. Thank you, Phyllis. I think I will go home now. If you hear anything, if anything happens here, would you page me?"

Phyllis nodded. "Oh, sure. Okay. You know, I'm really sorry . . ."

But anticipating those words, that *sorry,* Meera turned from the counter, walking toward the automatic doors, hoping that air, real air, would change all this, would lift this feeling clinging to her and lift it all away.

The Volvo still smelled like baby, Meera thought, breathing in soft particles of powder and shampoo. Sanjay's baby had been here, sitting right here, she thought, rubbing her palm on Ari's smooth plastic car seat. She sat down, turned on the ignition, and looked out the windshield. There had been nothing but fog and clouds and rain for days. Meera remembered her early frustration with sunflowers, tomatoes, and peppers, angry at the wilt and mold, the soggy flower stalks and black bruises on the tops of the fruit, desperate for the heat of her mother's Delhi garden, the steady sun and changeless air that pulled plants from the ground like miracles. But Deirdre had helped Meera, showed her how to cultivate the plants inside in empty egg cartons, then small pots, bringing the plants out only when the sun and heat were sure to be there, early May, the vegetables and flowers growing and blooming in fast rhythm to the quick summer.

"It's just different than India," said Deirdre. "If you want tomatoes, you have to adjust. But you can always plant other things." Deirdre brought over special California rhododendrons with names like "Countess of Haddington," "Atoon Van Welie," "Countess of Sefton," and "Saffron Queen," helping Meera mix the soil just right. When Tyler and Kate sauntered through the backyards, Deirdre would whisper to Meera, "Don't look now, but there go the Saffron

Queens." Meera laughed, moved closer to her friend, their dirty hands touching, and learned about the deep shade of her backyard, the cool caves made by the oak and bay trees, the humidity and soft clay soil, the very things that with time and compost brought forth yellow and pink rhododendron blossoms the size of a child's face.

Maybe she had learned all Deirdre could teach her by the time Deirdre withered away from cancer, first her body, then her brain. But sometimes even now Meera looked at the wet ground and thought, *I should ask Deirdre,* or *Deirdre will know about this plant,* almost walking to the side of the fence to peek over, anxious for Deirdre to look toward her with her brown eyes, her long body kneeling at the foot of a tree or at a row of beans.

Meera wished she could ask Deirdre something now, walk into Deirdre's kitchen, sit at the long farmhouse table, and wait for a cup of tea. Deirdre would be talking, brushing her hair behind her ear, and pulling boxes of tea bags from the cupboard. She would smile, pat Meera's shoulder, pull perennial catalogs from drawers, and array them on the table like Japanese fans, her eyes full of the potential of the Monte Veda soil they shared. Deirdre might complain about the girls, calling them "those little pills," laughing at how Tyler hid her homework under the sofa; or she might ask Meera about Jaggu and Ari, wondering about baby teeth and sleeping patterns and the mystery of boys.

Suddenly, Meera wanted to thank Deirdre, wishing she could say, "No more. You have given me so much already. What can I do for you?" Meera wanted to go to Deirdre as she had when Deirdre was sick, sit on the chair next to the couch and read. Most of the time she knew Deirdre was asleep, her breaths deep and even, but Meera read on. She believed that she could slide herself and her sick neighbor into another world, one of different lives, the lives on the page before her. For minutes, maybe hours, they were both in England, walking London streets, buying flowers for a party that night, thinking of love and loss and the beauty of children. Together they were in Sri Lanka, watching a grandmother make rice balls and frying sweet bread for her granddaughter. This was how Meera loved Deirdre; this was how she repaid those hours of help and attention.

How could I hide this baby from her? Meera wondered, feeling the itch of secrecy between her teeth. Even though she wouldn't want to make a story of real life, Meera knew she'd have to tell Deirdre that they had taken Kate and pulled her into their family without asking.

❧

As Davis left the hospital, told finally by Detective Johnson, "Look, just go home. The social workers and doctors are still with the girls and the baby. It's a little too late to give them advice anyway," he found himself holding his breath, pushing air slowly out of his nose, keeping as much oxygen in his lungs as he could, just so he could make it to the glass doors that had let him in.

Davis had been at Mt. Diablo for hours, sitting in the small, airless room, answering questions and filing complaints, his heart pounding to all the different news: Kate, Sanjay, the new baby, the new Deirdre. He knew Detective Johnson had kept him in the room while Sanjay was questioned and taken to jail, maybe worried that Davis would run down the hall and put his hands around his neighbor's neck, choking the breath out of him. Davis wondered if he would have done that, wondered what it would feel like to fit his hands around Sanjay's neck, pressing down on his windpipe, taking and withholding the air Sanjay needed to live. He imagined Sanjay pressing back, his hands around Davis's neck, taking and pressing back, the two of them, responsible, culpable, dead and gone, leaving Meera to clean up the mess of their lives.

Davis also knew he should probably wait until the interviews and reports were completed, the girls ready to leave for wherever they were sending them, but he watched himself react to Detective Johnson's command, relief as well as memory pushing him toward the door, the parking lot, the car, keeping him from doing what he should.

Davis avoided the faces of visitors, patients, and doctors, moving against the wall until he reached the door, and then air, breathing in the wet sky in front of him, breathing out stale smells of death and sadness, the same air that hovered over his wife during her last week. Later, after the doctors had convinced him to turn off the machines, Davis wondered if he had missed something, if Deirdre had ever told him not to keep her alive until the very last moment. Would she have agreed to the ventilator tube down her throat, the oxygen in her nose, the electrical connections to the monitors? What would she have endured to come back for a minute, an hour, a day? He wondered if he should have gone to her, pulled her to him, all fragile, papery skin and stiff hair, reached his nose and lips to the tender skin behind her ear, and asked, "What now? What do you want me to do?" Maybe if he had done that, and then waited by her side, still and soft into the late hours, Deirdre would have moved her hand, touched him as he laid his forehead against the blue sheets, brushed his hair back, and given him the right answer.

"Mr. Phillips," said the young doctor, a woman with black eyes, eyebrows, and hair that seemed to jump off her luminous skin. She waited for him to meet her eyes, and then flipped through the chart, clicking a ballpoint pin with her right hand. "Listen. When your wife's heart stopped at home—from the stress of all the chemotherapy, we think—she was deprived of oxygen for too long a time. The last EEG we did indicated that there is no measurable brain activity."

Davis had stared at her, thinking, *No brain, no brain*. "But what about all the movement she's doing?" Deirdre almost seemed to writhe on her bed, her head moving back, her eyes rolling, her feet twisting as if she were propelling herself through water.

"Yes, well, if you've noticed, even that movement is getting weaker. We call that *de cerebrate* posturing. It is a signal from the lower brain to stand up. It's from our earlier days as a species. It's a survival mechanism, that's all."

Davis felt the blood pulling away from his face and the cold, antiseptic air crawl across his skin. All along, all week, he had thought Deirdre was pushing herself to consciousness, telling him to stick around, to wait, to make sure he was there when she broke through the surface of the water.

Davis looked back into the room, his sister Gwen, Kate, and Tyler sitting by the bed, Gwen stroking Deirdre's hand and hugging Tyler, who sat in her lap. Out in the waiting room, Gwen's husband John, Rachael and Bob, Meera and Sanjay, three women from the cancer support group, and his boss Steve sat in clumps on fake leather couches, talking quietly, their eyes, he knew, on the door that would open soon and let them in to say good-bye. "What . . . what do you want to do?"

The doctor rubbed her forehead, her eyes still on the chart. "We want to take her off the ventilator."

"Will she . . . will she breathe on her own?" asked Davis.

"It's always possible. But truthfully, I don't think she will."

"So, she's going to die," said Davis, holding his body straight with his arms, hoping he wouldn't fall down in front of everyone.

"Yes. She's going to die," said the doctor, looking up. Davis thought her eyes were shiny with a layer of tears, but he couldn't look long into her serious face.

"Okay. Okay. When do you want to do it?"

The doctor looked toward the room. "Your family should probably go into the waiting room with the others while we take out the tube. Then you can all come back and say good-bye."

Davis nodded. "So right now."

"Yes. The nurses will come in as soon as I talk to them."

"Okay," said Davis, walking back to the room to tell his family. But before he walked into the room, he stopped, seeing what he knew he would see for the last time, his family, all together, even if Deirdre was really already dead. Her small reptilian brain was trying to tell her to be human, to stand up, to survive, but even that wasn't working. Maybe, he thought, this minute could last longer than it should, stretch out into a better memory, and he could imagine that Deirdre was awake, laughing about the strange night when her heart stopped and then was started again by paramedics in blue, putting her hand to her chest, thankful that she was alive and suddenly getting better, the cancer scoured from her bones and blood with poison, that finally everything could go along as it had before.

Outside Mt. Diablo Hospital, Davis breathed in nothing but sadness, the air as dark as his thoughts, the forever picture of his dead wife on her last bed surrounding his face like a caul. During the worst and last moments of her life, when she was in her bed at home, her brain and body slowly turning off, he hadn't been with her, hadn't held her as that invisible thing inside her flickered and shut down. Where had he been? Watching television? Turning down the girls' beds? Eating a handful of Planters peanuts over the kitchen sink? He couldn't remember. He had only been there later, as Deirdre's body, somewhat and mistakenly revived, was taken to the hospital, and then later, as it lay on the bed writhing in ancient human impulses. What had he been saving and holding on to? Davis wondered. What could he have possibly done for his wife then?

It was the same now; he had done the same incompetent, shitty job with his daughter as he had done with his wife. Was there anything he could do? What would it take, what could he barter or sell or steal, he wondered, for it to be 1981, and instead of Kate, it was Deirdre who was the new mother in this same hospital? Davis unlocked his truck and wished he could retravel all those old years and stop the future from ever happening.

❦

Kate held Deirdre against her shoulder, rocking in the way she had discovered put the baby to sleep, back and forth, side to side, over and over again. She listened to the baby's breath, waiting for that smooth pattern of sleep, waited for the little body to go limp, to relax, finally ready for a mattress. A new nurse—Raylene long since gone home—had brought a rolling, plastic bassinet from the nursery and had taken Raylene's old place in the corner.

Kate eased Deirdre into the bassinet, slowly pulling her fingers out from behind her back and her chest, pulling the hospital blanket over her.

The nurse looked up, and walked over, both of them watching Deirdre sleep.

"She sure sleeps good," whispered the nurse. "You're lucky."

Kate walked with the nurse away from the bassinet, and they both sat on the couch. "Well, it was hard, the first week especially. I mean, I felt I was up almost every twenty minutes or something. But now things are better."

"That's good. It just gets easier," said the nurse.

Kate looked at the nurse, wondering if she was just being nice. Or, Kate thought, in a moment of fatigue or malice, stupid. She wondered how it could get easier. She hadn't seen her father or Tyler all day, just the nurses, Cynthia De Lucca, Detective Johnson, and the doctors. Kate knew that something bad was going to happen—she just didn't know what it was exactly. Everyone asked too many questions about her father, Deirdre's feedings, her pregnancy. No one would be paying her so much attention unless they wanted Deirdre, her best thing of all.

As Kate thought, Cynthia De Lucca walked in the door, her face looking smudged and worn, her collar askew, one point headed toward her ear. Kate noticed the zipper on the back of her skirt wasn't completely up, a small swatch of satin underwear peeking out.

"Okay, Kate. They've done all the blood work on the baby. She got all her medicine. Everything is fine. She's doing good."

Kate, who never thought anything would show up, shrugged. "Good."

Cynthia put down her purse and a large bag. "This is going to be hard for you, but this is what the court ordered. I want you to listen to me. I am really tired, and I know you are, too. We just have to do this, and we can talk about it more tomorrow."

Just then a police officer walked in quietly, standing by the door, his hands at his sides. Kate felt something rise through her chest and arms, and she stood, walking back to the baby she had just so carefully put to sleep, and picked her up, placing Deirdre's small, heavy head against her shoulder. She pulled Deirdre closer to her, feeling the baby's head and back tight against her hands. She saw Cynthia and the police officer talking, but the conversation was coming to her in static gray blots of sound and picture at her eyes and ears. All she could focus on were the fast pulse beats in her own body.

"Kate? Kate. The judge on this case has ordered you and Tyler to a residential facility," said Cynthia, putting on her coat. "And I got you both a space, together, in a great house, run by an old friend of mine."

Kate blinked. Her mouth was dry; her lips stuck together like chewed gum.

"And the baby is going to a safe place for now. You'll be able to see her every other day, at least, supervised. You can still nurse her, and I brought you this breast pump."

Kate shook her head. "I'm still nursing, Cynthia. She needs me every two or three hours," said Kate, breathing deep to find air to carry her words.

Cynthia ignored her, pulling a pump out of her bag. "Put the milk in these Baggies and put them in the freezer. Ruth will show you. She knows about these things. I'll call over tomorrow to arrange your first visit."

Cynthia walked over to Kate, seeming to will the baby from Kate's arms with her level stare. Kate turned and faced the wall. "No, you can't take her. She's my baby. I took care of her. She's fine. I'm doing a good job. Even Meera said so."

"Kate, I haven't spoken a harsh word to you all day, have I?" asked Cynthia, looking to the police officer, who stepped slowly toward Kate.

Kate turned and stared steadily in Cynthia's eyes. "No, you can't take my baby."

"Kate, put the baby back in the bassinet. She needs to get settled. I don't want to fight and I don't want Deirdre to get hurt," said Cynthia, backing away from Kate.

Kate rocked the baby, who still slept. "I wouldn't ever hurt her. I've done everything for her." Kate closed her eyes and put her cheek to Deirdre's blanket-covered head, feeling her wet eyelashes beat against flannel.

"No, you haven't. You risked her life and your own by having her in secret. You and your sister were lucky, but it could have been a disaster. Deirdre needed to be seen by a doctor the day she was born. You didn't do that for her."

Kate, stung, began to cry at the harshness of Cynthia's words. "But she's fine. I've done everything else okay. She has her shots now and everything. There's nothing you can do that I can't."

"Kate, give me the baby. Give me Deirdre. You don't want me to have to ask Officer Dillon to help me, do you? You don't want anything to happen to her?"

Kate shook her head, burying her nose in Deirdre's neck, breathing in the new, beautiful smells of life, and soap, and all the care she'd given her child. "Am I going to get her back?"

"I don't know, Kate. That depends. The court needs to investigate your father's and your actions for a while. You know, the people losing out here are Tyler and Deirdre. And Sanjay's family."

As Kate listened to Cynthia, she felt the room become quiet, and

Cynthia's words had clear, sharp access: *actions, losing out,* and *Sanjay's family* colliding into her, almost knocking her down. Kate knew, as certainly as she had known she would keep the baby when she found out she was pregnant, there was nothing she could do. How else could she, Sanjay, Deirdre, her father, Tyler, and Meera move back into their lives without rules and orders and harsh papers telling them what to do? How would it be possible to go home, now, tonight, with Deirdre and Tyler, move back into the secret routines of the last nine months, avoiding the next-door neighbors and hiding from teachers and friends and family?

Kate looked down at her feet. She was wearing the same shoes she had put on this morning before dressing Deirdre, white thick-soled Keds that made her over an inch taller. When Kate had put these on, she was a mother at home with her baby, and now she wasn't. She had made too many mistakes, and they were going to make her pay and pay and pay for the hurt she'd done to everyone. Kate knew Cynthia and Detective Johnson and the doctors thought she deserved to lose Deirdre, this beautiful girl; they thought her unworthy of the love that flooded from her baby's small body.

Kate looked at Deirdre, brought her face to her baby's forehead, and knew that they belonged together. More than anything, Kate knew she would do whatever they wanted in order for Deirdre and her to stay connected.

"This is so wrong," said Kate, but she walked over to the bassinet and laid Deirdre down softly, just as she had done earlier, whispering small sounds, tucking the blanket around Deirdre's hands and feet.

Cynthia didn't say a word as Kate patted the baby, expecting, Kate thought, something else: hysterics, flinging arms, anguished wails. Kate thought of the Middle Eastern women she'd seen in a video during social studies class. The women wailed at a young man's funeral, voices so repetitive and sad that they made a constant sound of sorrow. "Ululating," her teacher had said. "This is how their society expects grief to sound."

Cynthia moved slowly over to the bassinet and watched Kate, waiting for her to move away. Kate looked into the social worker's eyes, wondering what was inside her, what face Cynthia had to paint on to do this kind of thing, to make decisions, hard decisions, decisions that changed lives. Then Kate almost laughed, thinking, *I've made those hard decisions, too, knowing that really, if your mind is set on what you think is right, you can do anything.*

Cynthia picked up Deirdre and cradled her against her chest, arranging the soft cotton blanket back over the baby's head. "That was the right choice, Kate. You made a good decision just now." Cynthia looked to the officer, who picked up the bag, and they walked away with the baby, the police officer holding the door, the new nurse finally putting away her *People* magazine and watching Kate.

Kate thought that when Tyler had cut the umbilical cord, she had felt it, the slicing of metal on flesh, the tearing away of major veins that connected her to Deirdre, that had connected them for nine months, their bodies beating and breathing together, all day, all night. But now, Kate knew that it hadn't been cut till the door shut, and she was alone, alone in her body, her chest as carved out and empty as her womb. There was nothing left to slither out of her body, nothing but a black feeling that pooled in her lungs. Kate wondered if she could push that feeling out, if she could change it into sound and push it into her throat, lift her voice, and wail over and over, birthing the grief her body held like water.

❧

It was nine-fifteen. Meera sat in an empty hospital lobby, her legs crossed at the ankles and pushed under the chair. She was still wearing her doctor's coat, not taking it off when she returned home to Jaggu and Ari, not taking it off as she heated up hot dogs and canned corn, as they watched television, not even taking it off when her friend Momta came to watch the boys, hugging her as she walked in the door.

"Oh, Meera. What is going on? You sounded most upset on the phone," said Momta, taking off her coat.

Meera could not look her friend in the eye, staring at Momta's sari instead, made of blue rayon, good for this time of the year. She saw a peek of Momta's solid brown middle and wished she could lean into her friend's flesh, for a minute, just to hold herself up. "It is terrible. Please come into the bedroom so the boys don't hear."

Meera and Momta walked down the hall, Meera listening to the swish of her friend's steps, the comfortable pad of her feet on the carpet. They sat down on Meera's bed, Momta reaching for Meera's red-nailed hand.

"What is it, Meera?"

"I am so ashamed."

"No. What could you have possibly done? It cannot be so bad."

"It is not me. It's Sanjay," said Meera.

"Sanju? What? What is it?"

Meera pulled her hand away and rubbed her forehead. "I cannot believe it myself. He has had an affair, and the woman, rather, the girl, has had a baby."

Momta began to launch into sympathetic sounds, but Meera put up her hand. "There is more, unfortunately. Sanjay has been arrested because the girl is not yet of age. I have called the lawyer, but now I want to go to the county jail to understand what is going to happen. Maybe I can see him."

Momta was silent. Meera looked at the carpet, running her feet across the perfect light brown, a color that matched the wallpaper exactly. "I hope you can stay with the boys. Maybe all night. I know you will have to tell Rama. But if you could, wait before you tell others. They will know soon enough."

Momta leaned over, finally giving Meera the support she needed. Meera put her face against the sturdy fabric, feeling the older woman's firm shoulder, smelling perfumed skin, lavender soap, whiffs of curry and cinnamon, breathing in the smells of home even while knowing she was nowhere near.

Meera left her house, thinking she was on her way to the county jail in Martinez, but soon she found herself driving to Mt. Diablo Hospital, parking in her physician's spot, locking the Volvo's doors. Outside, the stars had broken through the clouds that had hung in the sky all day like a headache, and the air was sharp and filled with moths. Meera imagined the bulbs and seeds beneath the earth—oxalis, purple coneflower, daylilies, lettuce, soon corn and pumpkin—

shooting out thin roots and green leaves, the summer leaves, flowers, and fruit only weeks away.

Meera walked into the hospital, the security guard giving her a brief wave, the automatic doors closing behind her. She walked to the lobby by the room she knew Kate was in, and sat, listening for anything, looking down when nurses walked by, ignoring how they stared, lifted their eyebrows, slowed down, then sped up. Soon she heard voices and then the door closing, the social worker walking by with the baby, a large bag, and a police officer behind her.

"Mrs. De Lucca," said Meera, standing up, walking toward Cynthia.

Cynthia stopped, backed up a bit, almost imperceptibly, but enough for Meera to notice. "Dr. Chaturvedi. What are you doing here?"

"This is strange. I . . . I think I want to see the baby again."

Cynthia shook her head. "I'm taking her to foster care now. She is fine. All the tests came back good. She is a healthy baby."

"I know that. I just want to look. Only for a minute."

Cynthia looked behind her at the police officer and then shrugged, her face full of the day, exhaustion hanging under her eyes in black circles. "Okay," she said finally, adjusting the baby in her arms. "But let's do it somewhere else. An examining room?"

"Please, follow me," said Meera, leading Cynthia and the officer in tow to the pediatric ward, just down the hall. Once in the small room, Cynthia laid the baby on the table, Deirdre still asleep, her fists curled up at the sides of her head.

Meera pulled the blanket away and stared at the baby's face. If she didn't know this baby was a girl and that Kate was the mother, Meera could imagine Deirdre was hers, Jaggu or Ari, the baby's skin as soft as theirs, as smooth, a color she wanted to put her tongue on.

When her babies had slept, Meera used to sit by the crib, watching and listening to the sweet steady breaths that brought them more into the world, more into her family, more into her. Indeed, they had both been inside her for nine months, but it was living that really brought Meera to her children, the combing of their hair, the washing of the skin, the holding of their small bodies. And here, Meera thought, was another small body, but one that was not hers yet part of her, part of Sanjay who was part of her, part of Jaggu and Ari who were parts of her as well. What was she supposed to do with this?

"Dr. Chaturvedi, I really have to go. The foster parents are waiting," said Cynthia, gently pulling the blanket from Meera's hands.

Meera looked up. "Of course. Certainly. Thank you," she said, backing away, resting her hands on the swivel chair by the desk. "Of course."

Cynthia took the baby and left, the silent officer still behind her. Meera sat down, listening for the last sounds of their footsteps before leaving the room herself, breathing deep the still hospital time, the lowered lights, the occasional footsteps, silence bouncing off the high sheen of linoleum floors.

Meera turned the corner and saw Kate and Tyler walking toward the automatic doors, another officer and a woman, another social worker perhaps, at their sides. The woman had her arm around Tyler's shoulder, but Kate walked slightly apart from the group, her legs mechanical, her tennis shoes squeaking on the scrubbed floor. Meera felt her knees lock but the rest of her body pull forward, her hands wanting to catch them all and stop them, her joints solid and fused and keeping her feet square and still.

Once, Meera had read a story about an Indian woman whose husband had an affair. In the story, the woman eventually searched out and discovered her husband's mistress and draped her with her favorite jewelry, her most beautiful clothing, pure silk saris, aqua, pink, thinking, *If my husband loves her this much, then so must I.* Now, Meera watched Kate, skinny, tired, her hair dirty and hanging down her back in sad dark strands. Meera wondered if she ever thought Kate lovable, if she had ever really considered her a woman, someone more than just Deirdre's girl, her oldest girl, someone more than Jaggu and Ari's baby-sitter. *Can I love her?* Meera thought. *Can I share my husband with her, anoint her with flowers picked from my garden, dress her slowly in my special, one-for-festival silk saris? Can I love her as much as I will have to?*

As the doors opened for the group, Meera pulled from her spot, words forming on her tongue like prayers, gifts she could give them all, words that could stop it all now. But then she slowed and stood still, letting them all go, realizing there was no special gift, no anger or sorrow appropriate, no touch acceptable, no fabric or words that would catch and hold them all before they fell.

The police officer and the new social worker, Susan, sat in the front seat of the police car, discussing directions and routes to the residential facility almost twenty miles away in Antioch, a city more than thirty miles from Monte Veda. Kate slumped in the back, her face to the window. Tyler listened to the adults from behind the screen that separated the seats, staring at the rifle that hung behind their heads.

"Now, to get to Antioch house, we take the 680 to 4. We make a left on Mariposa, a right on Salida, and it's a half a mile down. I've been there before."

"Okay. Sounds good," said the officer, turning on the car. Just as he was about to put the car into drive, there was a tap at the window.

"Oh, for Christ's sake," said Susan. "Just keep going! You'd think there was something better to do at this time of night. But no, they want to put in an 'on the scene' report."

The officer put the car in gear and drove off. "Who was that?" asked Tyler, looking to see if Kate was paying attention.

Susan turned around. "Oh, don't worry. It's just this reporter from Channel Seven. This is his beat. He's that annoying, 'All the way around the Bay' guy. He won't follow us."

"News guy? What does he want? What is the news?"

Susan looked at the police officer and then turned back to Tyler, her eyebrows raised. "Well, it's probably that Mr. Chaturvedi was arrested. Now, don't worry about it anymore."

Susan turned back around and began talking to the officer again. Tyler watched the dark night slip past the car. During all those months in the house, Tyler had come to believe, after she'd eliminated everyone else, that Kate was involved in a tragic love affair, something so painful Kate couldn't even tell Tyler, her only sister. At night, their father gone and Kate deep in pregnant sleep, Tyler lay in bed and imagined her sister's lover, someone young and blond who looked like Brad Pitt, tight body in expensive clothes, young enough to be cute—dimples, cleft chin, soft, shaved, scented skin—but old enough to have a job, money, and expensive car. She'd met him one night in the city, Tyler believed, and he'd taken her to the Hyatt for

a drink, a beer that Kate sipped carefully. Later, he'd taken her dancing, his body tight and coiled, and Kate had fallen in love with everything about him. Of course, he was rich and powerful, and thinking
that Kate was much older, twenty, twenty-one, he had taken her to
his bed, teaching her all there was to know about love. Then he'd
disappeared. Maybe he'd had to leave town on business or he had to
divorce his wife so that he could marry Kate. But he would come
back—Cory, his name was Cory, Tyler decided—Cory would come
back. Cory would eventually show up, in the knick of time, save
them, take them for drives in his Porsche, buy the baby clothes from
the expensive boutiques on Monte Veda Avenue, take care of Kate,
take care of the baby.

But instead, all along, it had been Sanjay. Just plain, old, next-
door Sanjay, who never said anything, who nodded and smiled,
hunched at the back of a room somewhere, his hands in his pockets,
wearing his same old white shirt and khaki pants. *He's so old,*
thought Tyler, anger flaring up her face, into her mouth and nose
making her want to snort. She turned to Kate and hissed out of the
side of her mouth, "Why didn't you tell me? I can't believe you
didn't tell me. All this time and it was just Sanjay."

Kate didn't move her head, her arms folded at her chest. She
stared straight ahead, whispering into her sleeve, "I couldn't tell you
or anyone. I mean, look what happened anyway. I didn't want Meera
to find out, and she did, and here we are."

"Well, *I* wouldn't have told her. I didn't tell Dad, did I?" Tyler
felt the weight of six silent months on her chest, the rock-heavy sentences she'd wanted to say to someone, the power and heft of her
fear for Kate and the baby and herself. "I did everything, and you
couldn't tell me that . . . He was right there. You made me do everything."

Kate looked blankly at Tyler. She was holding herself around her
chest, almost, it seemed to Tyler, shivering. "I'm sorry."

"Well," said Tyler, still whispering. Her words sliced the air like
soft knives. She slid closer to her sister, slipping quietly across the
leather seat. "That's just great, huh, huh? Here we are driving off in
a police car to some rat hole. No Deirdre. We're arrested. And what
about Dad?"

Kate stared at her, then said, "What about Dad?"

"He's alone. In trouble."

Kate almost laughed, then lowered her voice. "Oh, come on! Tyler, we've been alone for months. He's the one who left first."

"So is that why you did it? To get back at Dad? That is so stupid."

"What are you talking about?" said Kate.

Tyler laughed, pushing her hair back on her head. "Yeah, that was smart. Now he'll really come home for good. Like things weren't bad enough before."

Neither of them said a word, the night pushing by them like a dark ocean. Tyler felt the car heater's stale hot air and leaned her head back against the seat. Sometimes, when she was lying to the salespeople at Second Time Around or withholding the truth from her father or even when she held baby Deirdre's head in her palms for the first time, Tyler imagined her mother watching it all. It happened enough that sometimes Tyler would stop and look behind her, feel the urge to say, "I'm sorry. I'm lying," or "Mom, help me," or "You tell him, please. You can tell him." Now she wondered what her mother would say, how her mother would want her to act.

Tyler looked at Kate again, some deep ugly energy forming on the top of her skin. She knew that even if her mother were here, she'd feel just like this. She'd still want to slap some smugness off her sister's face. "You're so stupid. This is all your fault. And I told you. I'm always right."

"Stupid? Just shut up. You don't know what you're talking about."

"No, you shut up! You don't know what you're talking about," said Tyler loudly, punching Kate, her knuckles hitting shoulder bone. Kate flinched and held her shoulder, dropping her head down.

Susan whipped her head around. "Girls, girls. You've been under a lot of stress today. Don't fight. You'll be able to talk to someone tomorrow. Just try to relax."

"Right," said Tyler, but she sat back, her eyes walls of water, her anger pulsing smaller, smaller until she could feel only her heart, first fast and panicked, as if she were on some roller-coaster ride; then as the miles and towns went by, it steadied and slowed. She watched the two heads in front of her; Susan's graying old lady bob and the officer's short black curls. The air was still and smelled of leather; she couldn't hear the tires hit the asphalt or street noise outside. She remembered late-night drives with her parents from friends' houses, dinner parties lasting past midnight, the rides home long and tinted with the inside car light, her mother's face bending over her, whispering, "We'll be home soon. Go back to sleep."

Tyler breathed, wondering what her father was doing, wondering if he had gone to Hannah's or if he was walking through their empty house, looking at the crib, the baby clothes, the diapers—all the things she and Kate had collected and bought, all the hard work they had done. She wondered if he'd even seen the baby.

He hadn't been there when they left the hospital, and Tyler hoped he wasn't in jail. He must be, she thought, because otherwise he would have waited for them. Now her father seemed as gone as he had been ever since their mother died.

"If you hadn't done it, we wouldn't be here," whispered Tyler as she looked straight ahead. "I told you. I told you I was scared."

Kate whispered, "You're right. We wouldn't be here," and then was silent. Tyler felt her sister's dark body beside her as they drove through the night. Tyler envisioned Kate moving with Sanjay in a way Tyler had only read and talked about. He had always seemed so odd, so removed from them with his coldness and dorky sentences. To Tyler, Sanjay had always seemed upset as if everything was just a little off: the lunch Meera had packed for a picnic, the cloudy weather, the day's headlines. Whenever she baby-sat or helped out with the boys, Tyler walked around Sanjay, trying to ignore his lowered eyebrows, his soft flat voice, the disappointment that filled the house like gas from a blown-out pilot light.

Tyler was glad when Kate said one day, "You know, I'm not going to baby-sit for the Chaturvedis anymore. It's too weird over there."

"What happened?" Tyler had said, thinking of the spending money Kate and she made, thinking of the shopping trips they had on the weekends in Oak Creek, the runs they made on Nordstrom and Macy's.

"Nothing happened. It's just that, I don't know. When they fight, I don't like being there."

Tyler nodded, knowing the sharp quiet of that house on some

days. And after three or four calls from Meera, Kate saying, "No, I can't sit," and "No, I don't think Tyler can either," it was over, the connection cut. Meera eventually found other neighborhood girls for weekend nights and a day care downtown for the boys during the week, Sanjay driving them there in the morning, the boys waving at Tyler from their car seats.

At the time, Kate's explanation was enough for Tyler to let the Chaturvedis go, forget the money, the long-ago summer barbecues and dinners, forget the voices of Meera and her mother together in the yard as they conferred over soil or fertilizer or weather. It was easy enough to move into her own life, her friends, her cheerleading, her schoolwork, at least until Kate told her she was pregnant, and then it was all gone. Everything.

Tyler couldn't imagine how Kate's body moved toward his, how her arms pulled him to her body, how she kept everything, all of it, a secret from just about everyone. Tyler wondered if her own body would ever breathe with someone else's, their bodies together on a mattress, a floor, the back of a van. Would she fall in love with someone surprising? Did she, Tyler thought, have the same need as Kate, something that needed to be touched and held and opened? Would she ever be able to reach for anyone other than Kate or her father?

Tyler sighed. There had been nothing except darkness all day, first in the cubed dull rooms at the hospital, and now this, this rushing invisibly on darkened freeways. But her heart beat quietly and the water in her eyes dried, and she lulled herself by listening to Susan and the cop talk about the weather and their kids, kids who were home asleep in their own beds. Soon, as the freeway looped into another, leaving them headed southeast and so far from home, Tyler felt her sister's hand on hers, and Tyler took it, as she always had, all their lives.

※

Davis sat inside the dark house he had once shared with his wife. The only light came from the flashing numbers on the answering machine one, then two, now four, five; Hannah, he thought, putting down his beer, or the cops, or, somehow, the girls. He turned to the machine, watching the green flash, followed the eerie light through the dining room as it reflected off polished oak, Haviland china, Deirdre's grandmother's silver. He should listen to the messages, he knew. They were all important, nobody of insignificance calling him, all his friends, his colleagues, his boss calling Hannah's first, even phone solicitors. "They find you anywhere," he said to Hannah one night, laughing, hanging up on a man trying to sell insurance. But he turned back to his beer and the four empty bottles in front of him, thinking, *There's always more in the fridge.*

Davis stood up and walked silently to Kate's room, drinking as he walked. He turned on the light to her room, and then turned it off again, frightened he might have alerted Meera to his location. He knew he couldn't face her. Just a week or so ago, he and Meera had spoken while Davis fiddled with a broken sprinkler head, Meera in a gardening apron and a big hat that reminded him of a nun's wimple.

"Hello, Davis," she said, dusting dirt off her hands and apron. "How have you been? I haven't seen you in some time."

"Oh, the same old thing, you know. Work just keeps going on," he said, standing up, realizing how small Meera really was. Her head didn't even reach his chest.

"How are Sanjay and the boys?"

"Everyone is very well, thank you," said Meera impatiently. "I have something to say to you, Davis."

Davis shifted his feet, knowing there was a lecture coming, just like Rachael's. He brought his hand to his eyes, rubbing them with thumb and forefinger, wishing he could squeeze this woman away.

"What is it, Meera?"

"I know that your personal life is not my affair, but the girls . . . We have not seen the girls lately, and it seems that they are often home alone."

Davis flushed and turned his head away from her. "They're big girls, Meera. Kate's seventeen. And anyway, I come home. I'm here now, aren't I?"

"I don't want to bring my training into this, Davis, but they are only teenagers, children still. Who knows what kind of trouble they could get into if left too much to their own devices?"

Davis turned back to face Meera, and almost flinched at her hard, intense gaze, the set lips, her most forceful doctor face. "I hear you. Thanks for the concern. But I think I've got everything under control. They're both just fine," Davis said, walking stiffly back up to the garage. "I'll see you later."

Presumption, he thought. *Bitch,* he thought. *She should pay attention to her own life.*

Now, in Kate's room, he wanted to hit that foolish, arrogant man, pull him into the house, this room, and show him the sad crib he'd found just this evening in Kate's closet, the piles of baby clothes, the boxes of diapers, the baby supplies he remembered from when the girls were little: pacifiers, tiny toenail clippers, teething rings, baby wipes. He'd show that front yard idiot what was really going on in this very house, lift his daughter's baggy shirt, touch her stomach, round and nine months hard, tell him to take her to the doctor's, now, now!

He might even pull the idiot by the scruff of the neck to Meera's doorstep, beg her forgiveness, ask her to help him fix this mess, make it right, bring his daughters home. Davis would force the idiot to say, "This time I'll stay home at night, every night. I'll be a father, I swear it. You were right, I never imagined what trouble they'd be in."

Davis sank to the carpet, holding a bottle and a blanket he'd found on the floor. He recognized the old blanket from when Tyler was little; it was so faded that the pink was almost white. But it smelled like it always did, Ivory soap and baby. *How sad,* he thought, *here I am, a baby with his bottle and blankie,* and he put both down, leaning against the wall.

He closed his eyes, and then opened them, thinking, *I am a grandfather? How stupid,* he thought. *Right,* he thought. *Of course,* he thought. He could just hear Deirdre laughing, saying, "Hello! Anybody home?" But it was something more than just knowing that the word *grandfather* belonged to him; it was the fact that his body had moved into other flesh, new flesh, combined with the bodies from next door, made a little girl he had not even been allowed to see, Detective Johnson scared he might make a scene.

Deirdre had always talked of being a grandmother, even before they had children themselves, even while she was dying. "I want to hold a baby until I've had enough, and then give it back to its parents," she would say, laughing. "That's the way to be a grandmother." But Davis had known then that she would never give a baby back without being asked, holding the child through tears and illness and long sleepless nights, just as she had with Kate and Tyler. All those nights, he'd awakened as she swished back the blankets, her bare feet on the hardwood. Once Davis realized that Deirdre liked getting up for the night feedings—or, at least, when he convinced himself she did—he'd never gotten up, never held the night-crying babies and a bottle full of breast milk. "Don't worry," she said. "It's just easier this way. I don't have to pump any milk for a bottle. Besides, I like it. It's quiet. Just the two of us."

Maybe he'd missed something by sleeping, by letting Deirdre take that time alone, Davis thought. *She made it easy for me to let go. I've never known either Kate or Tyler the right way. And now it's too late.*

Davis stood, picking up the blanket, and walked to the window, peeking through the levelors at Meera's house. He could see lights on in the living room, the flicker of the television, the blue glow of the pool. Davis shook his head. How was he ready to do anything better? Here he was, a grandfather, grandfather to a baby with neither of her parents with her; no parent to hand her to; no grandparent able to hold her in the first place.

For a second Davis couldn't breathe, sadness filling his lungs like pool water. He turned from the window and walked out of Kate's room, his house, and into the night. He still couldn't breathe, so he started walking, moved up Wildwood Drive until he stood on the sidewalk parallel to the Chaturvedis' picture window. The room glowed like the inside of a pumpkin, their house all black shadows, the lumps of shrubs like frozen animals. Davis walked onto the lawn, perfectly mowed as always, stepping softly on the wet blades, occasionally feeling the crackle and slip of snails under his shoes. As he neared the window, he stopped suddenly, remembering all of Meera's plants, and he looked down, his whole weight on something white, a lacy leaf. He picked up his foot carefully, and the plant lurched back to shape, as if he had never been there at all.

His eyes on the ground, Davis slid next to the window, pushing aside Japanese maple branches and fern fronds, creating a space where he could stand unnoticed. Inside, a woman he had met once or twice before at the Chaturvedis', Momta, sat on the couch, both boys curled at her sides like puppies, warm in their footed sleepers. The woman had been crying, he saw, big raccoon eyes of mascara under her eyes, but now she looked glazed by television. Davis studied the boys. They were dark, with black hair and brown skin, and eyes, he remembered, the color of caramel. Davis especially liked the youngest, Ari, who, at the age of nine months, could say, "Hi." Once, Davis had walked into the Chaturvedis' living room, and Ari looked right up at him, smiling, and said, "Hi," as if he were two or three. Davis sat down on the floor by him, and felt that he saw the adult Ari would be right there, on the floor, surrounded by blankets and stuffed toys.

Neither Tyler nor Kate spoke that early. Kate had waited until she was almost three, but then sentences came out of her where there had only been smiles and sounds before. Deirdre had been making break-fast one morning, and Kate said, "I would like a piece of toast, please," as if she had been ordering at restaurants since she was born.

"Davis? Davis? Why are you in front of my house?" said Meera from behind him.

Davis swung around, holding on to the small maple tree for sup-port. "Oh, Meera. Oh." Davis looked into her face as he carefully pulled himself out of the plant bed. He thought of words to say, and could find none. So he looked down, ashamed, glad darkness cov-ered his face.

Meera, ignoring his silence, stood before him, wearing her coat, her hair uncombed, her eyes slightly closed. "I was at Mt. Diablo," she said. "I saw the baby again, and then they took Tyler and Kate away. There were reporters in the parking lot."

Davis stood on the lawn, suddenly remembering his beer breath. He tucked in his chin and breathed down and away from Meera. "The detective told me to go home. To stay away until the hearing. He said I'd done enough already."

Meera stared at him. Davis knew she deserved to come at him with fists, her deft brown hands curled into knots of anger. Meera deserved to spit and scratch, attack with words sharp enough to slice into him the truth that he had done nothing right. He held his breath and waited for her words.

Meera watched a car drive down Wildwood, and then make a perfect, swift turn into a driveway, back up, then drive past the house again. Her hair and eyelashes glinted in the car light. She sighed. "I do not know what to do, Davis. I think to call the lawyer or go to the county jail, and I find myself at the hospital. I want to go inside to my boys, and I find myself here, pulling weeds, and then, seeing you by my window."

Davis bent to the lawn, his knees full of nerves. Meera sat with him. They watched the empty street, full only of parked cars and garbage cans. Mayflies and gnats flitted under the streetlights like small rainstorms. "There are messages on my machine I can't answer. I haven't called my girlfriend. I was scared to turn on the lights because I didn't want you to come over and tell me you were right all along."

Meera nodded, silent.

"You were right, Meera," said Davis.

"Of course I was! How could you have left them there to fend for themselves? Deirdre would not have approved. She loved those girls."

Davis started at Deirdre's name, the name of the new baby, the two joined forever. "I love them, too. They're all I have left."

"What a way to show it! Your daughters had no one to guide them. You just left them there, even when we tried to help you. All of us. Rachael. Deirdre's friends," said Meera, her voice shaking.

"She hid it, Meera. I never would have guessed," Davis said, his voice defensive.

"How could you have guessed, Davis? You weren't around to see anything. Kate was nine months pregnant a week and a half ago! I can't believe it. What a ridiculous situation. . . ."

Meera closed her eyes, her palms stretched tight on her thighs. "Yes. Oh, yes. I was right. I was so right. I predicted it all. But we didn't see it either. At least I didn't."

Davis imagined Kate's body, the round pregnant stomach, the full breasts. He saw her clothes, big, dark, and baggy. He saw her quiet, stern face, her pallor, the puffiness under her chin. He saw Tyler reaching inside her sister for new life and finding it, loosening the flesh grip of Kate's womb. He saw the sad days that the three of them were alone, the quiet of the dead house. "I did a terrible thing. You were right all along, Meera."

"Yes. Oh, yes. And look how much that has helped me with my own marriage."

Davis blushed and then froze, thinking of the marriage betrayal and then of Kate with Sanjay. "Deirdre would be disgusted with me," said Davis, putting his head in his palms. "Deirdre would never have let this happen."

"No. She wouldn't have. And, most likely she would be disgusted with us all. My husband seduced her daughter. You didn't notice what was occurring. I didn't do anything to help Kate. But she is not here, Davis. She is dead. And we have done as we have," said Meera, not meeting his eye, focusing on the lawn and then pavement before her.

Davis shook his head, bringing his hands to his cheeks and ears as if to stop his movement and Meera's words. It had to be that, somehow, Deirdre was still with them, watching the yards, the houses, the people inside them. She must have seen it all: the seduction, the birth, the arrest. She must have seen her girls leaving the hospital without him, taken to a strange house. She must have cried, her arms outstretched, pulling on Davis and Meera, begging them to look, pay attention, save Kate from loneliness and Sanjay. How could she have not seen, when she was so alive, so much a part of his life, the girls', even Meera's? Davis could look around this yard and see the plants Deirdre had brought Meera, showing her what grew best in this climate, helping Meera prepare against wind, fog, and months of rain. His own house was like a Deirdre museum, he thought, wallpaper, carpets, curtains, shades, and upholstery all her choices. And how could Deirdre not see when Kate looked so like her, her fingers and arms moving to her mother's old rhythms? Anything as vital as Deirdre left traces in skin and flesh; in fabric and wood and paper, in plants growing from the warmed dirt.

Meera was still looking ahead, her hands tired and still on her lap. He wished he could touch her somehow, a hand on her cheek or shoulder, but he slumped inside himself and cried. He cried for himself, wet and drunk on Meera's front lawn, for his wife betrayed in death by those she loved, for Meera, who was alone now because he

himself couldn't stay home, couldn't will himself back into his bedroom because he missed his wife. Davis cried for the horrifying moments he had missed, his own child's blood, his other child's fear as
she held a bloody newborn in her hands.

Later, Davis would wonder how long they were on Meera's lawn,
under the streetlight, but what he would remember was her silence,
the way she helped him grieve by not saying anything at all. All day
long, he realized, he had been trying to work out a party line, a sentence to use when he had to, when it was time to explain to colleagues or friends, "Oh, it was a horrible shock. The neighbor
seduced her when I was at work. So awful. We've pressed charges.
He'll go to jail for what he did." Every word Davis intonated pushed
the blame elsewhere, not on him. But this night air and Meera's solid
silence said, "No, think again," and he did, and he thought, and the
night folded around them like a blank page.

Meera sat on her couch next to the sleeping Momta and listened
to the drone of the television, a rerun of *Matlock* spinning out in
dramatic sounds and voices, whispers and anger. She had carried
first Ari, then Jaggu to bed, curling them into their blankets, leaving
the doors slightly open, and then she had come back to the couch,
sitting down slowly, softly. She had not taken off her shoes or her
coat, and they and her dress were wet from sitting on the grass with
Davis, and her eyes were dry, stretched open and burning. Meera
imagined the red veins, the darkening sclera, the glossy look, and put
her fingertips under her lower lashes, tenderly patting the puffs of fatigue and sorrow.

Meera sighed, rubbing her forehead, feeling her stale breath
pass through sticky lips, habitually reaching for her lip balm in her
left-hand pocket and spreading it over and over her upper and
lower lips.

Everything had been a lie, and now she understood it had been
she who had been lying, so she didn't have to see. She and Sanjay had
never been the family she imagined, successful, professional immi-
grants moving up in America, understanding it, taking it on, their

marriage and then their family moving with the pulse of this enormous place, bolstered by American universities and American jobs, everything in the past and everything from Delhi now only food and custom and weekend ritual.

Meera took off her shoes and brushed grass bits off her feet onto the carpet. She stood up, finally taking off her doctor's coat and laying it on the couch, smelling the almost unknown scent of her underarms, dark and peppery. Meera sat back down, and Momta sighed and turned, her sari twisted around her middle, her toenails painted pink, her skin as brown as toast.

What should I have done? thought Meera. *What did I need to do to keep Sanjay from pulling away, turning to a girl-woman so unlike him that it makes me cringe to think of those two bodies sliding together, the sweat from each different elements, different chemicals, different fires.*

Meera thought of Sanjay when she first met him. He had made her laugh, bringing her bottles of unacceptable American wine, Almaden, Gallo, that they drank with even worse food, quick bean burritos from the vendor down the street, pizza thick and deadly with melted cheese. Once, Sanjay picked her up on a Saturday morning and took her to Bodega Bay, the place up the coast where that terrible, vicious bird movie was set. They walked along the bay at Doran State Park and ate at the Tide Water Inn, slurping thick clam chowder from sourdough bowls. Another time they took the ferry from Pier 46 to Alcatraz, walking in the halls of old crime, the wind whipping the sky clear of fog and clouds, sun beating down on them as they ferried back to San Francisco, the sunset in their hair and eyes.

At night, Meera touched him, warm and smooth, his quiet eyes radiant and holding her. How she had wanted to open to him, to shed everything, her work, her schooling, her family, her name, her skin, pull him, the air around them, and their bed into her body like food. But then it would be morning, five-thirty and a commute and an eight o'clock lecture, buses to catch, lunches to eat with colleagues, late-night rotations and thirty-six-hour shifts. It had always been the right internship and residency, the perfect letter of recommendation, the casual lunchroom advice that was important, the bedroom something to slip into only when there was time, desperate need, or practical purpose, and even then, Meera felt herself thinking of patients and the hospital, the work world etched in her brain like an ongoing recording.

Later, as scheduled, there were the children, the pregnancies followed to the letter, the right vitamins, the correct amount of sleep, the perfect nursery accoutrements. And as the boys grew, Meera followed them like clinical studies, measuring height, weight, and development at home, determined to never see a blip, an abnormality, something to take her and them all off course.

What she hadn't expected was Sanjay's secrets. What she hadn't watched for was the needs his body held inside, the arguments in his averted face, the sad desire and longing wisping up from his skin like perfume. All this time Meera believed he was right behind her, that what she wanted was what he wanted, that they had both agreed to this life, here in Monte Veda, these children, these jobs, this day-in and day-out pattern of meals, and temple, and friends, the comings and goings. Meera stood up, her coat slipping to the floor, and stretched her back, knowing she was lying now. Sanjay had often been silent, long before Kate. He'd snap back at her, anger on his face, and then there wouldn't be words for days. What should she have done? Gone to counseling? Confided in a colleague?

Meera thought of the men who had asked for her body over the years—Oscar Garcia, Doug Jones, Inyoung Kim—men who had wanted but not received sex: nights of shared coffee and cold pizza while on call, talks in the staff room, hurried kisses in the pharmacy annex. Even now there was Jim Ziegler from radiology, his eyes on her legs and breasts, reminding her of the boys who had followed her home from school. But not once, not on the school path, or during her residency, nor now, had she ever thought to pull them to her, breathe in their smells, smells so different from Sanjay's. Meera almost laughed. Should she have? Had she been missing something this whole time, something that Sanjay found and took and took again, something she would wonder about her whole life, never knowing if she had made a mistake by saying no, and no again. And again. Was it too late now? she wondered. Could she go back, search in the bodies of men to find the answer?

Meera slid to the window in her sweaty nylons, wondering where Davis had gone. Was he still scared to go home and feel what he must, that house empty and silent since Deirdre died? Was he still outside, wandering the yards, wishing that everything was just fine? Meera knew she might have slapped him, would have been right to, part of her body wanting to pull him to the earth and pummel him with her small bony fists. It was easy to blame him for all of this, and earlier today she had, whispering phrases to herself as she drove: "You have ruined all our lives . . . I told you what would happen, and it did. It did! Why didn't you listen to me, Davis? You foolish, stupid man."

Yet another part of Meera had wanted to slide into his big, strange chest and shoulder, lean away from all the problems, sliding her hands over his wrinkled shirt, breathe in his terrible day, the sadness and beer he had taken in equal parts, merge his sorrow into hers, make their sad bodies as connected as Sanjay's and Kate's had been.

Instead she had given him what she herself wanted: silence. The swirl of no words and no judgment because Meera hadn't decided whom she could truly blame for all of this, and she didn't want to start now because she imagined it was she who was at fault. Instead Davis's cries and the wet lawn had left her empty and unsure but hopeful that she might soon find a way to figure this out, to package it so it would fit in her hands.

Momta stirred and sat up, brushing her hair back over her face, pulling her sari up tight on her shoulder. "Meera, I did not hear you come in. How is it with Sanju? What is happening?"

"I didn't see him," said Meera. "I went to the hospital instead. I saw the baby again."

Momta said nothing, looking at Meera with a still face. "She reminds me of the boys. How they used to be when they were infants. She has Sanjay's face and eyes, I think."

Momta reached for Meera's hand. "What will happen to her? What will happen to Sanju?"

Meera shook her head. "I am not certain. I am not certain what will happen to any of us."

Sanjay was dressed in Orange County jail clothes, the ones he had always seen on Channel Seven's six o'clock news, suspected criminals led in and out of courtrooms, hands tied behind their backs, sometimes their feet chained. No one had put handcuffs on him, at least not yet, and now his lawyer—Zack Samuels, a brother of a colleague of his at the refinery—sat opposite him at a metal table, pulling papers out of his briefcase and adjusting his laptop computer.

"Well, the bad news is that they just passed a law for mandatory jail time for statutory rape. It's all the child-abuse cases, the Megan's law, the Polly Klaas abduction. The Sund kidnapping. Christina Williams. You know."

Sanjay felt his body want to spit itself up, bile and flesh and acid pulsing into his throat. In the nine long months since that last afternoon with Kate, he had never thought himself an abuser—naive, shortsighted, selfish maybe, but definitely not in the same league with pedophiles and murderers. Was he himself one of those men that made him lock and double lock Jaggu's and Ari's bedroom windows? Was he as bad as the men he saw walking into the adult bookstores down by the refinery, slipping in after work in their three-piece suits?

"What will that mean in terms of sentencing, exactly?" asked Sanjay, finding his voice.

"Well," said Zack, "that's what we've got to work out. There are mitigating factors, things that can sway a judge and jury. For instance, did you or she initiate the affair? Was there any force or manipulation on your part? That kind of thing. But hopefully, we won't even go to trial."

"What will happen to the baby?"

"From what I know so far, the baby has been remanded to temporary foster care pending an investigation. The mother and her sister will be sent to a home-care residential facility. Probably, the father will have to go to court to reestablish custody for them and the baby."

Sanjay wondered what time it was. It could have been minutes or years since Meera had said, "This is too much, Sanjay." And with this all in front of him, he could hardly remember Kate's warm skin. Was that what started this all? Who else could he blame for this? Meera for her expectations? Davis for never being home? Kate for her long-limbed bones? Couldn't he just blame it all on Deirdre for dying in the first place, leaving everyone without her? How could he blame himself for the shape these people's lives were now taking? How could he live with the fact that the moment he opened himself to what was necessary for him to exist, he wrecked everything? Sanjay could not even think of his boys, probably sitting in the clean white kitchen with Meera, eating dry cereal and watching American television, a purple dinosaur dancing in front of the screen, singing songs to keep everyone from thinking.

Sanjay put his head on the cold metal of the table, his forehead feeling greasy. He wondered what the shower procedure was here, almost smiling when he remembered his first American friend, Alex, saying, "Gosh, you gotta bring that soap-on-a-rope to the dorm showers. It's like prison. You don't want to bend over. Ya know what I mean?" Sanjay moved his head from side to side, suddenly hoping that the old joke wasn't true.

"We're going to do a paternity test, too. Just so we can get a jump on that aspect."

Sanjay sat up. "There is no need for that. I am sure I am the father. In fact, I am sure she had never been with a man before me."

Zack looked up from his notes. "Listen. We've got to make sure. You don't know what went on after you ended the affair. She and the sister could have had boys over there every night. You can't know everything that went on over at that house. Their father was never home. Who knows?"

Sanjay stood up. "All you have to do is look at the baby to see she is mine."

Zack nodded. "Sure, sure. But the court will want to know scientifically who the father is, not just base an important decision like that on a visual skin color observation."

Sanjay walked in small clipped steps from wall to wall. "I understand. But I do not want to make Kate out to be someone . . . despicable." Sanjay almost said, "Someone like me," but·said instead, "This is not the way I want things to proceed. I do not want to aggravate the situation."

"Listen, Sanjay. This isn't just a situation. We're talking about your life. Your family. Your job. Where you will be able to live after this is all over. Maybe jail time. You might have some vestiges of feelings for the girl, but you have to put those aside. This is about you and your family," said Zack, his black eyes earnest, like a friend's eyes, someone who cared.

"The baby is mine, though," said Sanjay, remembering her small body, the tiny signs of life under the skin, her heartbeat like a small tap against his chest.

"Fine. Of course. Now, sit down. We're going to go ahead with the test. Just so we can rest easy."

Sanjay did not sit down, walking from corner to corner. "You know, this is all my fault. I can find no one to blame but myself. Just because Davis was not home and she was receptive to my attentions does not mean I could do whatever I wish. I made this happen. I was the adult in the relationship. I want to plead guilty."

Zack leaned back in his chair. "That all might be true, Sanjay. Sure, we can go into the judge tomorrow morning and plead guilty to statutory rape. But what would that get you? You'll end up on the sexual offender's register, and you don't want that. It's going to be hard work keeping you off that. If you plead guilty, you'll be sentenced immediately, maybe get some serious time. But if we have a case, I can work on reducing the jail time. Or keeping you out of jail altogether. Keep you off the list. There are mitigating factors. It is not entirely your fault. There was another adult, her father, who is partially to blame. . . ."

Zack kept talking, and Sanjay leaned against the cinder-block wall, his chest opening up to the dark, the harsh legal words, the sad idea that he would never be able to repair all these relationships, that he would be lucky to save his marriage, lash together his feelings and Meera's and hope they didn't sink. He thought about the baby, that tiny girl body he'd held for only ten minutes, how her new skin smelled like clean sand, how she made small sounds at his neck, how his hand curled over her back, fitting it like armor.

Sanjay sighed, remembering that he felt the same way with both his boys, first Jagdish and then Ardashir. They smelled just like this new baby, Deirdre, made the same sounds, made his body curve over them in protection, too.

Sanjay knew that nothing would be the same, no matter what Zack did. Meera would never be able to forget, and neither would he, especially because there would be a child, waiting for him to one day claim her. By tomorrow all his coworkers at the refinery would know the story, retold gently, but with feeling, by Zack's brother Jordan. And then it was just a matter of time before all at the temple and the grocer and the Sleepy Hollow Tennis Club knew. Meera wouldn't even be able to shop at Safeway without whispers and stares, ugly looks that said, "There she goes, the wife of the pedophile, the rapist, the sick man who impregnated a girl. A girl!" And Sanjay also knew that a reporter from the *India Journal* was probably already on the scene, waiting somewhere in the building or even at the hospital, hoping for a story, something awful to report. Just last week there had been a story about a poor Indian family in New Jersey. The father and mother worked all day at minimum-wage jobs, barely affording their one-bedroom apartment. Their two children, a seventeen-year-old boy and a twelve-year-old girl, had slept in the same room, and one night they began having sex. The girl was now pregnant, and Sanjay and Meera watched the details unfold on the Indian channel *Namaste American* and read about the sad family in the *Journal*.

His story would be just as interesting, except even more shocking, he from his wealthy family in New Delhi. Sanjay envisioned the story sailing across the world and streaming onto the blank pages of *Ajj* and *Pragati*. His shame for all to read. Sighing, he knew it would be even worse for his family if he pled guilty, acknowledging publicly what he had done with Kate.

". . . I've got to let you know that we're going to have to discuss the seduction, show how she was willing, that she participated, that she liked it. This might be hard for you, but you want to get home to your wife and kids. Think about your family, Sanjay."

Sanjay turned and nodded, walking back to the table. He sat down and looked at Zack, wondering how one made such deals and, then, how one lived with them. He would give them both up, Kate and the baby, so he could go on with the life that wasn't right but the one he had, the one that fit. "All right."

"So let's get going," said Zack, adjusting his tie and turning on his laptop. "Go ahead and tell me how it all started."

At night, the county jail shook with the echo of too-much sound pushing at the walls, the beds, the bars. All night there were shuffles, clacking of metal doors and bars, yells, sobs, a secret conversation. The sounds pressed around Sanjay's head so closely, he wondered if they were coming from within him, from inside his heart. But then the noise would disappear, memories instead clanging in his ears, the past as ugly as any noise breaking over him as he lay on a pallet covered by a stiff tan blanket.

He would never sleep, he knew that. Not tonight, and not for the nights he would be in here until his hearing. And then, how would he sleep at home, Meera knowing that her bed had been taken by a girl, however briefly, taken and used. Sanjay tried to keep his mind blank, free himself from the thought of anything, tried to force the gray nothing of life and sound around him into his head and body, but he would slip, forget his vigil of nothing, and he would think of Deirdre.

Before this night, before Kate, when Sanjay thought of Deirdre, when he dared to, he remembered her hands. As he watched her pour milk for the children at a dinner table or pull yellow oxalis from the spaces in between fence slats, Sanjay imagined there was something mysterious underneath her skin, not just bone but a direction, a force, that put her hands on the right things, made children thrive, made her house beautiful in ways he couldn't conceive, couldn't imagine Meera doing all by herself. He saw the deft flash of bone under Deirdre's tan rounded flesh, but there was more, some kind of magic that he could not divine.

"Ah, Sanjay," she would say, laughing, placing her palm over his shoulder when he asked her questions. Her eyes were the color of gold in the sun, so bright he had to avert his own. But how he wanted to look up, stand straight, bend into her, holding her against his chest. Sanjay was almost positive she would have pushed him away, and he never would have risked that rejection, knowing he would have forever lost her smile, her palm, the warm nights of conversation where he could almost block out Davis and Meera.

Once, Sanjay had thought he'd seen something else, a glimmer of attraction, a spark of fire, a recognition of his own feelings. They were outside a crowded downtown restaurant, the Casa Orinda, waiting for Davis to get the car parked down by the movie theater. Meera, pregnant with Ari, was in Los Angeles at a medical conference, and Tyler and Kate stayed at home to watch Jaggu, who was only one. *Waterworld* was the main film on the marquee, and people walked by them, laughing, trying to figure out what the movie meant, the clack of shoes and conversation pushing Deirdre and Sanjay together against the restaurant wall.

Sanjay found himself talking, but not about anything in particular, just a patter so that he could look at her for as long as he could. Maybe she was not beautiful. Certainly, she was not as beautiful as Meera, her body heavier and fuller, her skin blotchy in that way of Americans and Brits, red on the cheeks and by the nostrils, but then she would smile, her eyes bringing her face into perfection, some light he had never seen brushing across her face, a feeling he imagined he could touch with his fingers.

That night she nodded and looked at him, her hand reaching out for his, reaching into the curl of his fingers, and pressing on his palm. He took her hand and squeezed back. Maybe she thought he was comforting her about her illness, which had been just diagnosed. But maybe it was more.

She pulled his hand to her cheek and left it there. "Sanjay," she said. "If you only knew."

His heart had opened and lurched, air tightening in his lungs, but a crowd of moviegoers walked by, and then Davis pulled up and tapped the horn, Deirdre already by the BMW's passenger door, slipping inside and closing the door even as Sanjay still felt her skin on the back of his hand, something burning and alive and so real he would look at it still, years later, and think there should be a scar.

But she never said anything else, and then she was sick, so sick, and all he could do was remember what she had been like before. Sometimes at night, Meera and the children asleep, he would lie awake in bed and imagine how it would be to touch her, this wife of his neighbor, this woman who had taught his own wife American customs, taught her how to dig in the American soil. Even in his fantasy, he caught his hand up short, poised just over her full, lovely breasts or rounded stomach, holding himself back even then, unable to blend into her body even in dream.

So he would imagine that he was Davis, suddenly taller, suddenly freckled, moving along the flesh of his everyday wife, tucking her warm body into his at night, holding whatever part of her he wanted to. As he thought this, Sanjay would pull Meera to him, listen to her tight night sounds, feeling his body pulsing with thoughts of another lovemaking. Slowly, he would glide his hands along the thin slope of Meera's buttocks, imagining they were filling and elongating, turning into the long full curves of an imaginary wife, a wife he would never have, a wife he could never touch or understand.

When Deirdre's illness became so obvious no one could ignore her tired, ashen looks, Sanjay was initially relieved, her body no longer magic, something poison eating her from the inside out, her hands closing tight to bone, the magic all but gone. When he saw her, though, later, trying to go outside to dig in the dirt after a round of chemotherapy, he sucked in air, guilty, so guilty, wishing he could put the hair back on her scalp, the weight underneath her skin. Sometimes he saw her walk across her patio and stop, hold on to whatever she could, waiting for a dizzy spell to pass, her head down between her shoulders, her grip tight. Maybe, he thought, maybe I could hold her now. Maybe she would let me press her head against my chest. Maybe she would take my hand again and tell me what it was she wanted to say. But instead he would wave, smile, ask, "How are you? Are you all right?" or say, "What a nice day to be outside." He would walk over to the house with portions of Meera's cooking— matar baneer or puri sabjee—hand them to Kate or Tyler, crane his neck to see into the living room where Deirdre rested. "How is she?" he would ask, hoping Deirdre herself would answer.

Sanjay was sure Meera never knew how he felt, and he never let her see all the tears he had for Deirdre after the funeral. He told Meera he had to go to the refinery, grab a few files from his office, and instead he drove the car down the Highway 24 until he almost disappeared into unfamiliar country, parts of Contra Costa County he had never seen, strawberry and tomato farms rolling by his window like bucolic picture postcards.

Sometime later, he couldn't say when, maybe months, a year, he turned to Kate as she laughed at once of Jaggu's silly jokes, and there Deirdre was again, alive in younger form, her same long body and chocolate eyes, her brown hair holding her body like dark arms. Of course, he knew Kate wasn't Deirdre because unlike her mother, Kate came to him, leaned her body next to his, took his hands and face and body and asked for more, but in the afternoons, with the light off, he could feel her mother, Deirdre, under his hands, rub the very skin he had always been too afraid to touch.

The Way Her Body Opened

There were three twin beds in the room, but only Tyler and Kate were to sleep there, another girl having left just that morning.

"It's how these things always work out," said Ruth, flying a sheet over the bed like a sail and then tucking it into sharp triangles under the bed's edge. "Here, hand me that other sheet . . . and the blankets. Anyway, she gets to go home, and if it isn't three hours later that Cynthia calls me. She says, 'Ruth, I have two girls for you.' And it was nice to tell her I had space, a separate room. Cynthia and I go all the way back to high school."

Kate thought to smile, barely listening to the woman speak, trying to concentrate on keeping her breasts from leaking, willing them to stop, stop the milk. Tyler stood by her side, laughing with Ruth, handing her linen and blankets. Kate shot a look at Tyler from under her half-closed lids, wondering again how her sister could be happy and laugh even as Deirdre was somewhere in Concord being lulled to sleep by some other woman, a woman Kate never wanted to meet. She never wanted the woman to pity her, the sad girl who couldn't do any better; she didn't want to be judged by a person the court decided was better qualified to take care of her own child. She shook her head, wishing Tyler would shut up, just shut up.

"What is it, honey? You don't look so comfortable," said Ruth.

"Well, you know I've got a baby, and Cynthia gave me this pump. She was in a rush. She said you'd know how to help me."

Ruth finished tucking in a blanket, walked over and put her hand on Kate's shoulder, and then turned to Tyler. "Why don't you get ready for bed? The bathroom's right there across the hall. There are two kids sleeping in the two other rooms down the hall, so walk like a mouse. And, Kate, you follow me."

Kate walked behind Ruth, following the woman's round rump down the hall, noting her swing, one cheek up, the other down, her elbows high behind her with each step. "Okay, come on into my room. Close the door. You have the pump?"

"Yes," said Kate, handing the strange plastic pump to Ruth.

"Well, isn't that nice of CPS to provide the highest in technology? No, really, it'll do. In a couple days, we'll have you producing like my brother's favorite Brown Swiss. Did you get any Baggies or should I go to the kitchen?"

"She gave me these," said Kate, holding the Baggies in her hand.

"Okay. Now, this is like a sporting activity. You got to get the correct gear on, and the correct gear is no shirt and no bra. Don't mind me, either. I've seen my share of everything."

Kate flushed, but her breasts pulsed like drums, so she took off her coat and her shirt, unhooked the soaked nursing bra, and then stood in front of Ruth with her arms crossed. "Now, you've got to imagine that gravity is your friend. You got no baby to make the milk come, just habit and gravity. So, stand like this." Ruth stood with her legs slightly apart. "And bend down, so your breasts are hanging. Just like a cow. Okay. Now, put the pump right over your nipple. Yes. Then slowly pull the bottom down. Got the suction?"

"Yes," said Kate, feeling ridiculous and pathetic as she bent over clutching the plastic pump to her breasts.

"All right, now, pull, and then push it back, then pull. Get a rhythm going," said Ruth, standing about four inches away from Kate's breast, staring at the pump.

"I feel something," said Kate, surprised at the pump's grip.

"A bit's coming out."

"Oh, jeez," said Kate, relaxing into the tingling of her milk flowing to her nipples. "I had no idea it came out like that!" Kate watched her milk squirt like the sprinkler heads her dad installed in the front lawn, hitting all sides of the pump bottle.

Ruth sat down. "Now, you've got the milk down, the other side'll be easy. The letdown's the hard part. The rest is just manual labor. You can sit down, honey," she said.

Kate worked her way over to the bed, pumping as she walked. "It's almost full."

"You just tell me when, and I'll pour it in the Baggie and you can do the next one. . . . How old's your baby?"

"Almost two weeks," said Kate, focused on the yellowish milk. *It's like there's cream in it,* she thought, amazed at her capability.

"So your milk's been in for a week or so. That's good. Your baby was nursed that first important week. Antibodies and all," said Ruth, taking the full pump and pouring the milk into a Baggie. "Look at this, enough for a whole feeding, almost. You got to do that other breast, though. You don't want to get an infection. I'll just go put this in the freezer. You get a move on. I bet you're tired. Be right back."

Ruth took the milk to the kitchen, and Kate pumped her left breast. *It's sort of like sex,* she thought, the in, the out, the in, the out, the liquid squirting from her nipple in pulses. It was so different from when the baby nursed. All Deirdre had to do was yawn or burp or make a small squeak, and the milk came down, ready to drink. This was obscene, fake, plastic, not at all how it should be, her baby at her breast, first one, then the other. Kate liked how Deirdre fell asleep finally, her mouth opening, her small tongue still trying to suck. How could she be gone? Kate wondered, feeling the weight of her empty arms. How could they have taken her?

Kate shook out of her head the movie that had begun to play during the ride here in the cop car. It was the story of a girl screwed over by life, one who had every living thing taken from her. Kate saw herself on screen, alone, the wind blowing, some melancholy cellos playing in the background. Nothing happened but that view, the camera moving closer and closer, Kate against the gray sky, no baby, no mother, no father. Not even Tyler, just alone, alone, alone flashing under her image like a subtitle.

"Oh," Kate said, "stop it." She wiped the tears off her cheek and put the pump down on Ruth's nightstand, next to a farm-implement catalogue and a *National Enquirer.* She looked around at the paisley wallpaper, brown with tan squiggles, the pictures of horses and lambs, an orange cat curled up at the foot of the bed. Kate realized she was cold, and put on her blouse, buttoning over her flattened breasts, pressing on them, thankful she was not sore or engorged anymore.

"Okay, let's take this one to the kitchen. Come on," said Ruth, popping in the door, then disappearing. Kate picked up the pump and followed her down the dark hall, to the light of the kitchen. "We'll just make a little pile of these in the freezer, and we'll take them when you go visit the baby. We'll bring a cooler."

Kate sat down, exhausted, her dirty hair hanging in slick dark ropes around her face. "Kind of like a picnic," she said.

Ruth smiled. "Yeah, you could say that. But the social worker will take them to the foster home when she returns the baby, and the foster mom will feed her your milk. That way, when you get her back, neither of you will have missed a beat."

Kate looked up, her eyes suddenly clear of the long, terrible day. "You mean I'll get her back? They'll let me? When?"

Ruth closed the freezer. "Oh, honey. I don't really know. I shouldn't have said that. My job is to take care of just you and Tyler. But don't give up."

"Oh," said Kate, wishing there was one person on the planet who could answer her questions.

"You just need to let Cynthia do her job. She's good at it," said Ruth.

"Yeah, she took my baby from me. Out of the bassinet at the hospital. Right in front of me," said Kate. "She didn't even listen to what I had to say."

Ruth turned from the sink and looked at Kate with soft eyes that Kate wanted to believe in. "It's not easy taking a baby from a mama. She's not a mean person, but there are rules she has to follow. I've been taking care of kids for years, and I'm telling you, it just takes time. The problem is time. It takes so damn long to get through."

Kate looked up, watching Ruth as she washed out the pump with hot soapy water and let it dry on the counter. Kate wondered why Ruth let kids like Tyler and her stay in her house, with all their problems and things like sore breasts and bad letdown and worse families. Kate wondered if Ruth could tell her why this had happened to her family. Maybe, because Ruth had seen it all before, all the sad kids with problems, she could tell Kate what strange current lifted Tyler and her to this house on this night, without the baby, without their father, without their mother.

"Ruth?" said Kate, wanting to see her turn around, to look at her brown eyes and freckled skin, strong hands and wrists emerging from her red sweatshirt.

"Yes?" said Ruth, wiping her hands, waiting, it seemed, for these very questions.

Kate swallowed, her throat tight and dry. "Can I take a shower? I feel terrible."

"Oh, sure, honey. Let me give you some towels and such. Follow me. We're all done here anyhow."

Kate showered for almost half an hour, soaping her body, trying to scrub off hospital smells, sweat, oil, and the smell of milk that seemed to float around her like perfume. She washed her hair three times, watching as thick dark strands fell into the drain. She knew that would happen after the baby was born, but it was something else to lose, the full black hair that sprouted and then tumbled down her back during pregnancy. Kate scoured her face with some acne soap she found in the shower, circling and circling, imagining the oil that she was whisking away. Finally, she turned the hot water off, and stood under the cold, letting it hit the crown of her head, her breasts, and all her pores, shrinking everything and taking away her breath.

Kate wrapped a towel around her head and one around her body, turned off the light, and felt her way to her door. Tyler was in bed, asleep. Kate finished drying herself, and pulled on the pajamas Cynthia had asked another social worker to pack, along with jeans and T-shirts, underwear and bras, sweaters and windbreakers. Kate wondered how it felt to walk into someone else's home, open drawers, and guessing, okay, this has got to be the sock drawer, and which toothbrush is it? But everything was here, her lotion, her toothpaste, even the maxipads that had been hidden behind the toilet.

Kate sat on the bed, combing her hair, looking out at the moonlight shining on fields of barely sprouted plants. She stopped moving, realizing she couldn't keep her arm up any longer. Kate lay down, pulled an afghan over her, certain that it would just be for a second, and let the moon splash across the landscape of her covered body.

She opened her eyes. She sat up panicked, forgetting where she was, the dark room glowing blue with late-night moon. *Deirdre,* she thought, *is she crying? She needs me!* Kate stood up, her feet cold on the floor, and then it all rushed in, the long day, the hospital, the police car. And Deirdre. Deirdre was gone.

Kate looked at the clock and realized only an hour had passed, but she felt as if she'd slept for more, her body quick with nerves, her stomach prickly and upset. The house was quiet, no plumbing noise, no light seeping from under the other kids' closed doors. Kate could hear Tyler's breathing, but her sister was still.

Kate pulled back the afghan, walked to the window, and saw the shadow of a barn, some fences, a truck. She quietly cracked open the window and breathed in animal smells, hay and manure, and wished it were daylight so she could go outside, pet the animals, just as she had done when she was little and her parents took Tyler and her to the petting zoo. She wanted something small and warm to hold and touch, a rabbit, a lamb, a kid who would slip its mouth into her palm searching for food. When she was little, after they had seen the spotted leopard and the water buffalo, her parents paid the admission to the petting zoo and bought Tyler and Kate ice cream cones full of green food pellets, and the goats would follow them, biting the hems of their dresses, looking up with wet eyes. So they fed the pellets and then the cones to the goats, the lambs, and the musk ox, sometimes even to the warthog that stayed in the corner of its pen, glaring at them with evil dark eyes. And there was a smell, urine, hay, alfalfa, dung, dirt, human bodies sweating, that mixed together, and Kate smelled that same thing now.

"Tyler," whispered Kate. "Are you awake?"

Tyler rolled over, her eyes glass in the dark room. "Yeah. I couldn't sleep."

"I can't sleep either."

"Do you want to talk?" asked Tyler, sitting up on one elbow.

"No. Listen, there are animals out there. I can hear them. Let's go see. Let's put on our shoes and go see."

Tyler rolled back, pushing her hair out of her eyes. "What?"

"It's like the petting zoo out there. I think there are lambs and cows. Chickens. Things like that."

"Kate, we shouldn't go out there," said Tyler, yawning.

"Okay. I'll go."

"You'll get in trouble. What if we get sent away from here, too?"

"I'm just going outside. I'm not running away or anything. Stay if you want," said Kate, tying her Keds and putting on a sweater.

"Okay, okay. Just give me a minute. God, what is it with you, anyway?" said Tyler, reaching down to find her shoes.

Outside, the moon had slid behind a stand of firs. Bats churned by, twisting and circling blindly, and Tyler moved into Kate as they walked, careful feet on cold ground.

"That's got to be the barn. There's a light there. See?"

"Yeah," said Tyler. "Let's go see the animals and go back to bed. I'm, like, freezing."

"All right. Careful," said Kate, feeling lumps of soil under her shoes.

In Monte Veda, with the streetlights on Wildwood Drive, there weren't nights like this, clear and dark, sky cloudy with stars. Kate was used to the Big and Little Dipper, the North Star, Mars, and Venus, but here were twists of stars, everywhere, so many they blended together.

"Look, a shooting star," said Tyler, pulling her sister still. "And another!"

Kate looked up, remembering a spring camping trip to Christina Lake in Canada with her parents, two years before her mother got sick. There were stars like this at night, and mountains holding the lake like cupped hands, and the air was cold and felt like snow.

"Come on, girls. Get in," said her father, running into the lake. "It's warm, I promise."

Tyler, Kate, and Deirdre had stood on the beach shivering under thick towels, watching Davis dive under and stand up, his hair slicked back, his body shiny with water. "Just come and test it," he yelled, diving under again.

The three of them went to the water, putting white toes into the ripples, smiling as they felt the warmth. "All right. For once your father isn't pulling our legs," said Deirdre, and they threw off their towels, and walked in, splashing themselves, finally diving under just as Davis had done.

At nightfall, Davis built a fire from the wood the forest service cut and stacked just for campers, and they watched the sparks, the stars, told scary stories. "Once, a long time ago, there was this grave-yard . . ." Davis began, Tyler and Kate leaning next to Deirdre.

"Davis. Do you want everyone sleeping in one sleeping bag tonight?" warned Deirdre.

"Okay, how 'bout this one. Once upon a time in this toy store, there was this certain aisle, D2. It was the Barbie aisle, the little tiny dress and shoe aisle, the Malibu camper aisle. At night, when all the employees went home, boxes started floating from the shelves. Each morning, when the employees came back to work, they'd find some-thing moved, a Barbie taken out of her box and posed in some strange way on the floor. You know, legs in splits, stuff like that. Sometimes, when an employee would walk the aisle, stocking it or something, he'd feel the floor move under him, almost knocking him down."

"Dad," said Kate. "Is this true?"

"Of course. Now, finally, the store decided they needed to pay one of those ghostbuster-type groups to get rid of this ghost. So they set up a camera at night, and put a Malibu Barbie Corvette in the middle of the aisle. All night the camera watched, and finally, the Corvette began to zoom up and down the aisle, Barbie's hair flying after her. Searching. Searching. And finally the car stopped, and the Barbie got out, and climbed up the shelf, and stopped by the exqui-site figure of Malibu Ken, buffed and tan."

"Dad!" screamed Tyler and Kate.

"So, the ghostbuster team restocked the shelves, putting Malibu Barbie and Malibu Ken together, and all the commotion stopped. The End."

"Dad! You are making this all up. Dad!" said Tyler, and Kate could still hear her voice, still hear all their laughter around that fire, sparks flying and curling up and over the firs, all the way to the stars.

"Someone's in there," said Kate as she and Tyler neared the barn door. "I see something moving."

"Me, too. I'm scared. Let's go back to bed," said Tyler, pulling on Kate's sweater.

"No. Wait. It's some guy." Kate and Tyler stood by the barn, their hands on the rough wood, eyes next to cracks and knotholes.

"Who is he?" asked Tyler. "He's feeding an animal, a sheep I think."

"Yeah," said Kate. "And look, there's a lamb, too."

Tyler and Kate pulled open the door and stepped into the yellow light of the bulb hanging from a barn rafter. The boy looked up and stood. "Who are you?"

Tyler stopped moving, pulling on Kate, trying to tug her back into the night. "We just got here. We're staying at Ruth's. You are, too, right?"

The boy nodded, picked up a large black flashlight, and then walked by them without lifting his eyes or saying a word. He grabbed the door handle as he walked through and slammed the door behind him.

"Jeez, what an asshole," said Tyler, shaking her head. "This is such a joke."

"What are you talking about?" said Kate, walking over to the lamb and watching its mother lick its small face.

"Hello! This. Being here. Have you really thought about it?"

"What?" asked Kate.

Tyler sneezed, rubbing her nose. "God. I mean, this is almost funny now," she said.

"Bless you . . . what? You mean we're out here in a barn in the middle of the night? In some strange part of the state with weird kids who don't talk?"

"Yeah. That and our lives are ruined, and the baby is who knows where. Dad's in trouble, Sanjay is arrested," said Tyler, kicking straw on Kate's shoe. "You know, basic soap opera stuff. Except it's us. It's real, Kate."

"It isn't that bad, Tyler," said Kate.

"Hah! Really? You're kidding, right? Are you living in some kind of dream world?"

Kate walked away from the animals, scared to reach too close, to disturb the new baby struggling to maneuver ever closer to its mother. "No. Yes. I don't know. I just don't want to think about it. I can't stand it. She's not here, and I don't know how she is, if she's sleeping or what. It's like it was when we'd leave her at home when we were at school. Every second, I'm thinking about her."

Tyler nodded. "So it is that bad. Just like I said."

"Stop it, Tyler! Just stop it! I don't want to think about it," said Kate.

"We have to think about it," said Tyler, moving toward her sister.

"What's the point? They'll just do what they want to do, like always. They'll make decisions and not ask or tell us, and then we'll just have to live with it. Don't you see? We don't have to think because it doesn't matter what we think."

"It's bad, then. It's as bad as I thought," said Tyler.

Kate brought her hand to her eyes, wiping them angrily. "Yeah. It is. And I promised you it would be okay, and it isn't. It won't ever be okay. I've ruined everything."

She sat down on a bale of hay, and Tyler sat by her, scooting across the scratchy surface to get closer to her sister. "We are still together. They haven't split us up," she said, pressing her thigh against Kate's, matching their bones together.

"Yet. Yet. They can do anything they want," said Kate.

"No, they can't. And next year you'll be eighteen. An adult. You'll be able to do what you want and live where you want. You can have your baby back then, I'll bet," said Tyler.

Kate was silent and still, the air around her heavy and full of tears. "Yeah, I guess. But I have to stay alive until then."

"Don't say that. Don't ever say that," said Tyler, dropping her forehead into her palm. Kate reached over and around her sister, pressing their chests together, until it hurt her spine. She hadn't hugged her sister like this in a long time, years maybe. There was nothing between them now, no stomach bulging with baby, no lies, and Kate could feel Tyler's bones, her firm, solid flesh, the same flesh Kate held to herself when they were little girls playing house, when Kate was the mom and Tyler would do everything she was asked to. *She's never changed,* thought Kate. *She's always been there, doing what I asked even when it brings her to this, this dark barn, this cold night.*

"All right. I promise. I won't say anything like that again. And we'll just think that Deirdre's coming home to us." Kate shook as she spoke, hoping, even as she said them, that her words were true.

Tyler pulled away from her sister, wiping her eyes, leaving her hand on Kate's shoulder. "When were you going to tell me about Sanjay, Kate?"

Kate kicked the straw off her shoe. "I didn't want to ever tell you. I didn't want anyone to know. Because . . . I was scared of what would happen."

Tyler looked up to the light hanging from a rafter, squinting her eyes and shaking her head. "But how did it start? How did it happen without anyone knowing? Didn't he wonder and try to find out why you weren't baby-sitting anymore? Did he ever call?"

"No. He broke up with me. Said he felt too guilty about Meera and the kids. And he kind of just let me go. He didn't call, just Meera. You know. I just kept saying, 'No, I can't. I can't baby-sit any-more.' "

"Why, though, Kate? Why Sanjay? He's so old," asked Tyler.

Kate breathed in the smells of hay and alfalfa, dirt and animals. She didn't know how to tell Tyler how she constantly thought about Sanjay's hand reaching to her that day in his living room, asking her a question she'd never been asked before. "I don't know. I don't know how to explain it."

Tyler took this in, waiting, Kate thought, for more, some finer answer. *But, really,* Kate thought, *there isn't one, nothing more than Sanjay's open hand, his invitation.*

"Let's get out of here, okay. I am so tired, and I don't care about animals anymore, you know?"

"Yeah, okay," said Tyler. "I'm tired, too."

As they turned off the light and left the barn, holding their breaths for a minute and listening to night noises, Kate suddenly thought about Jaggu's stuffed bear, the soft fuzzy child smell almost crushed between Jaggu and her as she read him to sleep. Once, long before last summer, she had been reading nursery rhymes to Jaggu and Ari, both boys and the bear in her lap. When Sanjay came home from work and walked in the den, the boys jumped off her and ran into his legs.

"Da, Da," said Ari. "Look, we're reading. We're reading the words."

"That is amazing, Ari. Has Kate taught you how to read today?" he said, winking at her.

"Yeah, Da," said Jaggu. "All the words on that page. I can read them. See?" Jaggu pulled the book from Kate's hands and, holding the book crookedly, read, " 'Mary had a little lamb, the fleece as white as snow.' See?"

Sanjay bent down to his boys, and Kate knew she was invisible to him and the boys now. But she didn't care, sitting close, listening to the boys' voices as they told Sanjay about their day, the books, the food, the television shows. And she watched Sanjay's head, bent down and low with his boys, watched him reach around to hold them, all three scooting closer, closer, arms and legs and knees moving together like one known animal.

When Kate and Tyler got back to the house, they went to the kitchen, following the streaks of light in the hallway. Ruth and the boy from the barn sat at the table under a copper lamp. They both looked up as the girls walked in the room, but neither was surprised to see them, Kate thought later.

"Hey. I guess you already met Adam. He's been with me for six months. Adam, this is Kate and Tyler." Ruth pushed her chair back on the wood floor and stood up. "I guess no one could sleep tonight, huh? What about some tea?"

Kate nodded. "Okay. You know, I thought I heard some animals, so we went out to see. There's a lamb in the barn. Was it just born or something?"

"Oh, yeah. Caused some commotion before you got here. I guess Adam here went out to check up on her. He named her Zena."

"What other animals do you have here, Ruth?" Tyler asked.

"Oh, sheep coming out of my ears. Two horses. A donkey. Goats. A couple pigs. Cows. Chickens. You saw my cat, right, Kate? But mostly, we are a pumpkin patch. Some Indian corn, too. This field over here"—Ruth pointed at the field next to the house—"is all pumpkins. Come September and October, and a bit into November, we've got kids coming by the busload. I set up scarecrows, and apple dunking. My brother takes them on tractor rides. Adam was here for most of last season."

Kate looked at Adam and wondered why he had come to stay at Ruth's, wondered what his long story was, wondered who had touched him in the wrong way or what adult had forgotten him. She worried about his six months, hoping that she and Tyler would not be at Ruth's for the next pumpkin season, that instead she could bring Deirdre, pick out a pumpkin to carve, show her the scarecrows and apple dunking, watch her smile.

"Let's see. Lipton's all I got. Nothing herbal, but I'll make it weak," said Ruth, filling the kettle.

"At home," said Tyler, "my mom used to buy all these weird teas, like, 'Drink Now, Go to Sleep Later' tea or 'Full Moon' tea. Once she brought home 'Afternoon Sun' tea."

Ruth laughed. "Sounds like you have to be really on time for all those teas. That's why I like Lipton. Always tastes good to me."

Ruth put four mugs on the table, draping the tea bags over the lips. "And cookies. Can't have tea without cookies. I've got vanilla wafers and Oreos."

Ruth filled a plate, alternating vanilla and chocolate, and put it on the table. "You know, I've always wanted to have one of those high tea things. You know, English style, with crumpets and raspberry preserves, and that wiggly custard . . . trifle. But I always just have Oreos and vanilla wafers."

Kate took a cookie and watched Adam. He didn't look up, biting down on his cookie under his red bangs. "Do we get to help with the animals?" asked Kate. "I would really like to."

"Oh, yes indeed. I didn't want to tell you both everything right away, but that's part of the bargain here. You don't have to go to the county facility, but you have to help every morning with feeding the animals, and in the afternoons my brother will ask you for some help, too. No way to get out of it, really, except if you want to leave."

"What about my visits with Deirdre?" asked Kate. "I have to go to those, you know."

"Of course, honey. We'll work out a schedule. And there's your homework. But the school district hasn't even gotten that message, so you'll be school-free until they get the information to me." Ruth poured water in the mugs and sat down, dunking her tea bag, one, two, three times, then pulling it out. "Do it this way, and you'll still sleep like a baby."

"Where does your brother live? Does he have children?" asked Tyler, taking a hot sip.

"Robert's got a house on the other end of the property. His wife died about four years ago. He doesn't have kids, but he's got three Border collies, mean as sin and just as ugly, if you ask me. Don't worry, you'll meet that whole house full."

Tyler curled a blond strand behind her ear and put down her cup. "Are you married?"

"Do you always ask so many damn questions?" said Adam, looking up, his eyes blue as frozen water.

"Well, Adam. How polite," said Ruth, turning to Adam. "You were just as curious, you know."

At Adam's question, Tyler shut her mouth, her lips a thin line, her eyes full of tears. Ruth patted her shoulder. "No. I'm not married. Too much going on around here for that."

Kate chewed her cookie, almost closing her eyes at the rhythm of her mouth, her head falling forward as Ruth and Tyler talked. "Well, seems like our little tea party is over. Let's get Kate to bed. Come on, Tyler. Adam, finish up. I'll be back in a flash."

Kate heard Ruth and stood up, even though she really couldn't see, almost falling into Ruth's arms, letting Ruth and Tyler walk her to their room. Kate lay down quickly, this time barely noticing the afghan come up over her, not feeling Ruth's strong hand on her cheek and hair as she said good night.

&a.

The house was finally silent, the lights out, Ruth's cat purring at the foot of the bed. *Happy for no special reason,* thought Ruth, *except for those things we take for granted.* She stroked the cat, Simon, and he turned over, exposing his white stomach, stretching out his front paws and yawning.

"Good kitty," said Ruth, brushing Simon's long fur off her hands. Ruth stood up, and pulled off her sweatshirt, folding it over the rocking chair. This was a sad bunch here tonight, those two girls, she thought, pulling on her flannel nightgown and red wool socks. The older one seemed almost unconscious at times, as if she were still pregnant, dosed by hormones. And her poor breasts, so engorged, so needing her baby to drink up all that milk.

When Cynthia had called Ruth in the morning, Ruth hadn't asked much about the girls, just happy to talk to Cynthia, who sent her clients, kept this little pumpkin patch afloat, kept Ruth busy helping people.

"I got these girls, Ruth. It'll break your heart," said Cynthia hurriedly.

"What's new? What is it this time?" said Ruth.

"Well, the father kind of abandoned them, and the older one got herself pregnant by the neighbor dad. He was just arrested. It's a big mess. The baby will be going to a foster home."

Ruth breathed in, always surprised how the word *baby* shook her. "Is it an ugly scene?"

Cynthia sighed. Ruth could hear the fatigue in her voice. "Not as ugly as it could be, I suppose. I've seen worse, but I've seen better, too."

And the girls were good girls, she thought, not angry like her other two, ready to bite the world's head off. But the older one, so full of motherhood and weepiness. Ruth rubbed her own breasts, remembering that feeling, like she would explode, even with the drugs the doctors finally gave her to dry up her milk. Ruth cried in bed for three days, wondering how her baby was, wishing she could have at least looked at it before they gave it to someone else.

"It's for your own good," said her mother stiffly, sitting on the hospital chair smoking a Camel. "You should have thought about this before. Before you *did* it."

Ruth had moaned, holding her empty stomach, knowing there had been nothing for her to think about before, before she was raped behind the bowling alley by two boys. "This is what you need, you queer. This'll change your mind."

She had never told anyone but Robert. And the day after the rape, sore and numb, her back full of asphalt and dirt, she cut off her long blond hair and never grew it long again.

*   *   *

Ruth walked into her bathroom and looked at herself in the mirror, not finding much of the fourteen-year-old girl in her fifty-five-year-old face. Now she looked tired and too tan, the constant sun from childhood accumulating on her face in three lines under her eyes, a wishbone crease around her mouth, two permanent worries on her forehead. *It shouldn't be a surprise to anyone that I'm out of circulation given the way I look,* she thought, turning on the hot water and splashing her face, rubbing in the moisturizing soap that the commercials said made skin "as soft as silk." More like linen or corduroy, thought Ruth, laughing, soap in her mouth. But she kept washing, then rinsed, patting her face rather than rubbing it dry, smoothing a palmful of lotion under her eyes, on her cheeks, chin, forehead, and neck.

Maybe it was ridiculous, she thought, to keep at this, the washing, the lotion, the night stares into the mirror, the worry about lines and creases and folds, the hope that despite the body's movement toward the ground that she was still there, still desirable, still a woman someone could love. No matter how many years passed, she was still that scared girl with her mother's sewing scissors in her hand, chopping off her hair, the gold strands like perfect thread on the floor, strands she would find for weeks in her bathroom, pushed against the toilet or behind the sink, a reminder of what had happened to her, the hair a symbol of how she was pulled and pushed and forced to take the bodies of others into her own, their grunting and spurting and ugly words. She took it all, and they seemed to walk away without a piece of her on them, not even her blood on their foreskins or clothes.

Later, at school, she would see them, seniors with lettermen jackets—football, basketball, swimming—the boys who, Ruth thought, had never seemed to notice her. But somehow they had, watching her from afar, finding her different, a difference that offended them, made them indignant, aroused their sex to anger, let them hurt her over and over again in the chill night of a bowling Wednesday.

When Robert had finally found her, still by the trash cans, her Levi's bunched around her hips, her back sore, her eyes full of nothing, he wanted to hunt them down and hurt them, skinny Robert with the cowlick and glasses. Instead she held him, let him pull her up, fix her clothes, take her to his car. Robert cried, brushing her hair with his smooth hand, muttering hate and violence under his breath, wanting to throw his slim body against the boys' muscles, let himself feel what Ruth just had but against his face, shoulders, gut.

"No," Ruth had said finally. "Let's go home. Please, let's just go home."

And that night Ruth had stared at herself in the mirror, watching her brown eyes, sad, pale skin, knowing that this was the face she would be watching for a lifetime.

"Well, Simon. Is it organic gardening with earthworms or 'Diana Talks from the Grave'? I thought so," said Ruth, getting under the covers and picking up the *National Enquirer* from her bed stand. She flipped through the pages, reading, then shut the newspaper, and stared at Simon, thinking, *Why do I read all this terrible stuff? Why?* She had Adam here, his father had left Adam's mother and her reaction was to drink all day while Adam was at school and rage all night, in one month's time breaking all the furniture and china in the house as well as Adam's arm. And then there was Virgie, pierced in every conceivable soft, tender, and hidden place, green-haired, tattooed, and broken, her father abusing her over and over, sneaking into her room at night like a pirate.

Ruth leaned back, putting down the paper, and turning off the light. She'd be up in just a few hours, throwing on her clothes and feeding the animals. She decided to let the girls sleep in, just this once, and as she had since she was fourteen, Ruth closed her eyes and imagined her bed was a boat with two giant oars. With each breath in, she pulled the oars back; with each breath out, she pushed them forward. The seas were calm tonight, and she moved quickly toward the horizon, the clear black water splashing beside her.

"Who used my goddamn Clearasil? It's almost fucking gone!" Kate opened her eyes. A green-haired girl was yelling in her face. "Who said you could use my goddamn Clearasil?"

Kate sat up and winced, her breasts huge and sore. "I'm sorry. I didn't really think about it. I just got here."

"Like that's a good excuse. Get your own damn stuff next time," said the girl, storming out the door and slamming it.

"Who in the hell was that?" asked Tyler, sitting up in her bed.

"I have no idea. I've got to get my breast pump. God, I feel like a Viking woman. I could star in an opera or something."

Kate stopped and stuck out her chest for Tyler, her breasts round and hard under her pajamas.

"It's like you've got one of those pointer bras on," said Tyler.

"If it could only last after Deirdre stopped nursing, right? I'll be right back," said Kate, leaving the room and walking toward the kitchen. As she turned a corner, she almost bumped into Adam. Reflexively, she put her arms in front of her chest.

"Uh, hi," she said, but he walked around her and kept going, not looking back.

Kate found the pump and the Baggies in the kitchen and went back to the bedroom. After she was done, Tyler laughing the entire time and calling her "Moo Cow," she went to put the full bags in the freezer. Ruth was in the kitchen, frying up some Jimmy Dean sausage and scrambling some eggs.

"Hey, Kate. Good morning. Listen, I've got some great news. Cynthia called and said she'd bring the baby to you today, rather than us going to her. What do you think?"

Kate sat down at the table. Thinking of Deirdre almost made her drool. She could smell Deirdre's body from memory, wanting to hold her skin, put her lips on her head, touch her fingers, toes. "When will she be her?"

"In about an hour. Apparently Deirdre's awake, and the foster mother called Cynthia and got it all organized. So eat and then you can get ready. You and Tyler'll get a day off from chores."

Kate felt something small start to well up inside her body: hope, or joy, or just satisfaction. She sat still and silent as Ruth rounded up Tyler and Adam for breakfast. The girl who had yelled her awake also stormed in, throwing herself into her seat and staring at Kate. Kate looked down at her lap, playing with her fingers and sniffing in tears, not able to ward off the girl's anger.

"Virgie? Why are your knickers in a twist?" asked Ruth.

"Somebody used up almost all of my Clearasil soap. Without asking, either," said Virgie, the stud in her tongue clicking on her top teeth with each word.

"Well, I said I was sorry," said Kate.

Virgie threw her arms on the table. "When I get zits will sorry take them away? Should I take a little bit of sorry and rub it on my face?"

Ruth laughed. "You are full of spit today. Listen, I think we can rustle up another bottle of soap. Just lay off a bit. Why don't you say hi first to Kate and Tyler? Girls, this is Virgie."

Ruth set plates in front of them and then platters of food. Kate suddenly felt enormously hungry and ignored Virgie, taking huge bites of sausage and egg, concentrating on the flavors of butter, garlic, cumin, and grease. She realized that it had been a long time since she'd eaten food other than what she or Tyler had made—macaroni and cheese from the box, melted cheese sandwiches, frozen pizza, chicken strips from Costco.

Kate looked up from her chewing and saw the girl, Virgie, staring at her, her fork full and poised in midair, making Kate wonder if she was going to fling the egg and sausage at her. Kate stopped moving her mouth, the food heavy on her tongue, and watched Virgie slowly move the fork to her mouth, sliding the food in, then chewing with her mouth open. Virgie put down her fork and stared at Kate, then Tyler, her elbows on the table, trying, it seemed to Kate, to figure something out without asking. Kate didn't take her eyes from Virgie's face, even though she felt herself grow warm with blood. Even though Virgie scared her, Kate wished she could be more like her, someone who could find a wrong and confront it, bring the problem to the one who caused it in the first place. She imagined herself going to Sanjay, waking both him and Meera up one early morning, yelling, "Who in the hell used my body? And now look! I'm pregnant. What are you going to do about it?" Kate then thought about driving to Hannah's house, barging through that bedroom door, waking her father and Hannah up, screaming, "You've left us and now look what's happened! How are you going to fix it?"

How do you do that? thought Kate. *How do you find the right words and push them loudly from your lungs? How can you make pain more than sound and motion, turn it into words that strike and change?* Had she ever been able to say anything?

Kate looked down at her plate, and then back at Virgie. She realized that Virgie didn't have one blemish on her white skin, her pores invisible, no pools of oil on her forehead and cheeks, just softness, a translucent plain from cheek to jaw. Someone could almost fall into that skin, thought Kate, but then corrected herself, because no one could get close enough to, sharp, dull metal on Virgie's lip, nose, eyebrow, both ears from tops to lobes.

"You have perfect skin, you know," said Kate.

"Yeah?" said Virgie. "Well, that doesn't mean I don't need my soap."

"You know, you're not the only one with problems," said Kate. Tyler looked up from her food, and so did Virgie, words and egg threatening to come from her lips, her eyes slit to lines of blue. But she took her eyes from Kate and ate her eggs. Kate felt Tyler's foot nudging her own under the table. She nudged back and then went back to eating, taking in the taste, the smell of the meal before her.

❦

"Give her to me," said Kate, quickly and without a smile, opening Ruth's door and holding out her arms for Deirdre.

Cynthia came inside, holding the baby and a diaper bag. She looked more put together than yesterday, her hair slick and styled, clothes ironed and tucked in, but she was obviously still tired, her face pale, her eyes heavy with dark circles. "Okay. Hold on. Let me put down this stuff."

Kate let her in and closed the door behind her, almost running to the couch. Ruth stood at the living room door, laughing. "Well, you'd think you'd been separated for years, not just hours. Hi, Cynthia."

"Well, I'm sure it feels like that," said Cynthia, handing Deirdre over. Kate held her breath, not wanting to wake Deirdre from the lull of the long car ride, at least not yet. Kate closed her eyes and thought, *I could find her in the dark. I could find her in a roomful of two-week-old babies. I could feel her toes and fingers,*

*and smell her hair and stomach. And I would guess right each time.
I know it.*

Ruth and Cynthia watched her for a time, the room silent as
Deirdre slept, her body fitting perfectly into Kate's. "Well, let's have
some tea," said Ruth, and she and Cynthia left Kate and the baby
alone.

Kate laid her head back against the couch, listening to the kitchen
noises, breathing in the quiet of late morning. She thought of one
afternoon last summer, Sanjay's head on her chest, his dark head
against her skin just as Deirdre's was now. Under the covers, he was
holding her waist, his breath smooth and quiet with sleep. Then she
had thought that she had never been as happy; she had never understood her own body as well, learning how things move and shake and
open. *No wonder they don't want us to have sex,* she thought, remembering the freshman year health class lesson "Just Say No." *But
maybe,* Kate thought, *teachers and parents really do want us to know
this, this having to give life to another, this opening of flesh and spirit.*
Compared to childbirth and the caring and feeding of a baby, sex
and Sanjay almost seemed like nothing.

At night sometimes Kate used to hear her parents behind their
closed door, light, rhythmic thuds against the wall, laughter, silence,
and then long, soft conversations, the mumbles finally lulling Kate to
sleep. She remembered her mother talking to her about childbirth
while Deirdre washed dinner dishes, the light above the sink glinting
red off her hair. "It hurts. There's no getting around that," Deirdre
had said, turning to Kate and drying the colander. "But it's worth it."

Kate sat at the kitchen table drinking hot chocolate, listening to the
water splash in the sink. That day at school, the teacher had brought
out the strange reproductive chart, listing the organs' functions and
uses, finally showing them how a baby emerged from the birth canal,
the small body twisting and bending like clay just to get out.

"So why do people do it? Why did you?" Kate asked, knowing
the answer already.

"Because you were worth it," said Deirdre, launching into the
story Kate really wanted to hear. "Your dad and I were at dinner. I
said to him, 'You know, I am going to have just a sip of wine,' and
then my water broke. Right there, in the restaurant. We were right

across from the hospital, so we walked over. Those poor waiters. But I was too nervous to be embarrassed."

"Then what happened?"

"Well, they sent us home because I was nowhere near ready. About two hours later, I made your father drive me back. And they sent us home again. Finally, about six hours later, we got to the hospital almost too late. You were just about to pop out right there in the car."

"And then?"

"So, they rushed me in, told me not to push, and when they finally set everything up in the delivery room, I opened my legs and whoosh, there you were."

Kate smiled. "And how big was I?

"Nine pounds one ounce, twenty-two inches long."

Kate took a sip of her chocolate. "So did it hurt?"

"Like I said, it was worth it," Deirdre said, turning back to the sink.

Kate felt something squirmy in her stomach, the beginnings of a question too strange to utter. She watched her mother move at the sink, imagining her and her father behind the closed bedroom door on Friday nights doing what the teacher diagrammed, the parts coming together in the right order, the two tiny sperm dots that would become Tyler and her moving fast up her mother's insides, trying to win the race. Maybe, thought Kate, it would be easier to just not have sex. "Mom," she asked, "why don't people just not have sex if it hurts to have a baby?"

Deirdre turned from the sink again, wiping her hands on her jeans. She raised her eyebrows and smiled. "Because it's fun. Because it's love, Kate."

Tyler walked into the room and sat down by Kate, but Kate didn't really notice, remembering her mother in the kitchen, focusing on the baby's face, her rose lips, almond eyes. Tyler bent over and stroked the baby's cheek with her index finger. "She's our little Dee Dee, isn't she, Kate?"

"I don't like calling her Dee Dee, Tyler. Mom never let herself be called that."

Tyler snorted. "Well, like, she's not Mom, is she? She's our little Dee Dee." Tyler brought her head toward Deirdre, her eyes closed, breathing in, Kate imagined, the same smells she had hunted for earlier.

Kate shrugged. "I guess. Oh, isn't she cute? I hope she wakes up soon so I can nurse her."

Adam walked into the living room and stopped at the couch, surprised. "That's yours?"

Kate looked up and nodded, trying not to look at him, imagining she'd see a raised eyebrow, a curving lip, a snicker.

Tyler looked at him, though, arching her back a little, Kate noticed, as she spoke. "Yeah, her name's Dee Dee, and I delivered her. Really. At home."

"Why would you do that? Isn't that dangerous or something?" asked Adam, sitting down.

Tyler looked at Kate and shrugged. "Well, yeah. It was. Like, you wouldn't believe how long it took. Kate was screaming, 'Pull it out!'" Tyler stopped at Kate's cautioning eyes. "But look, everything turned out okay."

"Right," said Adam, leaning toward the baby. "That's why you're here at Ruth's house." But his tone was softer, and Kate flushed, thinking that he was looking at the baby, looking at her, this strange boy with the wide clear eyes.

"Can I hold her?" asked Adam. Even with his bangs in front of his face, Kate could see his blush, red patches on his cheeks flushing upward. He looked up at her and cocked his head, his two slightly buck front teeth resting on his lower lip.

"You want to?" said Kate. "Why? I mean, really?"

Adam sat up straight. "Well, if you don't want me to, that's fine."

"No, it's, well, no one else but Tyler and me . . . and Cynthia . . . and the foster parents . . . Well, here," said Kate, holding Dee Dee away from her body, pressing the baby into Adam's arms softly. "Careful. Her head . . . okay. Okay."

He doesn't look awkward, thought Kate, at first waiting for his stiff elbows and straight back, but the baby slept in his arms just as she had in Kate's.

"My dad's new girlfriend had another baby. I saw her once. But I didn't get to hold her for long," said Adam, rocking the cradle of his arms slowly.

"Well, baby sheep probably aren't that different from a human baby. I mean, they want to eat and sleep. And they make all that noise. Last night they sounded just like babies crying in the middle of the night," said Tyler, scooting closer to Adam. "And you already know how to take care of them."

Dee Dee shifted, stretched, and opened her eyes, closed them, and then opened them again, dark gray-brown irises with pinpoint pupils. "Are you hungry? Are you hungry, little girl?" said Kate, taking her from Adam, who carefully leaned over and placed Deirdre back in her arms.

Cynthia walked in the room, handing Tyler a blanket she'd had on her shoulder. "You know, the foster mother said she took a bottle early this morning, so she should be hungry." She went back to the kitchen, and Kate began unsnapping her nursing bra, then stopped, looking at Adam.

"It's okay. I'll go," he said, walking back upstairs, his shoes thudding on the carpeted wood.

"He was a lot nicer than last night," said Tyler, now scooting closer to Kate, holding Deirdre's wrapped feet in her hands.

"You could say that again," said Kate as she began to feed Deirdre, relaxing back into the couch when her letdown came, this time something natural and not a mechanical, plastic exercise. She closed her eyes, listened to her baby suck and Tyler quietly cooing, "What a good girl, what a good girl. What a good little Dee Dee."

All she wanted, Kate realized, was this. A place to sit with her baby. A place to live with her baby, and feed her, and be with her sister. And her father, if he still wanted them. And, she knew, a place where she could forget about Sanjay and the summer before. She could not bear to look at their house, their yard, the clear glass doors and windows, that led into the life there, those people, their hearts. Those hearts that were not hers and never would be.

Sanjay remembered this room from the many times he had seen it on television. First, the suspect walked in with a court officer, and stood in the jury box. There was the television camera itself to think of, peering from the left corner like a wicked eye, seemingly unmanned but following the suspect as he walked. Sanjay could feel its plastic metal moves. The judge sat in her box, reading, not looking up, too busy with this day in and day out of arrested persons to notice a new one right away.

"Don't let it get to you," Zack had said, patting Sanjay's back as they walked down the long hallway together. "Look. You will be arraigned. I'll ask for the bail hearing, talk a bit, and you'll go home. Meera's ready with the bail?"

Sanjay nodded slightly.

"Great. That's great. Just hang on, now."

Sanjay knew that Zack's words were supposed to be good news, and he tried to smile, but there was a dull ache in his head and a sadness running from his mouth to his feet, pulling on him as he slipped through jail cells and court hallways. Maybe he would go home, but he would be out on bail like some wild animal let loose accidentally. He would go home to a disappointed wife, surprised and perhaps disgusted coworkers, and his own sad thought that nothing that had gotten him here was worth this. Not Kate's arms and mouth or the baby's soft skin. Nothing.

"Yes. Thank you, Zack," said Sanjay, following him in the room just as the television news had taught him, shuffling behind his lawyer, looking down, trying to avoid the camera. As an officer led Sanjay to the jury box, Zack sat down in a chair across the room and gave him a little wave, a high-five in the air, almost, thought Sanjay, as if this were a sporting event.

The room was full of fluorescent light buzz and the whine of the heating system. A bailiff sat at a desk, putting one folder on top of another, and Sanjay watched Zack stand up as the judge looked up from her reading, shifting on his feet, right, left, right, left. Sanjay felt his body shrinking away from the orange clothes, pulling into his bones, his thighs to femur, penis and testicles to hip and pelvis, and heart into spine. He knew if he stayed here long enough, he would disappear, flaking away into the courtroom, kicked into corners by lawyers and judges, suspects and convicts, onlookers and victims, finally swept away by the night janitor.

The judge nodded, and the bailiff stood up and called, "Case number 40702? Is the defendant present in the case of the State of California versus Sanjay Chaturvedi?"

Zack walked through the swinging oak gates and sat down at the table on the left. On the right, Sanjay realized, was the prosecutor, sitting quietly with her legs crossed, her papers already arranged. "Yes, Your Honor."

The judge nodded. "Is the defendant represented by counsel?"

"Yes, he is," said Zack.

The judge nodded again. "Will the defendant please rise?"

Sanjay looked at Zack and stood up, his legs almost buckling underneath him. Sanjay found himself leaning into the shoulder of the man next to him, trying to keep from falling, and was surprised to feel the man lean back into Sanjay's hip, steadying him against the words to come. The judge looked at Sanjay, closing her folder, a folder full of words about him, he suspected. He wanted to see the writing in it, suddenly, all of it, pull it apart and say, "My goodness! How they all have changed the story. You see, it was not like I raped her. You know the way the word is commonly known. It was a poorly thought-out affair with a seventeen-year-old girl. Yes, I understand, but let me point out she . . . she loved me. Yes. She loved me, and I her. I loved how she opened to me, as you might say, like a flower. A cliché, I understand, but so true, so very true."

Sanjay swallowed, also thinking, *I was older and I knew better, but I didn't know better and did it anyway. I did it anyway.*

"Mr. Chaturvedi, you have been charged with violating penal code seventeen, section 602," said the judge. "How say you?"

"My client is entering a plea of not guilty, Your Honor," said Zack, clearing his throat. "And we would like to request an immediate bail hearing so my client can be released on his own recognizance."

The prosecutor, who had been silent and unmoving all this time, stood up. "Excuse me, Your Honor, but we have some concerns here. Mr. Chaturvedi is not a citizen and there is a flight risk." She sat down, both her heels clicking on the floor.

Zack flicked her a quick dark look and continued. "Your Honor, my client has no prior record of conviction or arrest in a crime of this kind nor any other crime, for that matter. He has been employed for seven years by the same company, has a wife and two small children at home, and has strong ties to the community. His wife is a physician at Mt. Diablo Hospital with a strong private practice. This was an isolated incident, he poses no threat to the community, nor does he pose a flight risk."

The prosecuting attorney stood up again, looking at Zack and Sanjay. "Your Honor, we have another concern. While Mr. Chaturvedi has no prior arrests, he does live next door to the girl in question. When she is returned to her father's custody, the proximity may cause difficulties for both families, especially if the baby comes home."

The judge looked at both attorneys and Sanjay for a second. Sanjay wondered how it was possible to make decisions like these in seconds, minutes, lives moving one way or another based on words and the crack of a gavel, a wave and line of a pen.

"I don't think Mr. Chaturvedi poses a threat to the community or a flight risk, but I am worried about the living situation. Therefore, I will set bail at fifty thousand dollars, but Mr. Chaturvedi, we will impose a restraining order against you. You will not be allowed within one hundred feet of"—the judge hurriedly flipped through the papers—"Kate Phillips. If you are caught within one hundred feet of her, I will have you back in jail with no possibility of bail. Do you understand?"

Sanjay nodded. "Yes, I do, Your Honor."

"All right. Bailiff, see that bail is posted. Good day."

Before Sanjay left with the bailiff for the holding cell, and then the bus back to the county jail, Zack grabbed his shoulder and bent close to his ear. Sanjay smelled cologne and cigarettes, felt the man's rough face on his hair. "Listen, I'm going to talk to the DA now. I'm going to work really hard to get these charges reduced and keep you out of a trial. Go home and get back to your life. Do what the judge said. And I'll call. Don't worry."

Sanjay nodded and followed the bailiff, every square of linoleum a lifetime, the swish swish of his orange clothes as loud in his ears as music. He looked down, following the clink of the bailiff's handcuffs and clack of hard shoe, until he was behind the door, and in the hallway, closer than he believed—in these two short days—that he'd get to the outside world, to his children, to Meera, who was waiting for him, to Meera, who had negotiated the bail. To Meera, who had begun to wrap her mind around his affair with Kate so tightly, it was disappearing, even now, in a thin wisp of memory.

As he walked, Sanjay couldn't believe there had once been a time where he would get in his car, drive home, and walk into his house, calling out, "Da is home!" Sanjay closed his eyes, thinking of his boys, their small bodies always so willing to be picked up, touched, hugged, always so willing to give back, a pat on the cheek, a long kiss on his lower lip, small fingertips on his hair. Now, as he walked, his eyes half-closed, he pictured Meera in the kitchen, shelling nuts or talking on the phone, waving her small, neat hand in his direction. Or, he felt her arms around his waist, saw, as he sometimes did, her eyes on him with something he believed was love. But even now, even as he followed a gruff man back to the jail, even as he wore county clothes, even as his stomach was still full of dried county eggs and toast, he thought of Kate, he thought of how he never had to look for love, to question her face, to discern her motives. How, for those short weeks, he was looked at much in the same way Ari and Jaggu looked at him, but by a woman.

Sanjay shook his head and opened his eyes, breathing in quickly. *She's not a woman,* he thought. *She's not the right woman. She's not a woman at all, and that is why I am here.*

The guard turned the corner and stopped, unlocking a door and leading Sanjay into a holding cell. "Look, it's going to be a while. We have to see who else needs to go back. And then we'll get you all on the bus."

The guard smiled, then seemed to stop his facial muscles in midmove, pulling the door shut. Sanjay sat on the bench, squeezing his legs together and pressing his upper arms and elbows into his rib cage. He closed his eyes and thought of his father, Sundeep. In his mind, it was a festival day, and his father sat in the shaded backyard, wearing his silk pajama kurta, talking with other men, laughing quietly. Sanjay imagined himself, a boy, lying on the cool stone porch, watching and listening, the men's voices following the currents of the afternoon air, his mother, sisters, aunts, and cousins inside some-where, soft, scattered sounds of laughter and dishes echoed from the house. For this second, in the swirl of New Delhi and his family house, Sanjay breathed in some remembered rounded happiness, contentment, and he wondered what language he could possibly use to explain his story to his family, which words he could pick to de-scribe how he once had fallen in love with his own feeling of fullness and how he had lost it.

❦

Meera sat in the small dank waiting room on the first floor of the county jail, waiting for her husband to be released on bail. She had one small square of bench, folded in between two tired women wear-ing washroom slippers and raincoats. The air smelled like cigarettes, urine, and the sharp stink of fear. Meera had cashed out a small an-nuity and paid the bail bondsman, a clean, blond man of twenty-five, who shook her hand and wished her luck as she left his cramped Martinez office.

On the hard bench, her back against cement, Meera contem-plated loneliness. It was a word that worried her sleep like a night bug, something she had batted away since that first night alone in her bed, Sanjay's side still neatly made when she woke up in the morn-ing. She wondered how the word could have sliced open her life as if it were an orange. Meera thought she had never been lonely, in the sense of being alone. As a child she had gone with her family to the temple, sitting with her mother Divya and the other women, who talked about saris and bangles, wayward children and bad marriages. She followed them into the kitchen while they prepared meals for festivals and celebrations, breathing in sesame, curry, coriander, grease, hot bread, and cast iron. Later, she played with her four brothers and neighbor children on the smooth, cool dirt of some-one's backyard, running in circles and screaming into summer dusk skies. In school, she had always had a best friend—Sushma Shretha, Geeta Rathor, Romina Verma—girls she could talk to—quietly though, so quietly—while the tutor, Mr. Ranjan, scratched out prob-lems on the blackboard. And as she grew, her round chubby body growing long and thin from her waist, her hips pulling silk taut across her abdomen, there were always the protective eyes of her brothers, their gaze on her as she walked home from the tutor's house, neighbor boys behind her, hands over their mouths, whispering.

In college, in England and then the United States, she met colleagues, biology majors and premed students, thoughtful men and women she could study with and listen to, sometimes writing down ideas after she came home from a party or bar, ideas about biological theories or colleges that accepted international students or bookstores with the best selections. There was always someone to talk to, confer with, worry over, people in her life as naturally as there was air or food or water.

So when she met Sanjay, not a biology student but a chemical engineering student and so beautiful, his cat eyes, and thick, straight hair, someone she could talk to and hold at night, Meera thought she would never be lonely. Really, she never thought about loneliness at all, ever, especially after she moved to Monte Veda and the boys were born. She had a husband, children, neighbors, friends, colleagues, and patients, people in and out of every part of her day, so much so that what she often craved was the silence of an empty room.

This thing, then, that Sanjay said, this, "I think I was lonely," shocked and confused her, making her wonder if she had been living in the same house, walking through the same rooms, drinking the same water, sleeping in the same bed as her husband. What were the signs of loneliness? How could she watch for its shadow on her husband's face? Would she even be able to recognize it the next time?

Meera sighed, listening to the dense quiet of the waiting room, the only conversation coming from the *Days of Our Lives* actors on the black-and-white television that was suspended from the ceiling by a thick metal arm. She felt the vibration of her beeper, and looked at it—the hospital. Automatically, she reached for her cell phone, even while knowing she needed to be in this strange place in silence, watching, looking for her husband to emerge from a dark room somewhere.

"This is Dr. Chaturvedi," she said strangely, thinking how important that word was to her, how it showed who and what she was, encapsulated her hard work and status so perfectly. She had never tired of writing or saying it, even years later when it seemed redundant or silly, Meera with her white coat on, her stethoscope around her neck. Everything about her, she thought, said, "I know what I am doing."

As she listened to the nurse's voice, somehow catapulted and slung into the black square she cradled against her face, Meera felt the women next to her leaning in, holding their breaths, taking in everything, the technology, the words, the life outside these dirty walls.

Meera nodded her head, then clipped out orders, and hung up, dropping her phone in her bag, trying to pull her body separate from those around her. *I am a doctor. I know so much what to do,* she thought, *but nothing here, nothing at all.*

She thought of a boy she had seen in the office yesterday, Bernie, a four-year-old with wild, uncombed blond hair and excema, his skin red and dry, thin scabbed scratches from his itching at night.

"I tell him to stop it," said the mother, standing up by the examining table. "But he won't." The mother had looked down at Bernie, pulling off his red-and-white tube socks, the tops frayed, fabric strings like ribbon around his ankles.

Meera had walked to the table so close that the mother backed away, sat down, held on to the socks like a talisman. Meera brushed Bernie's hair, smiled, took his arm in her hands, gently sliding her palms over the sore patches, one on either arm. She looked into his eyes, brown and blue and green, heard herself ask Bernie, "Does it itch all the time?" but really breathing in the space around him, feeling his bones under his flesh, the mother's nervous shifting, the smell of his clothes, not quite clean, dog, maybe cat hair covering his striped shirt and shorts lying in a pile next to him. Meera breathed in the three-packs-a-day of his mother, saw the yellow nicotine stain on her middle finger, knew that the father was not around, maybe never had been.

"Yeah," said Bernie. "All the time. It hurts now." And Meera knew that, too, knew that it hurt him to ignore his mother and it hurt him to peel away his skin, fingers digging in at night as he lay in bed in the dark. She felt his fear and his tears, even as she moved to her desk to write out a prescription, even as she pulled pamphlets from the wall on allergies and asthma, even as she wrote out a referral slip for an allergist.

As Bernie and his mother walked down the hall, Meera watched them from the nurses' station, almost wincing from flashes of poverty and sadness and anger, knowing she might never see Bernie and his hazel eyes again.

Meera swallowed, then looked up, seeing her husband walk through the door, not his quick usual pace, but slow and hitched, a departure from the unusually smooth, clipped stride. *He walks like a man who doesn't know where he belongs,* thought Meera. She stood up, her body struggling as it had when she saw Kate days earlier, a pull to and then away from Sanjay, a yearning and then a disgust for. *How could he?* she thought. And then, feeling the hard knot of herself, how could he not?

Meera went to him. She felt him through his clothes and their sadness, hugged him though she knew the women and others were watching her, desperate for something to take them away from their vigils, something better and more real than a soap opera. He was still Sanjay, she could feel that, still her husband, and as she wrapped her husband in her arms, she strangled away all the strange smells of his last two days: the cold, the cement, the orange clothes, the ugly talk, the disapproving looks, and pulled him back where she hoped he belonged. She pushed aside the knowledge that another woman, Kate, had felt this same man in the same way, taken up Meera's place.

Meera ignored everything and pulled him to her, whispering, "Oh, Sanju, Sanju."

Sanjay shook his head against her shoulder, whispering, "I am so sorry. Forgive me."

Meera did not know if she would forgive him, but she knew she would watch for loneliness more carefully. She would study Sanjay as she had Bernie, as she had learned to observe all her patients.

Sanjay no longer smells like me, thought Meera as they drove through downtown Martinez and merged onto Highway 4. As she steered the Volvo through the beginnings of commuter traffic, she looked down at Sanjay's hands flat on his thigh bones, the nails slightly long and dirty. If she were at home, she would bring him to the bathroom, turn on the hot water, and bathe him, rub sandalwood oil into his steamy skin, take root powder and water and scrub his body down to new flesh, erasing the days in jail, his affair with Kate, the loneliness that started it all. But they were not in Delhi. They were in America, and Sanjay would take a shower standing up, by himself, use Head & Shoulders, Dove soap and a washcloth, and smell like he always did, as he had always smelled to her, as she herself now smelled.

Sanjay reached his hand over to touch her thigh, his fingers light against her dress. "What now?" he said.

Meera fought the simultaneous urges to flinch and melt, her anger and sadness equally at the surface. "I called the real estate agent just as you asked me to. She believes that we could get an excellent price for the house. And she said we could move across town, maybe to Monte Veda Woods or to Lafayette. To a better location, really. And we would make out well financially."

Meera turned quickly to Sanjay and then focused on the road, flicking on the windshield wipers.

"We have to move. There is nothing keeping us here," said Sanjay. "It's impossible."

It was easy for him, she thought. Just as easy as getting Kate pregnant in the first place. He just slipped out of everything.

Meera breathed in and wondered how long he would try to ignore the baby, Deirdre, who was theirs in a way, a person they needed to think about and care for. The lawyers were making all that easy by demanding child support, which they could readily afford, the money easing them out of responsibility. But someday, Meera knew, the girl, maybe teenager, maybe woman, would come to their door and ask for her father, demand to know him and be given the same rights as his other children, deserving to discover the flesh that made her.

"We are not going to move, Sanjay. We can't," said Meera.

She could feel Sanjay's stare, his surprise, his anxiety, and she welcomed it. She was in charge again, and it felt good, to know that she could say anything and he would have to agree. But now, she was not thinking about herself. She was thinking about the two Deirdres, one hovering over the other, a divine light in this murky mess.

"But, Meera, how can we? What about us?" said Sanjay, his

hands turning into soft fists. "I can never make up for what I have done, I know. I want us . . ."

"How would I know how it will work, Sanju?" Meera sighed and quickly looked toward him, reaching a hand to his hair, fingering the sad dirty strands. "I have no idea."

Sanjay half closed his eyes, turning into the passenger's window, watching rain fan across the glass. Meera breathed in the huge unknown potential of tomorrow and almost laughed at her notion that she was in control.

"It's not just about us anymore. It never was," said Meera. "We have to find a way to go about our lives, Sanjay. We have a home. Our two boys have known nothing else. I've worked that ground and made it mine. I don't want to leave, I can't." Meera gripped the wheel and could sense some understanding that she couldn't have just pleasure, that her life would be punctuated by painful moments, this being not the first, but the deepest, the sharpest, a scar that would throb all her life, to her last breath. But it was her life, and this new baby was her life. And so was this man, the man she had fallen in love with and would stay with because it was the right thing to do.

Meera drove on, ignoring Sanjay's silence, as she always had. Somehow, she would have to hold this discomfort in her body, and then she would share it with Davis and Kate and Tyler. She and Sanjay would not move away and leave the end of Wildwood Drive to the Phillipses. They would face strange days and silent backyards and averted looks. But Meera would be there, days, months, or years later, when Kate and her daughter came to the house. Meera would let them in, sit them down, and offer them tea and words. She would listen to it all.

❧

Dr. Meredith asked, "Do you ever talk about her? With Hannah?"

Davis shook his head. "No."

"With the girls?"

"No."

Dr. Meredith crossed her legs and sat back a little. "Tell me what she was like. What would you say if someone asked you about Deirdre?"

"I don't know."

Davis closed his eyes, brought a light fist to his mouth, and coughed. He wondered how long he could shut out Dr. Meredith, feeling the quiet of the room pound around him, the doctor waiting for answers. Outside, he heard water fall on rocks, a pool just beyond the window, bubbling and full of orange fish. If he kept his eyes closed, he might be able to drift away on the sound. But Davis almost shook himself, knowing he had to answer, had to talk in order to get his children back. "What do you mean?" he said finally.

"Can you describe her? Your daily life with Deirdre."

Davis looked up at Dr. Meredith from the black leather chair, his body slung into an S of sadness. Instead of answering, he scanned the walls, eyes running over the Mexican art—orange and red cats with purple eyes, dogs with fuchsia polka dots—and books: *Stop Obsessing, End the Struggle and Dance with Life, Beyond Prozac.* Davis wondered if there was a book for him, *Get Over It and Save Your Children.*

This was his second visit to this office. When he had first called for an appointment, Dr. Meredith talked to him for almost an hour, asking him general questions about the case; then she ran through a series of questions about his family, his mother and father and sister, what it was like growing up in San Francisco on the avenues. Davis had answered all her questions, no question too personal, no answer too sore. During his first visit, she questioned him about the chain of events just after Deirdre's death, what exactly happened to him, Kate, and Tyler. Dr. Meredith asked him about Hannah and her two boys; she asked about the Chaturvedis and their two boys. Therapy, Davis began to think, was nothing more than talking. But this visit was already different, and he looked at the doctor, who waited quietly for an answer. He shook his head. "I don't know."

"How long were you married?"

Davis almost blurted out eighteen years, realizing he still thought of himself as married. No one had officially ended the marriage. There had been no divorce papers or lawyers, no custody battles or alimony payments. All he had was a certificate of death and a permit for the disposition of human remains. His name was on both, but he never signed any document that declared he was done, it was over, he was leaving Deirdre behind. She hadn't wanted to go either, so how could he say he wasn't married? It didn't matter he'd dated and then lived with Hannah, sleeping with her for enough time that her body was becoming as familiar to him as Deirdre's had been. Dr. Meredith looked at him, threatening to ask the question another time, so he mumbled, "Fifteen years. It would be eighteen in October."

"I see. Well, in those fifteen years, what would you say were the things you liked best about her?" Dr. Meredith asked, writing notes even as she looked directly in his eyes.

Davis's forehead wrinkled into three bands of worried flesh. "What do you mean?"

"I mean, what was it that drew her to you in the first place? What kept you going home at night? What were her most wonderful personality traits? Her most annoying?"

Davis felt like he was being pushed out a door, but there was no stoop or even yard to fall onto. Once he left the wall he clung on, moving through the opening, he'd have to fall and fall and fall— there would be no stopping all that would fly past him, memories of Deirdre, her face, her laugh, her way of waking up in the morning with a tender moan. Her hands, smooth and short and round, her eyes, her hair, her smells, skin he could taste a mile away. He glared at Dr. Meredith, wishing she would leave him alone. "Why is this important?"

"Just try to tell me," she said, leaning forward a little in her black chair.

Davis could feel himself moving toward the open door, could see the sky outside. "She had small hands, round fingers. I used to tell her she had sausage digits. Sometimes she'd punch me in the shoulder, just kidding, you know. But I loved to kiss them. She had strong hands. She loved to plant. The yards. We had vegetables and flowers and trees."

Dr. Meredith shifted in her chair. "What else?"

"Her hair felt like cotton. It was dark and long but felt like it was thread against my fingers . . . She laughed all the time, even when she was mad. She'd just look at the kids fighting over a Barbie or something, and she'd lean her head back and just go at it . . . She laughed in bed. She laughed on the phone. I could make her laugh. She laughed at my jokes."

"What else?"

"What does this have to do with what happened?" asked Davis, staring into his water glass, feeling himself holding on to almost nothing, his body dangling in soft, clean air.

"Just tell me more about Deirdre."

Some large organ in Davis's gut ached. "Once when Kate was a baby, Deirdre fell asleep at a party. Right at the dinner table. She called me a shit when I tried to wake her up. 'Just let me sleep,' she said. 'It's my turn.' She never got a turn, you know," said Davis. "I never gave her a turn. I always slept in. She took care of them. I didn't know how. I couldn't do it like she could. She did it all, you know? She took care of them better than I did. I couldn't. I can't."

"You don't think you can take care of them?" asked Dr. Meredith.

Davis crossed and uncrossed his legs, his words clenched in his jaw.

"Do you feel that you took care of them after she died?" continued Dr. Meredith.

"No. No. Yes. Not like Deirdre. No one can. No one. Oh, God," said Davis, turning to the window.

"What else do you remember?"

"More?" said Davis.

Dr. Meredith nodded.

"She spent too much money. She didn't mean to. She just wanted to enroll the girls in classes or I'd come home and there'd be about ten flats of plants from Orchard Nursery. This was when I started at York and Prescott. She didn't want expensive cars, but we took a lot of vacations to Tahoe or to this lake in Canada. She loved those trips. She was on the Meadow Lane swim team when she was a little girl and she still swam like a fish. And with the babies. She was a good mom, a great mom. You should see her. . . . Oh, God . . ." Davis bent down, his head to his knees, thinking now that he held on to nothing at all, he could keep his body from opening up altogether. He tried to smash the sound jerking up from his chest. "Oh, God. She loved me. She loved me."

"Tell me more," said the doctor.

Davis sat up, holding his arm across his chest, trying to form words in his shaking mouth. "How can she be gone? I can't believe she's gone. How can she be dead? She was just here." Davis opened his hand, his palm over his heart. He wished he could leave, but he doubted he had the strength to lift himself out of the chair. It was as if Deirdre were on his lap. How could he leave when she was this close?

Dr. Meredith stopped writing on her pad. Hard rain, pushed by wind, smashed against the window. "What do you miss about your life with Deirdre?"

Davis looked up and breathed in, still clamping his arms to his chest. He looked at Dr. Meredith and beheld his wife and his grief, silence and shame blending and swirling around him like smoke. He couldn't wipe the tears from his face because he knew if he moved, he would scream Deirdre's name. "Everything," he finally whispered. "I miss everything."

❧

Davis sat at the front of a courtroom in the Martinez courthouse. His lawyer, Zoe Lundgren, and he sat at an oak table covered with her notes. Two weeks after Meera had driven everyone to Mt. Diablo Hospital, Davis was in dependency court for a hearing to prove he deserved Kate and Tyler. At a table next to him and Zoe sat a county attorney, Mr. Stevens; Cynthia, the social worker Davis recognized from the day at the hospital; and Dr. Meredith.

Davis had never been in court before, except for once, when he was eighteen and determined to get out of a traffic ticket. He'd put on a tie, his best pants, and prepared a case, showing why the cop could never have known he was going eighty-five on Highway 5 as he drove home from a visit to Los Angeles. But the cop didn't make it to court that day, so Davis's victory was short and easy. He walked through the wood gates without having to pay a cent or admit his guilt.

This time, twenty years later, he was also wearing a tie, but one made of pure silk, and his best blue suit. Zoe and he had talked for hours, and Davis wanted to show the judge that he could change, would change, that he had a right to his girls. He had told Hannah the same thing two nights ago on the phone.

"I'm going to get them back, Hannah. I can't believe it got this bad," he said when he finally called with time to talk, telling her everything about the baby, his therapy, the dark empty house, the sad cardboard crib.

"I haven't been able to get Kate out of my mind," said Hannah. "I just keep seeing her sitting behind the counter, hiding her stomach. I should have known."

"You? What about me? How could I have talked to her and eaten with her without knowing. Without seeing. God, I must have been blind," said Davis, feeling his head shaking against the phone receiver.

"You did everything you could for her," said Hannah defensively. Davis wondered who she was defending, him or herself.

"No, I didn't. I knew it. I should have been there. I feel . . . I feel so . . ."

"What?" asked Hannah.

"I feel it all," said Davis, realizing he did, and the pain was deep and full and there was no way out.

"I don't believe any of this," said Hannah softly.

Davis sighed. "I can't believe it either."

"No one could have known. I . . . I didn't see it. And I've been pregnant twice. You were doing a good job."

Davis lay down on his bed, staring at the wall, the phone in his hand. "No, I wasn't. I didn't do anything."

"What do you mean? You were there."

"No, I wasn't. I was with you."

"Oh, that's great," said Hannah. "So it's my fault? I didn't force you to stay here. It was your decision."

"I know. I'm not blaming you," said Davis. "It was all my fault."

There was a pause, and Davis imagined he could hear the boys playing in the background, small plastic cars on Hannah's carefully waxed hardwood. "Are you coming back? Are you coming home?"

"You know what Zoe said, Hannah. I can't," said Davis.

"We could come to you."

"What about the boys? I thought you said . . ."

"I know what I said. That was before. Things are different now."

Davis heard the desperation tensing her words. A part of him wanted to say yes. There was enough room for everyone, especially now, now that Tyler and Kate and the baby were gone, his house echoing like an empty heart. He wanted to fill it up with Hannah and her cooking and the boys' chatter. But wasn't that what he had been doing all along? Filling up the holes in him he couldn't bear to feel. Patching and repatching all the sorrow that ripped new tears in him despite his hard work at ignoring them.

"Zoe says I need to show willingness to change. Reestablish this as a home. For the girls and the baby. And Gwen's coming for a couple of months, maybe bringing her youngest boy Ryan."

"What? What do you mean? Gwen's coming?"

"Zoe says I've got to establish that I can turn it around here. Gwen wants to come. She's been worried for a while anyway." Davis didn't say that Gwen had told him months ago to pay more attention to the girls than to Hannah, Sam, and Max, finally hanging up on him one night after he told her, "The girls are almost grown up now. They're okay."

"So. When can I see you?"

"Zoe says . . ."

"I am so sick of Zoe! How can she know everything? Was she here when Kate was pregnant and no one knew? No one knew! Everyone will testify that it was impossible to spot."

Davis breathed in. "Well, she's a lawyer, Hannah. She's done this before."

"So can I see you?"

"I don't want to make any more mistakes. I want to do it right for a change," said Davis.

Hannah laughed, a harsh, bitter sound he didn't like. "I was a mistake."

"No. That's not what I said," answered Davis, thinking, *But yes, it was a mistake. It was a mistake to leave my house and my girls and move in with you.* But what could he say to her now? "I was hiding behind you? I love the smell of your skin only because it doesn't remind me of one damn thing? How I always knew I shouldn't be at your house with your children instead of my own?" Could he tell her that for a while her roof held him still like some sought-after, rare insect trapped by glass, metal, and wood? Was it ever possible to tell

Hannah that he slept with her and did not love her, held her hot
damp body against his after sex, put his tongue on her breasts without really wanting to taste her skin? Could he say that he played Go
Fish with her boys on rainy evenings, ate her paella with fresh mus-
sels and abalone, and sang "Happy Birthday" to her father at a
downtown Spanish restaurant and all along he didn't really know the
words to say good-bye and go home, home to Kate and Tyler and
memory?

Instead Davis said nothing, sighing into the phone receiver. He
smelled his stale breath, grief, lies, and warm beer against his cheek
as he waited for her voice.

"I think it *is* what you're saying, Davis," said Hannah before she
hung up, and he tried not to hear the sense of departure, of desertion in her voice as the phone clicked silent.

He didn't call her back, even though he wanted to. He thought
of Zoe and the case and the girls. And it was easier now, Davis
thought, without Hannah, knowing he could listen to Zoe and follow all her instructions without guilt.

"This is a no-brainer," she said. "I mean, we will have some hoops
to jump through. We will have to deal with the therapist's and social
workers' reports. And you are going to have to prove competency as
a parent. Your sister will be a help. But thirty days. Tops. They'll be
home."

"Are you sure? Can you guarantee me that?" asked Davis, wishing he hadn't as he watched her face fall into professional ambiguity.

"Well, no. I can't. But, from here, it looks very positive," she'd
answered finally, turning from Davis and organizing her notes.

He knew then that anything could happen, as it already had, for
the last two years, life just fracturing into unbelievable possibilities,
every option suddenly a disaster. And as he sat there, Davis could
barely contain his body, clasping his hands to control the shaking, his
shoulders tight and rising to his ears.

"All rise. Court is in session. The Honorable Judge Helmanski
presiding," said the bailiff as the judge walked up to his desk and sat
down. He shuffled through his papers, then leaned over and whispered to the bailiff, who wrote something down on a yellow pad.

"This is a dependency hearing for Davis Phillips, in regards to minors Tyler Jane Phillips and Katherine Diane Phillips. Mr. Phillips, are you represented by counsel?"

Davis almost answered, but Zoe grabbed his arm. "Yes, he is, Your Honor," she said.

Davis was embarrassed. Zoe and he had discussed the process so fully he felt he could imagine the whole hearing, from start to finish. *Then why,* he thought, *can I feel the sweat running down my ribs?* He and Zoe sat down, and he looked at her list. He knew that Cynthia would be examined by the attorneys and then by Zoe, the same for the therapists. Then came his witnesses.

"Who would be a good character witness for you?" asked Zoe early last week. "Who could show what a good father you are?"

Davis sighed, knowing that two years ago he would have asked Meera and Sanjay, neighbors who had watched him play with his children, protect them, bandage skinned arms and knees. Davis could have asked Rachael or her husband Bob, Tom and Jill Anderson, the other Girl Scout leaders, the woman who ran the cancer group. He would ask his boss, Steve, but he wasn't sure what he'd say, now that Steve had curtly said, "Look. This isn't good for the workplace. Take six months. Paid. And then we'll talk." Then he turned his back on the whole affair. After Deirdre died, Davis had pushed everyone away so there was no one to help him now. There really wasn't anybody who could tell the judge what kind of father he had been before the baby was born, not Hannah, maybe not even Gwen or her husband John. Finally, Zoe had mustered up school records showing how well the girls had done, pay stubs and bank accounts showing his financial solvency, an English teacher, and Kate's best friend Erin. Nothing and no one really showed Davis doing anything good at all.

"Mrs. De Lucca, could you tell me what the girls' condition was when they were brought to Mt. Diablo Hospital by Dr. and Mr. Chaturvedi?" asked Mr. Stevens.

Davis watched as Cynthia avoided his eyes. As she had walked to the stand, he had wanted to smile, but then didn't, desperate to avoid another wrong move.

"Well, the youngest girl was fine physically, except for being tired. She'd been responsible for at least half of the infant's care. The older—the mother of the baby—was doing fairly well, too. You have the doctor's reports which showed she had a checkup and a procedure," said Cynthia.

Mr. Stevens flipped through his notes, looking at Davis, and then moved in front of his table toward Cynthia. "And what about the baby? What was her condition?"

"She was doing well. She hadn't had her tests or shots. You can see that on the report, too. But she was healthy and fed and well cared for."

"What was the condition of the house when your office investigated?"

"It was fairly disorganized, except for the kitchen and the bedrooms. The girls had set up a nursery in a closet, which was supplied and clean," said Cynthia.

"To the best of your understanding, how long had the girls been living there alone?" asked Mr. Stevens, turning back to Davis. Davis looked down, not wanting to see the disgust in this man's face.

"It seems that Mr. Phillips had stopped spending the night there on a full-time basis about a year ago, maybe more. He did come home regularly to check on the girls, though."

"He did?"

"Yes. At least, that's what both the girls said."

"You never noticed anything peculiar about Kate's behavior?" Mr. Stevens asked Eugene Edgar, Kate's English teacher. Davis recognized him from back-to-school night in the fall.

"Not really," said Eugene, folding his right leg across his left knee and adjusting his tie nervously. "She was absent quite a bit after the first of the year, and I tried calling the house. We even met after class once. But she got her work in and it was good, not perfect, but good."

"Didn't she seem quiet or depressed?"

Eugene rubbed his hair back from his forehead, looking, to Davis, almost young enough to be a high school student himself. "I haven't been teaching that long, Mr. Stevens, but they all seem quiet and depressed, at least some of the time. They look at me when I ask a question, and I have to answer it myself. Some students want to talk, but it's not like most of them do more than show up and doodle on the desks."

"All right," said Mr. Stevens. "But didn't you notice anything different about her appearance? Her size? Her shape?"

"I guess you haven't been in a high school classroom recently," said Eugene.

"What do you mean by that?" said Mr. Stevens.

"Well, half the kids wear clothes that are too small, and the other half wear clothes that are too big."

"Meaning?" asked the lawyer.

"Kate could have hidden the entire football team under the shirts and pants she wore and no one would have ever noticed."

"You and Kate Phillips are very good friends, aren't you?" Mr. Stevens asked Erin, who sat chewing her lips and turning the stud in her eyebrow.

"She is my best friend. I mean, she used to be."

"Did your friendship change?" asked Mr. Stevens.

Erin looked at Davis and then sighed. "Yeah. We used to do a lot of stuff together. But probably in December or January, she just kinda went home after school. Said her dad had lots for her to do. We talked on the phone, though."

Mr. Stevens stood up from his chair. "So you are saying that you never noticed that she was pregnant?"

"Nope. I never did. Maybe I thought she was gaining some weight or something. I really just thought she didn't like me anymore. It was sort of like we broke up or something. Like maybe she had a new friend or something. Someone other than me."

"How often did you go to the house, Mr. Phillips?" asked Mr. Stevens. Davis swallowed, realizing that Mr. Stevens was not going to stop looking him in the eye—wherever Davis turned, there the lawyer was, asking him another question.

"I tried to go every day."

"But did you go every day?" asked Mr. Stevens, moving to the left, blocking Davis's clear view of the court doors.

"No. I didn't."

"And how often did you spend the night in the home, Mr. Phillips?"

Davis rubbed his sweaty hands on his pants legs. "Maybe once a week, every two weeks."

"Well, which was it? Once a week or once every two weeks? We have Detective Johnson's reports stating it was once every two weeks."

"It was every two weeks," whispered Davis.

"What? Could you repeat that please?" asked Mr. Stevens.

"Two weeks. Two weeks," said Davis, looking at Zoe, whose eyes were wide, urging him to calm down.

"Did you bring your girlfriend with you on those nights you spent at the home?"

Davis shook his head. "No. She has small children."

"I see. . . . Now let me ask you this. Did you notice any changes in Kate during what we now know was her pregnancy?"

Davis looked into the courtroom, over Cynthia and Dr. Meredith; over Zoe; over his sister Gwen, who sat in the back row clutching her sweater and purse as if she were ready to slip out the wood doors, leaving him, just as he had left his girls. He wondered if he had noticed, really, seen Kate's body for the changes that had to be taking place. Davis remembered Deirdre's body, her stomach pushing into fullness, her breasts suddenly ripe as summer fruit, her eyes luminous with some internal magic. He could trace her stretch marks from memory, still feel her lush, thickening hair. He missed this in his own child, the one who looked most, if not exactly like her mother. By being absent, he avoided seeing her pulled to Sanjay, missed the signs that a protective father, a good father, would have been keenly aware of. Davis knew he should have seen his daughter's secrets, her lies, her fear of being alone, without him, without her mother.

And maybe he did see. Maybe he saw it all, watched the whole thing in the rearview mirror of his truck as he headed back to Hannah's safe house.

"Mr. Phillips?" asked Mr. Stevens, dropping his notepad on the table and walking toward the stand.

Davis held out his hand, wanting the lawyer to stop and let the words come full into the courtroom. "I chose not to notice. I chose not to see a thing."

*   *   *

"After the sessions with Kate and Tyler and the sessions with Mr. Phillips, what are your observations about this case?" Zoe asked the therapist, Dr. Meredith, while drumming her pencil eraser on her yellow pad. Davis felt each dull thud reverberate through the table and into his body.

"The girls clearly feel a sense of abandonment. They felt that their father left them and that they couldn't rely on him."

"Why didn't they tell anyone about the pregnancy?" asked Zoe.

"Kate seems to think that if her father knew, he would leave them for certain," said Dr. Meredith. "It may also be that she thought a baby would bring him home."

"Is that what Kate said?" asked Mr. Stevens.

"No. That's one of my analyses."

"In your opinion, do you think Mr. Phillips would have left if he had known about the pregnancy?" asked Zoe.

"No. I don't. Mr. Phillips has shown a great deal of remorse and sadness over this event."

"So, in your opinion, why did this happen? Why did he leave the house and the girls?"

The therapist folded her hands and breathed in. Davis imagined the ideas in her head, full of big analytical words that would only show he was unfit for everything, not to mention parenting. He thought of all the books in her shelf, one that he hadn't seen, the one that recommended he be alone for life. Isolation therapy. Necessary for terrible people. Davis wondered if, in act, he was unfit for human contact in the first place; that he should never have married, brought children into the world, giving Deirdre, Kate, and Tyler the expectation that he could somehow take care of them properly.

Dr. Meredith turned to Davis. Her gaze made him want to weep because it was not full of accusation and horror but of compassion, something he had forgotten the look of, something he had been too scared to look for in her office, something he had certainly not seen in his own eyes these last two weeks, his own eyes inscrutable and cold.

Davis swallowed a cold bone of fear, his throat tight with the truth of her words, and he looked down at the table, wanting something to hold on to lest he slip away again.

*   *   *

After everyone had spoken and been questioned, Davis sat low in his chair, the sides of his shirt wet. Zoe stood up to conclude, her chair scraping against the marble floor. "Your Honor," she said. "You have heard the therapist's, social workers', and attorney's reports on this case. When listening to this story, we can't ignore or avoid some of the very sad truths about it. Davis Phillips was not in the home enough to notice that his oldest but underage daughter had become involved with their next-door neighbor, a man of thirty-six years. We can't ignore that the product of this relationship was a pregnancy and then a birth of a baby girl. Hardest to ignore is the fact that the girls were forced to deal with this situation themselves. They found themselves responsible for a situation we only deem doctors and hospitals worthy of handling. Because they were young, they made some mistakes, possibly endangering the child if not themselves."

Zoe stopped, turning to Davis for a moment, but then again faced the judge. "But, Your Honor, we can't ignore either what both the social worker and the therapist stated. These girls love their father. And all three—father and daughters—are still grieving the loss of a wife and mother due to breast cancer two years ago. Davis Phillips's reaction was to pull away, leaving girls he thought were old enough for some responsibility alone. Was this right? No. Was it understandable? Yes. We might also note that neither the neighbors nor the school nor their teachers nor Tyler's and Kate's friends noticed the pregnancy. These were people who saw them often, if not every day."

Zoe moved closer to the judge. Davis felt himself move along with her, wanting to believe her strong, positive words, wanting to ride them like a wave. "Your Honor, my client has employment that is backing him with his attempt to regain his girls, giving him paid leave for six months. He has moved permanently back into the family home, and his older sister Gwen is moving temporarily from Santa Rosa to assist him. He has already begun counseling alone and will do so with his family, and he wants his daughter's child to join them in the home. As the reports suggest, the house is in good order and can adequately support a family of this size. My client feels great remorse for this incident, which has hurt so many, and greatly wants to make amends in any way he can. Thank you, Your Honor."

As she finished, Davis realized he had stopped breathing, imagining his house as it would be when the girls and the baby came home. For the first time in two years, he pictured himself making breakfasts in the morning, sitting with Tyler, Kate, Gwen, her son Ryan, and the new Deirdre at the kitchen table, laughing, maybe arguing, maybe silently chewing, filling himself with the sounds he had almost forgotten. Davis started to shake, thinking, *I haven't been home in so long.*

When Zoe sat down, she took his hand under the table, squeezed it, the pressure still there when she let go. The judge looked out at the courtroom, nodding his head. "Thank you. I'll take it under advisement," he said. He struck his gavel to the desk and left, his black robe swaying as he stepped down off his podium and out the door.

❦

"Just come and get your stuff," Hannah had finally told Davis, the day after the hearing. "I don't want to see it anymore."

"All right," said Davis. Hannah could hear his nodding, his relief, through the line. With this call Hannah knew that she and her boys weren't worth enough. The scale was heavier in Monte Veda, those girls and that old life worth more than all Hannah had offered. More than her body. More than her love.

"When are you coming?" asked Hannah.

"Right now," said Davis. "I'll leave this minute."

He didn't argue, didn't protest, and the last year and months ended just like that, a soft click of a phone. "That little bitch," said Hannah now, wishing she could slap Kate, the older, quieter one, the one who had done this.

It was late. Hannah sat in her living room, the lights off, a glass of Pinot Noir in her hand. Outside, the downtown Oak Creek lights glimmered like landed stars, yellow and pulsing. Max had wandered out a few minutes before and was curled at her feet on the couch, asleep in his pajamas.

First Colin and now Davis, thought Hannah, looking at her free left hand, wondering why she couldn't keep anything solid in them. Davis had seemed like the right one, the one who would make it all different. There would be no more departures, no more affairs, no more lies. He would move into her house and fill it. He was perfect, tall and good-looking, and strong. Strong. Not full of Colin's needs. Despite all the processing that Colin always wanted to do, the checking in with their feelings every week, sharing fantasies and hopes, he'd left anyway. No, with Davis it was just life, everyday, normal life.

Max sighed and turned. Hannah finished her wine and put the glass on the floor. She closed her eyes and put her head back on the armrest. She might have known Kate was pregnant. *Maybe,* thought Hannah, *I saw it, the full face, the high stomach under the baggy shirts.* Maybe it was all the sleeping and mysterious illnesses and constant disappearances.

But Hannah knew that even if she had known Kate was pregnant, she would have left her in the house. She would have counseled her and brought food over and taken her to the doctor's. But she would have left them alone in that house. She knew she would have done anything in order to keep Davis.

Hannah stood up and carefully picked up Max, carrying his warm, soft body to bed. She didn't know why this flesh wasn't enough, why her boys alone couldn't sustain her. And as she slipped Max under his covers, she realized she was in shock. She couldn't believe she'd been passed up again. If she could break things without making a mess, she knew she would. She would rip the curtains from the wall, pull the rugs from under the tables and chairs, slash the pictures, and shatter every hand-fired bowl and plate.

Hannah imagined this action, this fever of breaking and throwing and killing off of all that was her, had been her, the her that didn't work at all, the her that no man stayed for. But she also knew that this house was all she and the boys had, all that kept them together, all that kept her family in one small crew.

Closing the door softly behind her, Hannah walked out onto the deck, a slight breeze pushing her hair. She felt like she was on a ship on darkling waters, no course, no whistle, no lighthouse pointing a clear direction.

The night before a chemotherapy treatment, Deirdre would have nightmares. Each time, though, Davis was surprised, waking from the deep sleep to her shouts, moans, and cries. *What now?* he would think, opening his eyes to the same ceiling he had fallen asleep to, re-membering, *Oh, yes.* Davis turned, held Deirdre, talked slowly in her ear, and brought her back to the dark night.

Davis was always surprised because during the day Deirdre cooked, talked to friends on the phone, called him at work to ask him to pick up the girls at school. When he and the girls came home, there were lasagnas in the freezer, one hot on the table, Deirdre just waiting for them to sit down, one of her friends, Rachael most often, walking out the door, waving.

But at night Deirdre's body tensed, flexed, finally felt as lean as it had truly become, her elbows banging into the mattress. Once she called out, "Not my knees! Not my knees! Leave them alone!"

"Honey," said Davis. "Wake up." He pulled her to him, and she cried tears bigger than he thought she had room for anymore.

"They were injecting my knees. The nurse stuck the needle in my kneecaps—she said it was my fault it hurt. She said none of my veins would work, so they went at my knees. It didn't work. It didn't work!"

"It's okay. It was a dream," Davis said.

"No, it wasn't. It's real. Oh, I want to see them grown. I want to see them as women, Davis," said Deirdre. "They'll grow up and for-get me."

"You'll see them grow up," Davis would say, stroking her ribbed back. "That's what the treatments are for."

Deirdre wiped her eyes and turned her head into Davis's armpit. "No. You're wrong. I won't. I won't see it. I'll never see anything."

Each night like that, Davis held her till she fell asleep, and then in the morning, the girls off at school, he took her to Mt. Diablo, where they waited for the drugs. First, it was the IV full of antinausea medication, and then a clear, invisible chemotherapy, Cytoxin, was turned on. During her first treatment, Deirdre watched the fluid sluice into her body, whispering, "Toxin. Toxin."

After the Cytoxin came the Hawaiian Punch, or that's what Davis thought Adriamycin looked like—a dark syrupy red sloshing in its vial. But the drug wasn't something anyone could sip on summer days; it was so poisonous, the nurse came in wearing gown and mask, holding the vial away from her body as she changed the IV and stood back, waiting for the red stuff to work its evil magic. If the drug touched skin, it would burn.

"Well, at least this one doesn't sound like poison," said Deirdre. "More like an antibiotic."

But when her first treatment was done, and they walked together out the hospital door, Deirdre shut her eyes. "Oh. Oh," she said, grabbing his arm.

"What is it? Do you need me to carry you?" said Davis, steadying her body and looking around for a nurse, doctor, someone.

"No. It's the sun."

"What? Do you want my sunglasses?"

Deirdre shook her head. "No. I can feel it, the chemo. It's tingling where the sun is. On my forehead. It's killing my brain cells."

Davis imagined her brain, hot, soupy, bubbling with acid, poison, her whole body, in fact, boiling and churning, the drugs killing everything.

The first day wasn't the worst, really. It was the fourth day after the chemo, the fatigue, the way Deirdre felt her body had been pummeled. "It's like someone took a hammer and banged me all over. And then handed the hammer to his friend," she said, trying to smile, falling back onto her pillow.

And maybe that wasn't really the worst, either. It was the clumps of her hair, the shrinking flesh, the way she looked out the window, desperate for soil, earth, plants between her fingers. It was the way she looked at them all, her eyes half-closed, tears just under the skin, looking at Kate, Tyler, and him as if she knew she was saying good-bye. The second week after the treatment, she would start to slowly feel better, knowing she had to do it all over again: the nightmares, the toxic pipeline into her body, the slow and painful recovery. And really, it was the second round of treatments, after the first had failed, tumors now in her lungs and bones. Then, for Davis, it was the stunning knowledge that the doctors, the drugs, and the cancer were taking his wife from him, slowly, killing her off and leaving someone else, someone who was going to leave him. In the dark, after Deirdre fell back to sleep, her bald head against his shoulder, her breath light and tentative and impermanent, he thought over and over again, *What will I do?*

❧

Two weeks after his appearance in court, Davis dressed to go see his girls at the residential facility they were staying at in Antioch. He had picked out a suit, then, no, just a tie, and Docksides, then went back to a suit. Finally, his sister Gwen walked in his room, carrying an ironed collarless button-down shirt and a pair of jeans. "This would look good, Davis."

"You think? I don't want the lady who runs it to think I'm not taking this seriously."

"I don't think a shirt will make the difference now," said Gwen. Davis could hear her thinking, *I told you already* . . . But her face shifted, and she smiled as he put on the shirt, just the same as when they were kids and she had to get him ready for church. "Gwen, you get Davis ready. Right now," their mother would say as she took another sip of black coffee and finished reading the bridge column. And Gwen would, making sure his shirt was tucked in and his belt was tight, his shoes polished so he could see his head's reflection when he bent over.

And now it was the same, but terrible. There was just so much wrong to fix, thought Davis, tucking in his shirt and then slipping on his shoes. Gwen and he had gone baby shopping after finding not much left from the girls' babyhood except the prized mementos Deirdre had saved in the trunk, and Tyler and Kate had gone through those already. So Davis and Gwen shopped for and bought an oak crib and a changing table at I Bambini.

"Look at these crib bumpers," said Gwen. "They're tie-dye!"

"Sort of infant Grateful Dead?" said Davis, trying to laugh as if this were a normal situation, happy father and aunt buying needed gifts for his daughter and grandchild. But even as he paid for them at the cash register, he felt the lies cover his skin like a cold, thin shirt.

They shopped for more, buying what they had not given before, toys and clothes and cute Winnie-the-Pooh snow globes. They painted the guest room light purple—to match the tie-dye—and bought a rocking chair and a bookshelf for Beatrix Potter and Dr. Seuss books.

And without Gwen, Davis went over to Hannah's and packed up his things while Hannah took the boys to the Heather Farms Park. "They can't take this kind of desertion again," she said stiffly, packing the boys into the car as soon as he arrived.

"This is only for now, Hannah. I just need this time," Davis said, meaning it, realizing, after seeing Dr. Meredith once a week, that proffered love was not something to ignore. But Hannah was frozen in anger and silence, just looking at him through the shiny tinted glass of her Dodge Caravan. He couldn't tell if she was crying. The boys sat in their car seats unmoving. Davis forced himself to look at them and smile, trying to see if they waved or smiled. He studied their faces and hands, boy bodies he had grown to love in the months he'd been with Hannah. But like their mother, Max and Sam sat still as if waiting for something impossible to happen.

As Hannah lurched out of the driveway and accelerated down the street toward the park, Davis knew he had to let them go, for now or maybe for always; he had to make amends to his own children, try desperately to make up for his mistakes.

In his ironed shirt and jeans, Davis drove Deirdre's old BMW up the highway, Gwen sitting next to him, scratching at a crossword puzzle. When the girls were first gone, and he was strung out by legal talk and fear, Davis cleaned everything he could find, the carpets vacuumed, the windows washed, and the car almost excavated of teenager detritus: 7-Eleven cups, corn-nut wrappers, and sadly, receipts from the Goodwill and Sears for diapers and knit sleepers. He might have looked here before, he realized, could have found all the clues he needed if he had wanted to, if he had wanted to see anything.

It hadn't rained in three days, sharp, new blades of grass and dandelion spitting from the ground, apple trees ripe with first bloom, flirting with their pinks and whites, color ready to emerge. When he was little Davis couldn't believe how one morning, a morning no one could figure out or decide on, the apple trees in the backyard just opened, flowers with thin almost transparent petals, more opening as the days went on, till finally there were small apples the size of olives.

Davis looked at Gwen, her newly acquired glasses down on her nose, wondering if she knew how dangerous this visit was. He didn't know if she knew he could lose the girls forever. The judge had allowed him this visit, but no one had yet said, "Take them. They're yours. Of course they can go home."

One night last week, he'd had a dream that Deirdre was knocking on the front door. He stood up and went to answer the knocks, the hall a dark tunnel that went on forever, her hard thrums beating in his ears. The pounding was so loud, Davis wondered if he had put his hands over his ears as he lay asleep in bed, trying to muffle the thuds on wood and Deirdre's cries of "I just can't get in anymore! Why don't you open the damn door?" Finally, Davis made it to the door, but when he opened it, there was nothing but the front yard air and sun and the silence of midday. When he woke up, Davis could still feel the loneliness of unshed tears on his face.

Now he had that same feeling, but the cold was in his throat, his chest, the fear as closed and hard as the door Deirdre beat on, the door she couldn't open.

❦

Right before Kate's father was supposed to arrive, Dee Dee grunted, her face red, and then her diaper was full. "Oh, God," said Adam who had been holding her. He held her in his hands away from himself and walked over to Kate. "Here. Take her. What happened?"

Kate and Tyler laughed at Adam's nervous face. "Don't worry," said Kate, walking toward the stairs and holding Deirdre away from herself, too. "That's what babies do."

As she walked up the stairs toward her room, she heard Adam say, "Well. I guess I'm glad I don't have one yet."

"Yeah, that's why I'm never going to have any babies," Virgie replied. Kate could almost imagine her hip slung out, her booted foot at an impatient angle.

Kate gave Dee Dee a quick bath in the sink, washing her with the tiny squares of baby soap Cynthia had brought. The baby looked up at Kate from her bath, her eyes a strange shade of gray, the color of pewter. She was growing so fast, thought Kate, thinking about yesterday when she had had the baby on her lap, lying facedown on her belly. There was no way Dee Dee's life could start all over again back inside her, Kate had thought. There was no way any of them could go back to the beginning and do it better.

As she dried her baby, Kate wondered how she would greet her father if she were Virgie. Probably she would storm in with her green hair moussed on end, a cigarette dangling from her lips, wearing a short-sleeved T-shirt to show off her *fuck you* and bleeding heart tattoos. Maybe Virgie would stamp her foot and yell, "You totally fucked up. Just like the tattoo says. You left us alone. I didn't even know if you were going to come home again. And you didn't help me. You didn't even notice."

Virgie probably wouldn't say the last, thought Kate, putting a clean diaper on Dee Dee, rubbing the tape firmly on the plastic so that there wouldn't be another disaster while her father and Aunt Gwen were there. Virgie wouldn't allow for anything too melodramatic and sentimental. But even so, Kate felt the skin rise along her neck and up her scalp. These were words she could say, the pain so true, the words breaking open the awkward silence of her family.

Kate rubbed her forehead, and then slipped one of the sleepers Tyler bought from Sears on her body, smiling as the baby looked at her. "Are you ready to meet Grandpa?" she asked. "Are you ready to see Dad?"

Kate picked up the baby and put her against her shoulder, realizing that Dee Dee was almost asleep, rubbing at her eyes and fussing. As she walked down the hall, throwing her legs in front of her as if they were tree trunks, things that didn't belong to her body at all, Kate knew she wasn't talking to Dee Dee, she was really just talking to herself.

❧

Tyler looked thin, her small bones points of light under her skin. Davis wasn't sure when she had gotten so tall either, her legs almost as long as Kate's. *What else have I missed?* he thought, holding his kneecaps with his palms as he sat on the couch in the home-care facility. Both his girls stood in front of him, Kate behind Tyler, the baby in her arms, Kate's face almost hidden in the shadow of the hall. Davis looked at Kate, wishing she would say something, but his older daughter stayed silent, her eyes down, shifting back and forth from one foot to the next, consoling the baby who wasn't even crying. Kate wasn't as thin as Tyler. Some of the weight he had ignored before was still under her chin and on her cheeks, and her body was still disguised by dark, baggy clothing. He looked at the baby, thinking, *Deirdre and me, and then Kate and Sanjay, and now a baby, this baby, named for my wife.*

The woman, Ruth, whom he had spoken to on the phone and the social worker, Cynthia, from Mt. Diablo Hospital, walked in from the kitchen. "Well, everyone's here now," said Ruth, pulling two chairs from the corner and arranging them close to the couch. "Why don't you sit down, Tyler, Kate?"

Tyler looked at Kate and then walked to a chair, sitting down, her thin legs pressed together.

"Well, give me that baby," said Gwen, standing up and walking to Kate, hugging her and the baby at the same time. Kate bent toward her aunt's shoulder and then pulled back, lifting Dee Dee into Gwen's open arms.

"Oh, my," said Gwen, moving back to the couch. "Oh, Davis, look at her."

Kate moved closer, just barely, slowly reaching for the back of a chair and then slipping onto the seat.

"Here," said Gwen. "Why don't you hold her?" Gwen smoothed the baby into Davis's arms. He looked at Kate, wishing she would say something, but his older daughter stayed silent and sat on her hardback chair, seeming only to want to refill her arms with the baby.

Davis bent his head toward the baby, holding girl baby weight that was palpable, firm. There was more than just his wife's body here, he knew, now remembering Deirdre's body in his arms, her long, substantial body, flesh alive and strong. Davis looked up and around, the difference of these two bodies in his palms at once. The silence of the room echoed with questions.

Ruth coughed. "Listen. Why don't you girls go for a walk? Show your father and aunt around. It's a real nice day."

Before Davis could really think about it, Kate was up, pulling jackets and a snuggly from the coat hook.

Davis looked at Ruth, the baby still in his arms. "What about the baby?"

Kate turned to him, her jacket already on. "She can come with us. I've got this." She lifted up the snuggly and began putting it on.

Tyler walked to her sister, sliding the fabric over her shoulder. "Here, Dad, give Dee Dee to me."

Davis sat up, carefully, holding the baby in his palms. He remembered sliding Kate and Tyler into this same kind of fabric holder, these cloth arms. Deirdre had taken the girls everywhere, one in a snuggly, the other holding her hand or in a stroller. Sometimes Davis thought it was as if Deirdre never stopped being pregnant, the girls connected to her always, by flesh or material, something umbilical always leading back to his wife's body.

Once the baby was snug, Kate tightening the straps, Davis turned to his sister. "Gwen?"

She shook her head. "I think I'll sit here and talk with Ruth."

Davis almost flinched, wanting his sister on this walk, scared of what might happen without her.

"You go on," said Gwen. "I'll be fine."

As Davis, Tyler, and Kate walked out of the house, Davis half wondered, half hoped that he would be fine, that they all would somehow be fine.

Outside, Davis breathed in deeply, trying to hide his gulps from the girls. They didn't seem to notice the movement of his chest or the sweat on his forehead, both walking toward the barn, eyes straight ahead, breeze blowing back their long hair. Dee Dee's ferocious head of black hair glinted like onyx in the sun.

"She's beautiful, Kate," said Davis.

Kate ducked her head and brought a hand to Dee Dee's head. "Thanks."

Now that they were talking, Davis knew he shouldn't stop, fearing that silence would just lead to more of the same silence that had taken over his house, filling it with secrets and pain. "If the judge decides you both can come home, I've promised them I'll take care of you."

"This time," said Kate, her head still down.

"Yeah, this time. I screwed up. I am so sorry," Davis said, turning to Kate, who still wouldn't look at him, then to Tyler, who would.

"Why didn't you notice anything? How come you didn't come help us?" asked Tyler, tears pulling her eyelashes into dark spikes.

"You didn't tell me. Kate didn't tell me. I didn't know," said Davis.

"You never knew? You never thought something was wrong? You're supposed to be the dad," asked Tyler.

Davis looked at his feet, pretending to watch for rocks on the path. "I don't think I really did. I've gone over it in my mind. But maybe . . . maybe I was scared to know more."

Kate's head jerked up. "You were scared? What about us? Me? You just left us there all the time. And then I was afraid you'd never come back if you knew."

"Maybe it seemed that way. Maybe I wouldn't have wanted to come home, but I would have, Kate. I'm here now. And I mean to be. Forever," he said, reaching out to Kate, who pulled away.

"Why did you leave anyway?" asked Tyler. "Why couldn't Hannah have brought the boys over some nights? Why did she boss you around?"

Davis stopped and breathed in hard. The girls took a couple more steps, then stopped, too, turning to face him. A flock of goldfinches unfurled in the sky like yellow confetti. "She didn't. I told her I would stay. It wasn't her fault. It was me."

"She never wanted to be with us," said Kate. "She just wanted you."

"That's not true. But I . . ."

"She's a bitch," said Tyler. "She's selfish."

"That's not fair," said Davis.

"Well, what exactly is fair, anyway? And why should we want to go home with you when you don't even want to be with us in the first place? Mom would never . . ." Kate stopped, her face red. "Now look, Dee Dee's awake."

They started walking again, Kate humming Dee Dee to silence and sleep with a song Davis recognized, a song Deirdre had sung to the girls when they were small, *Blackbird singing in the dead of night,* bringing him back to nights of crying babies.

Davis held that image away for a second and then breathed it in, pressing his lips together slightly, pulling air in deeply through his nose. There, in that full breath, was the past, his wife, a baby on her shoulder, the song echoing in his head as it had in the house. He felt tears in his jaw, his cheeks, behind his eyes but continued talking. "I'm so sorry. I know you may not want to come home. But I want things to be better."

The girls didn't say anything, Davis hearing nothing but the swirls of white-crowned sparrows and blackbirds in the trees. He looked down, watching all their legs move together, seeing the tiny, dangling legs of the baby moving to Kate's rhythm.

The barn door was open, and Tyler led them inside. "This is where we do a lot of work."

"What do you have to do?"

Kate and Tyler sat close together on a tight, square bale of hay. "We feed the sheep. Lots of work with the pumpkin patch, too," said Tyler.

Davis looked at Tyler and Kate, and knew he had been mistaken. Deirdre had not been the only one who was strong. She had made— they had made—these two girls, brought them to life, giving them the strength Davis thought they had all lost two years ago when Deirdre died. "I didn't know you were both so brave."

Tyler laughed. "I'm not scared of sheep!"

Kate nodded. "That's not what he means, is it, Dad?"

Davis rubbed his eyes with one hand. "No. I mean about the baby. I can't believe you did it, both of you. I wish your mother were here to see you, to see Dee Dee. You're right, Kate. She would have never done what I did. But she'd be so proud of you."

"Are you proud of us?" asked Kate.

Davis nodded, unable to push more than "I am" out of his throat.

Davis sat next to Kate and pulled her to him. At first her body was stiff, but then he felt her relax, felt her lean into him, felt the weight of her and Dee Dee against his chest.

"Dee Dee has your eyes, Kate. Your mother always said you had the most beautiful eyes."

"You never talk about her. You didn't take us to the cemetery after that once," said Kate. "It's like she disappeared and only Tyler and me remember."

"I remember," said Davis. "I've always remembered."

"I want her to come back, Dad. Why did she die? That isn't fair," said Kate, her soft, broken voice muffled in his body.

"I miss her, Dad," said Tyler.

"So do I," said Davis, crying, lifting his hand to find Tyler's shoulder, pulling his girls and his granddaughter to him, knowing that if the court and lawyers and social worker let them, they could float, they could all hang on forever.

Tyler sat on the back stoop with Ruth's cat Simon and a bottle of Coca-Cola. It was afternoon, and her hands were dark with dirt and manure, the underside of her cement-colored nails black and gritty. Back home, especially after the baby, Tyler would have cared more about her nails, running in to wash and moisturize them; or taking off the polish gently, pushing back the cuticles, and putting on a new coat of polish. But here, she thought, running her hands through Simon's orange fur, dirt was just part of the day, and somehow, she felt like her mother as she grappled with pumpkin vines and corn seeds.

Tyler took a sip of Coke and turned her head, watching a woman and two children ride down the dusty road on horses, the wind blowing at their hats and the horses' manes, their conversation turned into pieces of language that floated and meant nothing. Tyler had never ridden a horse—except if the pony rides at Tilden Park counted—but that was how she always thought of her mother, a galloping horse, a horse with warm, muscled haunches, a horse with quiet, mysterious eyes. Tyler used to watch her mother as she leaned on the kitchen counter, Deirdre's absent eyes looking out to the garden, the steam from her tea wisping past her face. Tyler was never sure what her mother was thinking, never exactly certain what to expect when her mother turned around. Sometimes, she'd clack down her mug and say, "Come on. I've got an idea." And they'd hop in the car, drive to the drugstore, buy birdseed and twine and glue, and come home to make a bird feeder. Or she'd snap back to Tyler, close her eyes to serious slits, and say, "Get that homework done, pronto!"

Tyler could rely on her mother to push her toward action, move her to the next thing and then the next, organizing, laughing, finding the way. There was always a way. There was a way to get her best friend to apologize for pulling her hair; there was a way for her second-grade teacher to give her more time on the spelling tests. Her mother would put her hands on Tyler's shoulders and say, "Tell me. Just tell me everything."

Tyler shook her head, wondering how she all alone managed to pull that baby out of her sister. How—without their mother—had she followed all the directions and rules and managed to not go totally insane, killing both mother and child? It was a miracle, or it was simply that her mother was still there, thought Tyler, still in their house, pushing them on, whispering, "Don't worry. You'll find a way."

Tyler closed her eyes, wanting more than just the air, wanting her mother's body to come back in the flesh, press against Tyler's back, and hold her up. But there was nothing but afternoon air, and then she heard a cough.

"What are you doing?" asked Adam from behind the screen door.

Tyler turned and squinted her eyes, peering into the dark of the house. She saw Adam's black skateboarding shoes, his baggy jeans, a chain hanging from his waist and looped into a pocket. "Just having a Coke." Tyler got up so Adam could open the door.

Adam pushed open the pine, mesh, and plastic of the door, letting free the smells of fried hamburger and boiled egg noodles. "Ruth's got a new lamb in there. It won't suck for some reason. She thinks she can get it to eat."

Tyler sipped her soda, feeling Adam's thigh against hers, his soft arm hair rubbing against her forearm. Tyler sneaked a look at him, taking a sideways glance of his red hair and freckled skin, his head closer to her than usual, their bodies touching on the poured concrete. Together, they looked out at the green hills leading up to Mt. Diablo, and then his hand moved and almost touched her knee, balancing on the thickness of air between them. Maybe he was waiting for a sign, and Tyler didn't move, breathing out only when he dropped his hand back to his lap.

"Do you want a sip?" she asked, handing him the bottle. Adam smiled, took the Coke, drinking with his eyes closed. Tyler felt the moment stop, the angle of sun from a movie shot, the warmth of another body near hers, unique, special, something she had been thinking about since she found out about Sanjay and Kate. Tyler wondered if this could be how Kate felt when she sat with Sanjay in the Chaturvedis' deep leather couch. She knew she could never ask her sister any of this right now, but Tyler wondered how you moved from close and clothed to naked and moving, how bodies slid together, how one could ever prepare for it, how it was supposed to end.

"Well?" said Adam, handing her back the bottle.

"Well what?"

"They called today, right? You found out you are going home."

Tyler nodded. Just before lunch, she and Kate heard the phone ring in the kitchen. A few minutes later, Ruth came around the corner, Tyler reading Ruth's expression, believing it tense, preoccupied, maybe angry. "Kate. Tyler. I've got a call for you."

Tyler looked at Kate. Kate was still and pale, her eyes on the dining room table. "You get it," Kate whispered.

"Why?"

"I . . . I don't want to," said Kate, standing up.

"Kate, get over here," said Ruth. "Come to the phone."

"What is your problem?" said Tyler as she pulled Kate into the kitchen.

"It's my fault," said Kate.

"Oh, shut up," said Tyler, grabbing the phone. "Hello? Hello?"

Tyler waited, listening to air, static, children in the background. "Oh, hello? Kate?"

"No, it's Tyler."

"Oh, hi, honey. Listen, I just got the call," said Cynthia De Lucca. Tyler could imagine Cynthia sitting at her desk, her blouse rumpled, a pencil holding together the bun at the back of her neck.

"The call?"

"Yes, *the* call. From your dad's lawyer, Mrs. Lundgren," said Cynthia.

Tyler turned to Kate and Ruth. "Cynthia got the call." Kate reached out an arm, a hand, held on to Tyler's elbow.

"Ask her. Ask her what happened. Ask her how it ends," said Kate.

"I heard that," said Cynthia in Tyler's ear. "And I'll tell you."

Tyler imagined the days as they might be, hot afternoons working on this farm, the animals, separation from her friends and family. She imagined Kate—without Deirdre—turning to fear and sadness and resentment. She imagined her father sitting alone in the house, nothing to remind him about who he once was. Or. Or it could all be different.

"You're both going home. Tomorrow. It's all settled."

Tyler dropped the phone and grabbed Kate, pulled her close, reached a hand out for Ruth, who was smiling. "I thought Cynthia sounded happy. I am so happy for you both," she said.

"I'm sorry, Tyler," said Kate, breathing into Tyler's neck. "I'm so sorry."

"Don't be. It's almost over," said Tyler, thinking that her life might come back to her after all.

Now, even with several hours to begin to believe that what Cynthia said was true, Tyler still felt the outcome was a dream. "Yeah. I can't believe it. It will be, like, so weird," said Tyler, a rush of blood under her cheeks as she thought about her room, her father, school, her friends in the hallways.

"The judge finally decided it would be okay. Things'll be different, though. My dad will be home more. My Aunt Gwen. You remember? She'll be there, too. And my cousin Ryan. And Deirdre, of course," she said, setting the bottle on the cement. "It'll almost be like . . . like before. When my mom was alive."

"Do you know what will happen with the father of the baby?" asked Adam.

Tyler shrugged. "Yeah, but Kate knows more. Well, they live next door. We're bound to see them. There is this restraining order against him. Like, he can't come within a hundred yards of Kate or something. But I don't know."

"That's really weird," said Adam, and Tyler didn't know what he meant.

"What? That he can't come near her?"

"Well, yeah. He's the baby's father, right?"

Tyler nodded, and then pushed back words because she realized Adam probably wouldn't want to hear about a perfectly good parent who was being ignored and thrust aside, a person no one really wanted to have around. Tyler knew that Adam would not be going home for a long, long time, not until his mother was out of jail, not until she didn't drink anymore. Tyler wondered if his arm still hurt, if he could feel where it snapped. "I'll miss you, Tyler. Maybe you could come visit sometime. With Kate and the baby," he said, avoiding her eyes, his hands fidgeting in his lap.

Tyler wondered if she could move her knee into his hand, wondered if it would fit just as she imagined it might, his palm the perfect size. She could almost see her mother's smile, her face framed by window light, the garden green and full behind the glass. Tyler almost head Deirdre say, "Well, what do you think about him?"

Tyler wanted her mother to answer for her, tell her how she should feel, but the kitchen vision disappeared, and she was back on the stoop with Adam, the sun glinting behind the house now, long shadows pulled and stretched from the roof and the trees, the warm air swirling around them. Tyler liked Adam, felt sorry for him, but she didn't need him, and she felt sad he needed her. All she knew for sure was that she would never see this certain sunset or this boy's face again.

Tyler imagined her mother's hand under her arm, holding it up as she moved her hand to Adam's hair, pushed it back, waiting for his eyes to turn to her face. Her skin on his flesh reminded her how she felt about Dee Dee. It was nothing like the dark, sensual movements she'd pictured when thinking about Kate and Sanjay. She moved her nose closer to his face, barely breathing in astringent and shaving cream, gently touching her lips to his soft, slightly prickly cheek. And even though this kiss was about caring and saying good-bye, Tyler knew her mother would smile at this gentle kiss, would lean over and whisper in Tyler's ear, "Tell me everything."

Kate was standing with Virgie, Adam, and Tyler by the fence, watching Ruth's brother Robert drive the tractor, making firm lines of wet brown soil in the soon-to-be cornfield. It was almost sundown. The animals were back in the barn and the pumpkin patch had been tended to—plants thinned, mounds of compost and manure put around each scratchy twisted vine. Ruth was in the house with the new lamb that wouldn't suckle, trying to coax it with soy milk and a rag.

"I told her to call the vet," said Robert, pulling up beside the fence, dust spraying around them. He took off his A's cap and rubbed his bald head. "But she thinks she's Doctor Doo-dee-lee-do."

Virgie laughed, jabbing Robert's shoulder. "Do you mean Doolittle?"

Robert shrugged. "Whatever. Come on, let's go for a ride."

Adam and Tyler followed him, the orange evening light sparking off their hair, Adam's a brilliant glow. Tyler laughed, holding her hands to be pulled up, and she and Adam both held on tight to the seat as Robert started the tractor and bumped into movement, their laughs and hair and waves trailing behind them.

Virgie climbed onto the fence and sat, her heels holding her on. She pulled a cigarette out of her pocket and lit it, her mouth pinched as she inhaled. "Sit down. They won't be back for a while."

Kate climbed up, realizing she had been using her body more than ever this past month, so much of her flesh working its way to her old form, her stomach flattening, her breasts easy with milk, her thighs slimming and hardening from five A.M. chores, bending and cleaning, and walking. Kate sat, hitching her own heels over the wood slat, and looked after the tractor, breathing in dust and manure and irrigation water.

"So what are you going to do? What's going to happen with the baby?" asked Virgie.

Kate watched the earth plume from behind the tractor, topsoil lifting to the sky. "We're all going home tomorrow. Tyler, me, and the baby. The judge said my dad could have us back."

Virgie nodded. "You're pretty damn lucky. Adam and me'll be here for years, I bet."

Kate looked up, following bird chatter. A dozen blackbirds flocked in a line, twirling and twisting like an unattended summer hose. "In a way, though, I don't want to go home," said Kate.

Virgie snorted. "Are you crazy? You've got this whole happy little family thing going on. What more do you want? Jeez."

"But it was so awful before. I mean, I didn't really think so at the time, but now, I couldn't go back to that, the way it was."

"Have you told your dad this?" asked Virgie. "I mean, I could never tell my dad anything, but have you tried?"

Kate shook her head, kicking the fence post with her heel. "I haven't really said too much to him, yet. I don't know. Maybe I will." She turned to Virgie.

"Best place to get scared is in a family, as far as I can tell," said Virgie.

"It wasn't when my mom was alive. Not at all," said Kate and then tried to swallow back a memory, her mother in the dining room, holding her arms around her body, rocking. Kate had watched her, hiding behind the living room door, waiting to find the reason for the movement, but her mother didn't stop and didn't stop. Kate sucked in her breath, some strange feeling ripping across her mouth and forehead, trying to find form in tears or moans. *What do I do?* Kate thought. *I don't know how to help her.* So Kate backed away from the crack of light, silently slipping into bed, pulling the covers over her head, and breathing into the silence. Now, Kate wished she could go to her mother, pull her thin arms open, take her mother's body in her strong, healthy arms and hold her, whisper, "Don't be scared. Don't cry. I'll take care of you."

But she hadn't done that or anything. She had been too scared to help either of them.

Virgie looked at Kate and then jumped down off the fence as they both watched the tractor stop, Tyler and Adam sliding off the tractor seat.

"My advice is to go home and stay alert. Just keep your eye on things. If anything weird starts happening, bolt. Get the hell out. Don't let anybody hurt you. That's what I would do."

"Have you ever gone home? And come back?"

Virgie walked faster, running her hands through her hair, the palest blond growing at the roots. "Yeah, I went home once, about five months ago. For a day. For a fucking day. I don't have the whole happy little family thing, remember?" She turned to Kate, and then ran back to the house.

"What's going on?" asked Tyler, breathless from her ride. She pulled on Kate's arm. "What happened with Virgie?"

"I don't know. We were talking and then she got upset," said Kate, waving to Robert and walking with Tyler and Adam back to the house.

Adam sighed and put his hands in his pocket. "Don't worry. It's just the way she is." He smiled and then started humming a sound that reminded Kate of a reveille, something to say good-bye with, a song to comfort the sun into the bodies of mountains and oceans and plains.

As they walked, the sky quiet, the birds silent, the light almost gone, Kate looked at Adam and wondered if after tomorrow, she and Tyler would ever see him again, if they would ever see Virgie. She wondered how it was that people came together and were pulled apart, how it was decided, what factors kept them all willing to try and try again, desperate to connect with someone else, so sad when it didn't work out. Like with Sanjay and Meera. Almost how it was with her father. How it might be with Sanjay and Deirdre, flesh and body, but awkward in each other's lives, at least for now.

Tyler smiled and turned to Kate. "I am so hungry. What do you think Ruth made tonight?"

"Lamb stew?" said Adam, and they all laughed, pulled for that instant into the same words, the same sound.

❧

It was late. Kate stopped trying to write under the dim yellow desk light and listened for the cows and sheep in the barn, waiting to hear the quiet lowing and baaing, imagining all the warm bodies rubbing together. Tyler was asleep, her breaths smooth and even, reminding Kate of Deirdre, reminding her of the way she'd learned, in the last month and a half, to listen for sleep, knowing its cadences, its rhythms, its beginning, its end.

Kate was writing a letter to Sanjay. So far, she had written: *Dear Sanjay—I think about the day you came to get Deirdre all the time. I bet you thought I was a bad person, having her at home and not telling anyone. But, I didn't want anyone to get hurt. I am sorry about what has happened to you. I hope you know I didn't want it to be like this, ever.*

All I can tell you is that your little girl is the color of gold. She is the most beautiful thing in the world, and someday, maybe soon, I hope you will know her and understand it was all worth it. I think so, even with all that has happened to us all. One day I hope you believe me. . . .

Kate stopped writing, even though there was so much more to say, so much that confused her. On her last visit to Deirdre's foster home, Kate had learned from Cynthia that Sanjay had been released from the Martinez jail, his lawyer somehow getting the charges reduced to misdemeanor sexual battery. Kate juggled that term in her mouth like knives, thinking, *It isn't what happened at all.* But it was done. At least for now.

Kate stood up and quietly left the room, walking downstairs to the kitchen. Ruth sat at the table, a mug in her hands. "Hey, you. Why aren't you asleep? Tomorrow is the big day," she said, standing up to get another cup, pouring the still hot water on a fresh tea bag.

"I couldn't sleep. I'm nervous, I think," said Kate, taking a cookie.

"Who wouldn't be? It's like a new life you're going into," said Ruth, sliding the tea across the table and smiling, her blue eyes brilliant against her darkened skin. "When you get back you're a full-time mom, full-time student."

Kate nodded, taking a sip of tea. "I can't believe I have to go back to school. That will be so weird."

"Yeah," said Ruth. "But just for a while. Then, it will be business as usual. Tests and lectures, you know. The whole thing."

Kate breathed in and put her mug down. Earlier, Adam and Tyler had done the dishes, and Kate could still smell the spray cleaner and dish soap, everything clean and sharp in her nose.

"You know, Ruth. I was thinking. I am writing a letter to Sanjay. I mean, I think there is stuff I need to say. My therapist thinks I have 'unfinished business.' Whatever that is."

Ruth nodded. Kate went on. "It's going to be really weird going home, seeing them and stuff. My dad and Cynthia have told me some of what's going to happen. Like Sanjay's agreed to pay child support. But what does that really mean, you know? How can I ask him what it means?"

Ruth looked to the ceiling, following the slight sway of the lamp over table. Kate tapped her fingers on the table, finding Oreo crumbs and smashing them together with her thumb and forefinger. Ruth made a clicking sound. "Oh, Kate. I don't know what to tell you, really. I sure don't know this Sanjay, and aside for some pretty bad judgment calls he sounds all right, I guess. You want him to be in Dee Dee's life, but that's going to take some healing, on all sides. You don't really need him in your life right now, do you? And when it all boils down to it, your dad can take care of you, Tyler, and the baby just fine."

Kate shook her head, and then wondered how it would be possible to stay separated when Sanjay would be next door. He and Meera would hear Dee Dee when she began to play outside, and Jaggu and Ari would be curious, peeking through the fence slats to see who was laughing. Kate could imagine Jaggu climbing the bay tree and yelling for her, "Kate, look at me!" What would she do? How would she introduce the children? As siblings? Friends? How would Meera look at her, or would she look at her at all?

"I don't know what it'll be like, Ruth. It'll be so weird."

"You don't have to know how everything will turn out all at once, Kate. That's the mistake I made when I was young. Trying to figure it all out pronto. I thought the perfect answers to everything were just around the corner and I had to chase it and wrestle it down." Ruth patted Kate's hand. "There is just so much time to figure everything out."

"I hope so," said Kate, though she was thinking, *Is there? Can you promise? Did my mom have enough time?*

Ruth stood up and walked to the counter, and Kate followed her, bringing her cup to the counter. Together, they looked out the window into the farm night. Kate sighed. "I just wish I could look at my own life and see it perfect."

But even as she said the words, Kate wondered if she were able to go back to that first afternoon in the Chaturvedis' living room, would she now say, "No, Sanjay. I don't want this!" Kate knew that without that day and the other two days in Sanjay's bed, there would be no Deirdre. And it would just be Tyler and her in the house again, all by themselves, no father coming home each night, again and again, just like he used to.

And so, here she was, Kate thought, here she herself was, some-one she had never been before: a mother, a lover, a sister, a daughter, a woman. A mother. She still couldn't believe the way her body opened and her daughter slipped out, alive, living, beautiful.

Kate knew she was going back to an old, imperfect life, but every-thing was new and different and somehow better, a life so strange and magic sometimes she could barely swallow while thinking about it.

PHOTO CREDIT: JAMIE WESTDAL

Jessica Barksdale Inclán teaches composition, creative writing, mythology, and women's literature at Diablo Valley College in Pleasant Hill, California. Her short stories and poems have appeared in various journals and newspapers. Ms. Inclán holds bachelor's degrees in sociology and English literature from CSU and a master's degree in English literature from SFSU. She lives in Orinda, California, with her husband and two sons and is currently working on her second novel.

Visit Jessica Barksdale Inclán's Web site at:

www.jessicabarksdaleinclan.com

HER DAUGHTER'S EYES

Jessica Barksdale Inclán

This Conversation Guide is intended to enrich the
individual reading experience, as well as encourage us
to explore these topics together—because books,
and life, are meant for sharing.

A CONVERSATION WITH
JESSICA BARKSDALE INCLÁN

❖

Q. *There are so many true, sad stories of young mothers abandoning their babies—what inspired you to write a novel about one who makes mistakes but struggles fiercely to keep her baby?*

A. A few years ago I read and saved a tiny newspaper story with the headline *17-Year-Old Can Keep Baby She Hid in Closet.* The article went on to describe, in only three sentences, the story of a girl who had a baby, hid it in a closet for two weeks so she could go to school, and was then discovered and charged with child abuse. Later, the judge gave the baby back to her, as long as she agreed to live with the baby in a home for young mothers. I was fascinated by the story because I could not get my mind around a mother doing that to her baby—and yet, there was some beauty, some strength in the mother that she kept her child, fed her, and made sure the baby had the best she thought she could provide.

Q. *How did this haunting headline evolve into a novel?*

A. Well, a few years after I saw the story, I found myself in a Napa Valley writers' workshop. My teacher was great and the class was fun, but I found myself looking at the teacher and thinking, *I can do this.* The only difference between the teacher and me (because I was a college teacher at the time, too) was that she had published two books. I mean, I knew that getting published was a big deal, but I also suddenly realized, *I can absolutely do this.* I realized that I needed to do it—I needed to have a book of my own, to be teaching a class. When our teacher gave us an assignment that day to write a scene between two characters in which one has a secret from the other, I went back to my friend Mara's beautiful Calistoga house, sat down, and wrote the opening scene of *Her Daughter's Eyes*. I suppose that all the mysteries of the article I had saved, all the unanswered questions of why something like this had happened, opened a door for me. I wanted to know the answers and so I started to write them. I didn't really know, at first, that the character sitting in the closet was Kate but I wanted to know what was going to happen to her, to the baby, to the father of the baby....

Q. *What were the questions you asked yourself as you started the novel?*

A. When I wrote the class assignment, I knew that Kate had secrets from her sister, but I could also see that Tyler had secrets as well. I wanted to know what was going to happen to them. Who was the secret father? Where were the parents? What about the neighbors? The school? How could this happen in the United States? As I answered these questions, I discovered how complicated and, at times, contradictory the answers could be. A mother can do stupid things even as she feels an overwhelming urge to protect and defend her child. And the same rule applied, really, to the other characters in the book. We are all so well-intentioned but flawed. I began to see how very gray right and wrong can be....

Q. *How long did it take you to write the novel?*

A. Twenty-four years! Well, not really, but in some ways I had been wanting to write a book since I was twelve and it took me until that moment in the writers' workshop to actually give birth to my long-awaited dream. So I count all the time between the initial desire up to the moment I typed *The End*. Annie Lamott told me, "Three hundred words a day and you have a novel in a year." It's true. I just started to show up at my desk each morning and say, *What's going to happen to my characters today?*

Q. *How much of this novel came from your own experience?*

A. Childbirth has provided me with the most intense experiences of my life. I have two boys and they were both born without complications. But there's still that amazing moment in childbirth where you feel it is truly *life or death*. The line between the two seems so fine. And it's such an enormous rite of passage: a girl becomes a mother, a fetus becomes a baby. So much of it is just genetic and instinctual, I think. I knew that from my own experience and I suppose I was able to refer to those feelings to help me understand Kate and Tyler's lives.

The other experience that really informed the novel was my father dying when I was fifteen. It wasn't too hard to imagine how teenaged girls, two teenaged sisters, would feel at that moment. My sister Sarah was 13 at the time, so we were the same age Kate and Tyler were when Deirdre died. Right after my dad died, my youngest sister, Rebecca, was diagnosed with diabetes, and between my father's death and Rebecca's life-threatening illness (she eventually died at age 26), my mother had her hands full. Sarah and I sort of drifted on our own for a while, so again, I could imagine what it was to feel "abandoned" by one's parents.

Q. *What are some of the secondary themes of this novel and how did they evolve?*

A. Marriages fascinate me. I have been married for eighteen years and I think what is said, and not said, in a marriage can be both blessing and curse. Both of the marriages in this story suffer from a lack of communication. Davis's job, in the end, is to say all the things he thought he couldn't. Only then does he begin to heal. Meera and Sanjay have grown apart—they love each other but have lost touch not only with each other but also with their own feelings. Only by saying the truth to each other, painful as it is, do they start to forge a stronger and more meaningful relationship. In my own marriage, I know that if I can muster the courage to say something true, it helps—even though it might hurt at first.

Q. *The neighborhood you created on Wildwood Drive is very multicultural. Why is that?*

A. It's American! I have always been interested in the way cultures exist, coexist, and clash in this country. My husband is Mexican, and during our time together, I've witnessed his family—generations of immigrant, naturalized citizen, and native-born American—deal with social, political, and cultural developments in the United States. When my husband and his family first moved here, assimilation was the norm, and my mother-in-law learned to cook and shop and live American. While a certain amount of assimilation is good, I think there's now much more of an emphasis on all of us retaining those parts of our cultures that make us feel whole. Part of Meera and Sanjay's feelings of emptiness and loneliness may lie in their desire to assimilate but their equally strong need to feel a meaningful connection to family traditions and heritage.

Q. *Now that you have written this book, what's next?*

A. When I was twelve, I decided to write a novel called *A Baker's Dozen*, about a family with thirteen children. I think I wrote about four pages! But writing has always brought me peace and happiness. Every day since that momentous day at the writers' conference, I sit down and write three hundred words, putting together stories that I feel compelled to finish, creating characters I want to understand. I don't always know where I'm going when I start but I know I can get there. And I feel lucky and proud I can do this every day.

QUESTIONS FOR DISCUSSION

❖

1. *New York Times* bestselling author Sally Mandel said, "Jessica Barksdale Inclán brings a profound understanding of human nature to her characters—each is flawed, each is heroic, and their lives are comic and tragic, often simultaneously." Why do you think she feels this way?

2. One of the most striking things about this novel is the lack of villains. Why do you think the author created characters who are less than perfect but also less than evil? Discuss how this applies to Davis.

3. Redemption is a recurrent theme in this novel. Discuss how each of the characters compensates for a previous failure.

4. Kate and Tyler's dead mother, Deirdre, who looms larger than life in this novel, is presented from varying perspectives. When you finished the novel, did you feel you knew and understood Deirdre? Discuss her strengths and weaknesses and her continuing importance in the family.

5. How do you imagine the lives of these characters progressing? Discuss where you think they might be—emotionally and psychologically—five years after the novel ends.

Notes

NOTES

<u>*NOTES*</u>

<u>*NOTES*</u>